From the award-winning auth
Winner of the *Global Ebooks A*
Finalist in *the Kindle Book Aw*
Cinnamon Press Novella Award **and** *the Chaucer Awards.*
'Evocative and thoroughly riveting. A vividly-written, historical saga.' *The Wishing Shelf*

'I highly recommend all four books. You will love this historical fantasy!' Autumn Birt, *The Rise of The Fifth Order*

'Fascinating history – the plot was terrific.' Brian Wilkerson, *Trickster Eric Novels blogger*

'You will not find any better historical fiction, nor a more powerful evocation of a vivid past than in Gill's brilliantly written series.' Paul Trembling, *Local Artist*

'A remarkable achievement. Every character, and that includes the horses, dogs and hawks, is bursting with vitality, and Gill's lush descriptions of Moorish palaces seduce you as they send you on a journey full of treachery, adventure and romance.' Deborah Swift, *Pleasing Mr Pepys*

'Gill's skill at moving from culture to culture, savoring the distinctive colors of each, is breath taking.' Elizabeth Horton-Newton, *Carved Wooden Heart*

Praise for Someone to Look Up To
Litpick Student Reviews TOP PICK Award 'A very moving book... superbly written'

'Thank you for the wonderful experience of being in a dog's head. I've often wondered what a dog's world was all about. Now I know.' Claire Stibbe, *The 9th Hour*

© Jean Gill 2019
The 13th Sign
ISBN 979-10-96459-11-7

First published in 2019

This is a work of fiction. Names, characters, organisations, places and events are
either products of the author's imagination or are used fictitiously.

For Anita Kovacevic
who loves the Forest as much as I do

Dwi wedi dod yn ôl at fy nghoed
Welsh proverb meaning 'I have returned to my trees'
(I have come back to my senses)

CHAPTER ONE

Why was the Forest forbidden? The very word was unmentionable. Yet everybody knew it was out there. Otherwise, how could children scare each other with whispered stories of what might be in the Forest? Gigantic sticky-buds, striped man-eaters, slithery poison? Their imaginations ran wild in a tamed world. But as each child reached Maturity and passed – or failed – the ritual test, the word *Forest* disappeared from the new adult's mind, like a leaf dropping in autumn.

Mielitta had tried to ask adults why the Forest was forbidden but the word tied her tongue in tangled roots and instead she found herself asking the way to the schoolroom, or some other question so ludicrous that she was mocked for her stupidity. She sensed magecraft twisting her words but she could not force a different path from the one required of good citizens.

Now she was the only child who'd seen eighteen year-cycles and still been told she was not ready for testing. Her old play-mates moved around the same halls as she did, girls in silken robes, boys in leatherette jerkins and long trews, while she still wore a tabard over a child's short britches and stuffed her hair into the coarse netting of a servant's ugly snood.

Flowers, thought Mielitta, as three girls in gowns like satin petals rustled past her. Grace, Felicity and Espoir had turned into a golden daffodil, a blue pansy and a violet campanula respectively. Mielitta knew these flowers from the books in the library, which she was tasked with cleaning each week. She remembered when the golden daffodil used to play leapfrog against the stable wall and when the violet campanula had linked pinkie fingers with her, swearing friendship forever. But even then, her finding had set her apart. All the other children had been born in the Citadel, not discovered as a baby by the Mage-Smith. She would always be a foundling, a freak.

'The stones be with you, Lady Grace, Lady Felicity, Lady Espoir,' murmured Mielitta, lowering her eyes. Barely nodding slender necks, expressions stonier than the walls they passed, the ladies swished past in silence, the better to ignore such a freak.

Had they forgotten her when they reached maturity? Or did they prefer to forget their broken promises, made by childish pinkie fingers?

As the chirruping gossip started up again behind her, Mielitta was warned of a potentially worse encounter by the brown scent of peat, a metallic clank and rumbling voices. She shrank into the shadows of an alcove, held her breath. Whichever route she took from her bed to the kitchen, there was always the risk of meeting Jannlou and his cronies.

She willed herself invisible, wished she had the powers to really be so. Children entertained each other with such stories and the books she read in the library, while she was supposed to be working, tantalised her with magical possibilities for every citizen. But adults never spoke of such powers outside magecraft. It wasn't a banned subject, like the Forest. More like a pointless train of thought, as if magecraft was the privilege of the chosen few, controlled, and those who lacked it were unimportant. Whereas the Forest was dangerous. How Mielitta knew this, she couldn't say. She just did. In the same way she knew that people like her had no magecraft. And people like Jannlou, did.

'My father says we must strengthen the walls of the western

2

keep.' His voice was deep and echoed in its confident authority but Mielitta knew the speaker was her own age. They had not linked pinkie fingers as children and if anything had been sworn, it was eternal enmity. Mielitta had no idea why Jannlou wanted to make her life a misery. It was just another fact of her cursed life.

'Is there a threat?' A smoother voice. Bastien, whose fast-talking explanations always put Mielitta in the wrong. She had never snitched, even on Jannlou, but Bastien's confessions had blamed her for a tipped bucket of water on precious books or a damaged bow in the archery yard. After all, the freak's clumsiness was legendary. Bastien himself had created that legend and Mielitta wore her reputation like a porcupine shirt, prickles inside.

He had excelled himself with his martyred performance after Jannlou accidentally knifed him in a schoolroom rough-house. When the schoolmaster returned and questioned Bastien about the cut, he 'couldn't say… couldn't tell on a girl…' and indicated Mielitta with his eyes. As the knife had magically appeared on her desk, there was little she could say in her defence. Not that she wanted to. Not when seventeen classmates apparently accepted that she'd caused the wound. Were they scared of Jannlou and his gang? Or genuinely magicked out of their memory? She preferred to believe the latter, but then why did such magecraft never work on her?

'There may be a threat,' Jannlou replied to Bastien's question. 'My father has had word from across the Wilderness. Of,' he hesitated, 'of something. I can't say more and especially not here. You never know who might be listening.' He turned his head as he passed the alcove, his nostrils flared and he held Mielitta's gaze in his own, red in the torchlight. Even though she looked down quickly she felt the heat, burning. If he wanted to, Jannlou could blaze light across the stone passage, reveal her. He walked on.

Like reptiles, thought Mielitta, as the young men passed. *Especially Bastien. Fork-tongue.* Chain-mail hauberks and hoods glittered like crocodile scales. Huge buckles on belts and backpacks gleamed and clinked. As they grew older and gained experience, those belts would acquire trophies, filling the spaces with symbols of achievement.

I would like that as a job. Engraving belt motifs. Next time I go to the forge I will ask Declan if I can work for him instead of this endless cleaning and table-waiting. If I am to be a child-servant until I die, then I should seek a position that suits my situation.

She followed this distracting line of thought as the last echo of boots faded and all she could hear was her heart pounding. Why hadn't Jannlou taken the chance offered? Maybe he hadn't seen her at all. It had just been her imagination. Burning eyes! Among the books she dusted and read, there was a section full of men with burning eyes. Clearly, she should take more care. Maybe she wasn't immune to all forms of magical influence after all.

She rushed along the passageway to the kitchen, where a cauldron of soup bubbled. Today it contained orange vegetables and would be called carrot soup. Maybe the diners could taste a difference because they saw a different colour and shape to the bits in their hot water each day but to Mielitta, the food always tasted the same. It tasted of salt and Citadel water.

She had learned from her own body, sweat and blood, that tastes could be different, and her palate found the daily sustenance dull. As if she knew that something better was possible.

The same was true of scent. The Citadel food had no smell, just temperature, tepid or cool. But Mielitta could distinguish all the scents around her; dusty books in the library, laundered clothes and bedlinen, smoke and molten steel in the forge. She could smell them and see their scents in colour.

That was probably why she'd received a year-cycle gift this morning, with the instruction that she should keep it secret. When she woke up, there it was on her bed, a carved wooden box with a tiny scroll and phial inside.

My parents, was her first thought. *Maybe they were waiting until my eighteenth year-cycle to tell me who I am. Who they are. Or who they were.*

But no, the sender was anonymous. The writing on the scroll was in spidery green ink and made no sense. A riddle.

When the bottle is empty, you will be full.
No life ends while The One lives.
In the year of the prophecy, choose well.

She'd scrunched up the paper and thrown it on the floor but she unstoppered the phial, curious. Her nose filled instantly, glutted, as she inhaled, savoured. Her untrained nose smelled immediacy and many layers. Book-words offered themselves: musk, attar of roses, geranium, sandalwood. She'd experienced none of these but their names waited for the day she did.

She breathed deeply. She *had* to find words for these scents. *A fruit bowl.* Not the kind she now carried into the Great Hall after the evening meal, as fake as the carrot soup, but squashed blackberries, apricot smoothness and lime zest. Bound with something unexpected, mild, creamy, yellow… banana. Yes, that was the word. Banana. She had no idea how she could identify each scent but she would bet a week's food on being right. If only she could have food scented like this instead of the usual dull sustenance.

There was more to life than this bland existence. There must be. She had dabbed the perfume on her wrists, wafted in a cloud of scented beauty, waited to be told there was something different about her. All day she had worn her cloud but nobody had noticed. She was still invisible unless she failed or disappointed.

'Stop daydreaming and give me that bowl!' the fat man at the table growled at Mielitta. 'The smell's driving me crazy with hunger and you stand there like an idiot!'

For a minute, Mielitta thought he meant *her* smell.

'Mmm, carrot soup.' He sucked his moustache with enthusiasm before giving the same attention to the bowl in front of him. 'My favourite.'

Bemused, Mielitta sniffed the other bowl of soup she carried. Nothing. As if she lived in a different world.

JEAN GILL

'Mielitta!' This voice was right in her ear and she jumped, spilling some soup. 'Idra isn't feeling well so you need to take her place. Take wine to the Council Chamber right away. They've eaten already and are meeting now.'

'Ten goblets?' asked Mielitta. Her heart pounded, knowing the answer. Ten Councillors, ten goblets. She was never tasked with the Council Chamber. The most powerful people in the Citadel wouldn't want to see a misfit, living proof that their rule did not have a place for everyone. Clearly the steward was willing to overlook Mielitta's unfitness for the task in view of her being available, now. And she knew her way around the Citadel, unlike the little ones who beamed as they served table. Had Mielitta ever been so young, so enthusiastic?

She was still pondering the question as, with a still-beaming follower, she carried a tray to the square tower of the keep, climbed the seventy-two spiral steps and waited. Chewing his lower lip as he carried out his instructions, her young helper gave three great taps with his stick on the oaken door and opened it for Mielitta. She touched the door, breathed in its musty toasted age, marvelled at the luxury of real wood instead of woodette. Apart from the stones themselves, little in the Citadel was of natural origin, and the real wood must have come from the Forest.

'Bring another pitcher every hour,' she instructed the little boy, who bowed and left, proud of being so useful.

Accustomed to the signal, the mages at the table didn't look up. Mielitta set down the tray, took a pitcher of red water, that smelled of nothing and tasted of salt, and began to pour. The steward need not have worried. Nobody in the Council Chamber had eyes for a servant, however over-age and odd, and smelling of bananas. An invisible servant who had eyes, ears and a remarkable nose, and who intended to make use of them.

6

CHAPTER TWO

The ten faces were known to everyone but usually Mielitta saw them from the back of the Great Hall, where she sought her usual invisibility. The Council of Ten would be on the raised podium at the other end of the Hall, either eating at the High Table or speechifying or both. This was the first time she'd been so close and the room crackled with barely suppressed power.

In her mind, she named them one by one, round the table, starting with Jannlou's father, Magaram. Grey hair feathered above his ears into a dusty black mane. No doubt it was once sleek as a colt's, worn in a warrior's queue, like his son's today. The same deceptive blue eyes, even more startling against the seamed shadows of weathered chestnut skin. The same smell.

Mielitta inhaled, tried to separate the human scents in the room until she could distinguish each person by smell but that was too difficult. She could only identify those she already knew – and two others, pungent and clashing.

Magaram was easy to recognise because of all the times she'd hidden from Jannlou, his earthy tang a warning. His father carried the same rich brown scent. Mielitta saw smells this way, in colours and book-words, though she had no experience of earth, any more than of blackberries. All her life, words had popped into her head to match each new experience, released from her deep thinking. She just *knew*. And she'd quickly realised that the other children didn't. Not even Declan knew the words she did so she learned to keep quiet about her sharp gold senses and her book-world.

To Magaram's right was Shenagra, shimmering in an aroma of cocoa, black braids erect in a fuzzy headpiece. Brown-scented, like Magaram, but with sweetness, milk and sugar. She sometimes came to the schoolroom, tested those children who showed signs of gifts. Mielitta had felt Shenagra questing in her thoughts and she'd hidden against the wall of her mind, as she did against real walls. Now, as Mielitta poured wine for Shenagra, the cocoa shimmer brushed against her, dismissed this oddity as of no interest, passed on.

Invisible thought Mielitta and smiled to herself.

A high voice fluted, 'I checked the seals and there was a weakness in the water gate.'

Hamel. Mielitta's nostrils flared and followed a scent she perceived in emerald loops, in metallic and leatherette binding, to their source, the least human-looking Councillor. Tiny, elevated by several cushions, Hamel seemed unaware of the instinctive repulsion he evoked.

His hands drummed impatiently on the table as he spoke, the spiked nails sheathing and unsheathing. Everything about him was pointed, from the tip of his bald head and his knobbly shoulders, to the leatherette boots hidden under the table. Many wore pointed boots as fashion but everybody knew that Hamel wore them to fit his feet. Or feelers. Nobody was sure what names were suitable for the green-skinned Councillor's body parts. And nobody was likely to ask him.

Rumour said he was the result of a magecraft experiment. Whether the experiment had been a success or a failure depended on your point of view. Mielitta shuddered.

'Is this a witch-hunt or a Council of War?' A woman's voice grated like Hemel's nails on the table. Mielitta scented the mage's scarlet trail: roses, thorns and one iron blood-drop. As dumpy and ordinary as her scent was glamorous, Puggy had bad skin, lank hair and gave the impression her robe was a punishment from which her curves were trying to escape. Nobody was hoping that they would.

Why would someone with so much power guard such an appearance? wondered Mielitta. If she were Puggy, she'd wear robes as scarlet and dangerous as her scent, smooth her skin to silver satin and drip honeyed words into the hearts of all who heard her, whenever she opened her mouth.

The two strong forces clamoured for Mielitta's nose. She could see them: an arabesque of bright emerald and an arrow-straight track of blood-scarlet, but it was the Chief Mage who replied to Puggy's question.

'Neither. It's not a Council of War – yet.' Magaram oozed calm. 'We mustn't overreact.' His glance swept the table, told them how invaluable each one of them was. 'But we must act. And we must be united.'

His next words made Mielitta doubt her ears. 'The Forest is gaining strength and Perfection is under attack.' Her hands trembled as she took the pitcher round the table, topped up goblets. But none of the Councillors even flinched at the forbidden word. Nor showed shock at the Citadel's very core being under threat. Perfection was the basis of their government, of their society and of Mielitta's day-to-day existence. Its tenets had been handed down through the generations, sanctioned by tradition and created from the wisdom of history.

Hamel repeated, 'I checked the seals and there was a weakness in the water gate. *Somebody* has allowed flow between the Citadel and the Forest.' He stared across the table at Puggy.

There was an uncomfortable silence. Then Puggy laughed.

'Oh no, you don't! Nice try but if there's a traitor in the Citadel – and I'm not sure there is – you're lighting a fire under the wrong chimney. Let Shenagra do her thing if you want proof.'

'Why not?' challenged Hamel. 'Unless the Chief Mage would

rather *not* find out where this trail leads, or rather to whom? Would rather not – act?' His tone was a mocking echo of Magaram's.

'Do it, Shenagra,' commanded Magaram, his face granite. 'On all of us. You can start with me.'

Mielitta stood very still at her post beside the trays, in the furthest corner of a room that was suddenly too small. She had not enjoyed Shenagra's tests in the schoolroom and she suspected this demonstration of magecraft would be a thousand times worse.

Shenagra shimmered in concentration as her black braids unwound, thinning into long fuzzy strands that extended until they reached her left-hand neighbour at the table. The questing hair hesitated, tapped Magaram's head.

'I am open,' he said, his eyes shut, his body braced.

The hair streamed into Magaram, burrowing in a thousand cocoa fissures that criss-crossed his skin into crackle-glaze earthenware. Each hair began to glow, a fiery link between Magaram's interior and the writhing mass of braids still coiled on Shenagra's head. Then sparks began to shoot upwards from the lines of hair, raining down in a flash of words that landed on Shenagra's burning head.

Mielitta could read some of them but they came too fast for her. *Leader. Loyal. Perfection and Citadel first. But Jannlou.*

Shenagra sat like a volcano, absorbing the lava instead of spewing it. The lightning rain of words ended, the sparks died down as the word *Future* buried itself in the coiled braids. Grey as ash, she retracted her hair, left Magaram shaking but unblemished, the cracks in his skin healing the moment each hair withdrew.

Within what was probably only minutes, Shenagra's braided headpiece was coiled impeccably on her head and behaving once more like hair. She was paler than before but her voice showed no sign of strain.

'You saw the words. Magaram our leader is loyal.'

Hamel frowned. 'Nobody doubts Magaram! But words can be interpreted different ways. Should the same words come from another Councillor, who's to say they mean he – or she' – a glare at Puggy – 'didn't tamper with the water gate in the mistaken belief that it was for the good of the Citadel, that it is time to open to the Forest.'

'They are not just words, Hamel,' Magaram pointed out. 'They are Shenagra's power and their meaning is clear to her, without ambiguity. We see part. She sees all. And she pays for that as we all do for our powers.'

'What if Shenagra is the traitor?' Hamel challenged.

'Then you shall have my place as leader, when you prove it.' Magaram glared. 'I stake my life on Shenagra's loyalty, not just from long friendship. You *know* she draws power from obedience to the Council and is incapable of using it against us.'

'We only have your word for that,' Hamel grumbled but was shushed.

'Next,' commanded Magaram quietly to Shenagra, who breathed deeply and turned to the Councillor beside her.

'I am open,' he said quietly, but before the test could begin, the Councillor on his left, next in line, spoke up.

'Perhaps it *is* time to open to the Forest,' he said. 'Why can't we benefit from its powers instead of this separation? We have such strength and yet we live such mutilated lives. Aren't you sick of bland food, bland surroundings, the same comfort every day, the same everything! Don't you long for something more? For contact with Nature again?'

The outcry around the table hid Mielitta's gasp. She only knew what Nature was from books but maybe that was what she wished for too? The *something* missing from her life: could *Nature*, whatever that might be, fill the loneliness that drained her each day?

Shenagra's braids shifted uneasily. 'Mutilated?' she queried, simmering.

The rebellious Councillor seemed encouraged rather than

11

impeded by the shocked reaction to his words. He rushed on, 'We can't even use our powers to the full, so we lead boring lives with endless meetings. We remove the spark from the children before they question the way things are and we perpetuate this dreary existence! I want to *live,* not just exist!'

Magaram gave Shenagra the briefest of glances. She nodded, tightened her lips, waited.

'You have forgotten what the world was like before Perfection, Crimvert, when all men went outside the Citadel. Risked leaving the canopy.'

Crimvert shook his head, long locks flying. *Did he have the same magecraft as Shenagra?* wondered Mielitta.

'*You* have all forgotten what the Forest is like,' Crimvert countered. 'Birdsong that hushes as you come near, then a flight like living arrows into the high branches of trees that whisper of shelter. You talk of our canopy as if it's a wonder but you've never seen the canopy of trees, as high as ten men, swaying in the breeze.'

There was more angry muttering but this time Mielitta was bemused, not shocked. She knew what 'breezes' were, from books, but why would you want a breeze?

'And *you've* never seen typhoons and tsunamis.' Magaram's reply was calm, tutoring naivety. 'If you'd spent as much time learning from the walls as you have enjoying your forage rights outside them, you would know our history and control this juvenile attraction.'

'I listened to the walls all my apprenticeship,' muttered Crimvert. 'They repeat themselves. The Forest never repeats. It dazzles, varies, enchants.'

This time, the room held its breath in silence at the blasphemy.

'You were trusted,' Magaram's voice grew deeper. 'You showed you could control your powers and resist temptation. You swore an oath of loyalty, on your life. But you betrayed us, left the water gate unwarded, allowed the Forest into the Citadel.' It was a statement, not a question. And it was a judgement.

'I did all that you asked me,' Crimvert replied between gritted teeth. 'My duty. I led the lumberjacks into the Forest and wiped their memories when we returned with wood. I never used the password unless I had a foraging party. All I did was observe the Forest and I realised we've been wrong! We could live Perfect lives *with* the Forest, heal this rift between men and Nature, between men and their own nature. What harm can it do to give a tiny passage from the Forest to the Citadel?'

'What harm it has done I don't yet know.' Magaram's tone was heavy. 'You have admitted your guilt. You broke your oath. Shenagra?'

Crimvert's eyes were wide as Shenagra's black braids uncoiled, sending tendrils past his neighbour and towards him.

'I am not open,' he gasped, as his throat was squeezed between tendrils that sought entry, tapping his skin.

Magaram sighed. 'We shall need you tomorrow, Shenagra. Save your strength.'

The black tendrils whipped back into neat coils. Magaram leaned thoughtfully on one hand, which glowed a sudden red.

Crimvert had barely drawn two clear breaths when he burst into flames, a blaze that made the mages flinch, although it threw no heat.

'A breeze is indeed useful,' Magaram murmured to the pile of ash remaining on Crimvert's seat. The Master Mage blew softly and a current of air picked up the ash, carried it over to the fire-place, deposited it neatly in the grate.

'A fitting end, don't you think?' Magaram asked nobody in particular. 'With the bits of wood he seemed so passionate about. Does anybody else wish for a reminder of our history? A lecture on the dangers of mixing with the Forest? On how we sustain this society as Perfect? Perhaps you question how we keep our citizens busy? Or why we limit our use of magecraft?'

Around the room, mages concentrated on not blinking, not looking down and especially not exchanging glances.

Shenagra risked making the first comment. 'We need new wards on the water gate and a new password.'

There was a ripple of relief that they were moving on to practical matters.

'A volunteer to take Crimvert's place?' asked Magaram.

Nobody looked at the empty seat or at the fireplace.

A Councillor with a metallic sheen on his arms and upper body, spoke up. 'I have no affinity with Nature. This is not a duty I will enjoy but I am a safe person to carry out such a role.'

General nods of approval were confirmed by Magaram's assent. 'Thank you, Veebo. Reset the wards as quickly as you can and I suggest a password in your honour. Radium. Reactive, lethal, barbaric – like the Forest itself and all you help protect us from. In a word, toxic.'

'I will try to be worthy.' Veebo bowed his head.

Radium, memorised Mielitta. *The way to the Forest by the water gate.* She knew where that was. She'd explored all of the Citadel open to non-mages and trespassed in a few places that weren't. In the curtain-wall underground, the water gate let in the Citadel's water supply, which was purified on entry and later channelled separately for washing, cooking and drinking.

'Let's all drink a toast.' The leaden atmosphere cooled a few degrees at Magaram's suggestion but all heads nodded.

'To our Perfect society!' Magaram raised his goblet and drank deeply.

'–our Perfect society!' All followed suit, with real or well-feigned enthusiasm.

'What about the damage done already?' asked Hamel, flexing his finger-blades.

'We don't know whether any damage has been done,' pointed out Shenagra. 'A little fresh air blowing through the water gate will be soon inhaled and gone. Maybe one or two of the younger inhabitants will be more troublesome than usual but I suspect that's all. I'll be vigilant in the schoolroom.'

'And I with apprentice training. Double time spent on wall history.'

One by one, the Councillors suggested ways they could step up their supervision of Citadel life. Magaram suggested a speech in the Great Hall to reinforce morale. The meeting was clearly coming to an end and Mielitta would be able to escape with a little new knowledge and a lot of new questions.

Magaram drained the last of his goblet.

'Wipe the servant clean, please, Shenagra.'

Mielitta's stomach heaved. The instinct to run flooded her but her legs turned to mush and she couldn't even lift one foot. She suspected that only the wall was keeping her upright as she tried to lean back further into the stone, disappear. But the black braids were unclogging, tendrils snaking towards her and the wall was just that – a wall.

She felt the first prickles on her skin, opened her mouth to say – to say what? She was no Councillor to declare that she was open. Nor was she a revolutionary to say she was not open.

Just a schoolroom test from Shenagra she told herself. And she'd evaded the last one. *It's just to wipe me clean not to… do that thing.* She turned her imagination resolutely from what had happened to Crimvert. If Shenagra wanted to wipe out Mielitta's memories of the last hour, then she should have what she wanted.

Mielitta built the wall in her mind, the one she'd hidden against during the schoolroom testing. But this time she didn't hide. She pictured herself knocking on the door, pictured that little boy who'd helped her, put their conversation on a loop in her head. She, Mielitta had no memory after knocking on the door, entering with a tray, pitchers and goblets. This time it was her memories that she hid in the wall. She tucked an hour's worth of memories into a bag, drew the strings tight and put them into a hole behind a brick. She put the brick back in place and re-ran the conversation with the boy, just as the first tendrils reached her inner core.

Knock knock, knock went the stick on the door. She played the scene as the tendrils quested around her. 'Don't forget to bring a pitcher every hour.' A tendril skittered along the wall but didn't pause. They were all over her, all into her. *Knock, knock went the stick on the door.* 'Don't forget to bring a pitcher every hour.'

'Clean,' a whisper commanded in her head but she didn't listen, didn't fall into the trap.

'She's clean,' the hairs were transmitting the message back up, up to the coiled braids, up to the follicles, to Shenagra. And then they were gone.

Mielitta opened her eyes and inhaled. A strong whiff of bananas. She must have sweated more, brought out the scent. But the Councillors seemed not to notice. Was she the only one in the Citadel with a sense of smell?

She picked up a pitcher and moved to Magaram's right side, like the well-trained servant she was, offering to pour. He covered the goblet.

'Enough,' he told her. She felt the blue gaze drill her meekly lowered head. 'You may go now.'

She looked up and let her surprise show. How fast the meeting had gone!

Shenagra nodded. 'Thank you, boy,' she said. 'Leave the tray. Someone will collect it later.'

So that was why they hadn't even noticed how oddly old she was. They thought she was a boy.

Mielitta obeyed. She knew that she'd forgotten something that was very important. And she knew exactly where in the Citadel walls she could find out what she'd forgotten. She only had to take out the brick and all her memories would be fully recovered. Her years traipsing round the towers and passages, carrying out pointless errands, had not been wasted after all. She knew every stone. And it seemed the walls knew her too.

She sensed a current of air against her cheek. *Wrong,* her senses told her. She walked steadily, not changing her pace, heading predictably for her chamber and her bed. The Councillors were checking up on her. There would be no memory retrieval tonight. She must choose her moment, not be caught.

Pff. She was a mere servant. They'd have forgotten her by the next day.

CHAPTER THREE

She'd started the day badly, dropping the little perfume bottle so the last of its contents emptied on her throat and down her cleavage. She reeked of bananas but nobody seemed to notice. After an hour's immersion in the sickly-sweet smell, her nose was so offended it stopped working. A blessing! Not that breakfast in the Great Hall had any pleasures for the senses. Hot liquid and granular 'bread' sustenance with vitamin spread. Then Mielitta, an alien giant, followed the other children to archery practice.

Usually, archery practice was her joy but today Mielitta was sloppy, distracted by the prospect of finding the brick in the wall where, last night, she'd believed some of her memories were stored. In the cold light of day, she thought it would be a waste of time following up such a childish fancy. She'd served wine in the Council Chamber and lost track of time while the Ten discussed boring politics. Her overactive imagination had given her stories to pass the time and now she was going to waste more time looking behind a brick that probably didn't even exist.

An arrow was still in the target from the children's efforts earlier and she made a mental note to speak to the little ones about responsibility for equipment. If she didn't pass on Tannlei's teachings, who would, now that the archery mentor was gone?

Tannlei's replacement only knew the mechanics of archery, not its soul, and had been as relieved to declare Mielitta a graduate, needing no further tuition, as Mielitta had been glad to practise alone. As if Tannlei could be replaced!

Mielitta always helped the children then waited till they'd gone before she honed her skills, exercising the mental discipline as well as the physical. Today, she'd been abstracted.

She could hear Tannlei's voice, challenging her to do better, to teach the children what she'd learned.

'You have mistaken the target, Mielitta,' she said, as clear today as she'd been when Mielitta was a little girl, answering in frustration, 'But I hit it, I did!' She'd had tears in her eyes. Couldn't this stupid woman see her arrow in the inner ring?

'What is the target?' Tannlei had asked gently. She'd shaken her head every time Mielitta replied it was the cork circle with rings and a bull's-eye.

'Think again,' the mage insisted.

Mielitta had practised and practised but still her teacher told her to think again. Then, one day, Mielitta was pitted in competition against one of her classmates, a red-headed boy.

When her teacher asked, 'What is the target, Mielitta?' the red-headed boy stuck his tongue out at her behind Tannlei's back.

Mielitta answered without thinking, 'To beat *him*!'

To her surprise, Tannlei nodded slowly and gave one of her rare smiles. 'You see, the target has changed. And yet you are still shooting arrows at the same circles.'

Mielitta owned up. 'But I didn't think at all when I answered.'

The creases deepened in her teacher's face but the smile remained and her black eyes were kind. 'That too is archery,' she said. 'When thinking happens deep inside you and does not seem like thinking, it shows the true quality of your mind. When you first held a bow, I had to tell you to put your hands here and here.' Tannlei placed her own hands over Mielitta's, correctly positioned on the bow. You had to think each time where to put your hands. Do you think about this now?'

QUEEN OF THE WARRIOR BEES

'No,' she realised.

'Because it is part of your deep thinking now, part of your true quality as an archer.' Without even turning around Tannlei told off the red-headed boy for meanness of spirit and let the two rivals shoot against each other. The fun of winning soon faded but Mielitta carried on thinking and not thinking.

From that moment on, whenever she was asked what the target was that day, she found different answers.

'To shoot over my shoulder.'

'To hold three arrows and fire them fast.'

Soon she was setting and beating her own targets in performance. Then she made another breakthrough, the day she answered, 'To kill someone!'

Ever gentle, her teacher had said, 'Then you will miss the mark.'

She had, of course. Arrows loosed in anger flew wide and the worse she did, the more her frustration grew and the more danger there was that she would break something.

'What have you learned, Mielitta?'

'That I'm useless!' Her sulky tone could have clouded a sunny day.

'When are you useless?'

'All the time.'

Tannlei just waited. Mielitta knew what her teacher wanted but she'd been too sullen to speak the words. So Tannlei walked away, at the measured pace in which she did everything.

Mielitta had come back the next day to return her weapons.

'There's no point me carrying on.'

'What is stopping you?'

'I'm no good.'

'And what makes somebody good?'

'Some people just aren't any good at archery.'

'What stops them learning?'

'They're clumsy or slow or whatever.'

'How will they become better?'

'Work, I guess. But it's not worth it.'

'So, what stops them learning?'

'Themselves,' Mielitta muttered.

'Now you understand. You know what limits you and you can choose what to do about it.'

Mielitta had gone back to the archery yard, back to work.

And here she was again, wondering who she was and what the walls wanted from her.

'What's the target today, Mielitta?' she asked herself as she prepared mentally for target practice, stilling her mental zigzags. She'd probably imagined the whole weirdness with the walls and she wasn't rushing to find out how foolish she'd been. She'd check out the hidey-hole later. Her brush with magecraft had highlighted the real problem. She couldn't go on like this, a woman with a child's status.

'You know what limits you and you can choose what to do about it,' she told herself. She shouldn't wait any more for somebody or something to change her life; she should do it herself. She would visit Declan in the forge, ask him to take her on as an apprentice. She'd waited long enough for him to ask her and she should take the initiative. Maybe that's what he was waiting for, the final proof on her part that she was ready for the role.

She marshalled her arguments and collected five arrows in her shooting hand.

She ran across the yard, turned and loosed the first, which at least hit the outer ring of the circular target. *One.* Declan needed an apprentice.

She faced the curtain wall, jumped and back-somersaulted off the wall to shoot. She felt the thrum of the bow with her whole body. Better. Sometimes more complicated was better: it forced concentration. *Two.* She'd watched him work since she could toddle. She was like a child to him, the natural heir. Nobody knew the smithy and its processes better.

She smoothed a flight straight and nocked the arrow, concentrated, ran again, let fly. A clean split of the earlier arrow. Much better, even if it had spoiled a flight! *Three.* He would say she was a girl, not strong enough. She would quote him. 'You always said technique and attitude compensate for strength as you age. That's true about being a girl. If I can beat your superior strength in an archery contest – and you know I can – then you have to concede that being a girl is irrelevant!' He'd have to concede.

Her grip on the bow was making a ridge in her hand. She had to relax the tension but the cork target was boring. She needed a different challenge. She unlaced one boot, loosened it completely and wriggled her foot until she could free her foot in one movement. Then she breathed deeply, nocked a fourth arrow. She spun on the spot, aimed in the air and sidestepped, pinning her empty boot with the plummeting arrow. She inspected the hole. *Pff.* They were workboots. A Mender Mage could fix the hole in seconds. Declan could do it, though he'd scold her.

Four. She was eighteen and stuck in limbo, ridiculous among the other children, barred from adulthood. Apprenticeship was the rational way to continue her life. No, that sounded selfish. Apprenticeship was the best way for her to contribute to the Citadel for the rest of her life. Of course she wanted to be a master smith but for now, she just needed a start.

'Mielitta! That was won-won-wonderful.'

Was there no peace! One of the older children was gazing at her starry-eyed, her stutter identifying her straight away as Drianne, Mielitta's little shadow. Drianne was not the first to tail Mielitta, worshipping her skills, wanting to be like her. At first Mielitta had been flattered, years ago, after she'd lost the last friend of her own schooldays. But as each wave of children reached maturity, those who'd worshipped her most, blanked her most. She belonged in their past, their childhood. Their snubs hurt her more than the daily slights of her servant role. They always hit their target, drew blood.

So she kept her distance with each new cohort of children, played teacher but avoided names. They were just little ones. She could help them but they were passing through a phase in which she was doomed to stay forever. But that didn't stop her playing.

'Drianne.' Mielitta acknowledged the child. But only because she wanted something. Not because this child was any different from the others. 'Can you shoot from there?'

'Of c-c-course.' The girl waved her bow above her head, took an arrow from the quiver slung over her shoulder. Like all the little ones, she was a static shooter. Mielitta kept her quiver round her waist, held up to six arrows in her shooting hand, for rapid release while moving. When she'd finished for the day, she would shift the quiver to her shoulder for convenience – and to keep it within reach.

'Good girl! I'm going to count to three, and on three, I want you to shoot me. I'll catch your arrow and aim it at the target.'

Drianne was young enough to have absolute faith in her hero. She nocked her arrow, took Mielitta in her sights and waited.

'One, two, three!' called Mielitta, knowing that if the child fudged the shot she might well be hit. She felt the arrow coming, judged the half-step, the catch – right-handed – twirled, nocked and twang! Bull's-eye. The fifth arrow, Drianne's arrow, had arced true. She always knew when she'd loosed a perfect shot even before the clean *thunk* confirmed it. *Five*. This was the clincher. *Let me show you,* she told an imaginary Declan. *I will make a knife fit for a Battle-Mage. Damascene steel with magical wards inlaid. I will earn this apprenticeship.*

She'd pictured it so many times. When she'd helped in selecting the metals, in making the steel sandwich that would fold a score of times, then a score more, and again. When she'd looked at a tree-trunk, pointed out the flaw that would crack the knife handle, selected grain that ran beautiful and strong. When she'd even been allowed to turn the steel in the forge. All under Declan's supervision. Why would he have let her taste such work if he did not mean for her to pursue it further? Small hands clapped her from above.

'B-b-bravo!' yelled Drianne.

'I couldn't have done it without you.' Mielitta cursed herself for encouraging the girl. It was hard to remember why she should not. But if she succeeded with Declan – and how could she not? – she could permit herself such little pleasures in future. She would have status of her own.

Buoyed up at the thought, Mielitta crossed the courtyard of patterned cobblette, which cleaned itself as her boots passed over. The balance between magical and human maintenance had been established so many lifetimes earlier that only children wondered why there was any need to work at all. It was just how it was, that servants were tasked with the Citadel interior but the outer keep maintained itself. Apart from in the forge, where Declan and the labourers who wielded hammers worked with only the magecraft needed to brand magical wards into the weapons they made.

The forge was open, allowing some heat and smoke to escape. Fire, sweat, and the tang of metal all told Mielitta's nose *hot* and she braced herself as she entered the dark haven.

CHAPTER FOUR

Blinking from the contrast, too bright and too dark, fire and blackness, Mielitta could see the anvil's dark stone in the red glow of a cooling blade. Declan was of course at the centre of the action, beating and turning the future weapon on the anvil, talking to a youth beside him. Six brawny men swept filings and dust out of the way, where they could not stick to and spoil the fine metal in the making.

Declan was singing his song of making and Mielitta waited patiently, her heart rising and falling, thrumming with the song that had been a lullaby to her in her parentless childhood.

Finally a pause. The metal cooling on its stand, already showing patterns in blue, dull as tattoos. Until the final polish, Damascene steel hid its beauty and its power.

Declan's attention left the weapon and his face lit up, red in the forge-light. 'Mielitta, I'm so glad you've come today. I want you to meet Kermon, my new apprentice. I've finally found someone!'

The youth beside Declan held out a polite elbow, his hands being grimy, and Mielitta held it briefly. He beamed at her. 'My first day,' he announced.

'I-I-I thought,' stammered Mielitta, looking from Declan to

Kermon. *Damn! I sound like Drianne!* She took a deep breath and smiled. 'I thought so,' she told the apprentice. 'You don't know how lucky you are.'

'Oh I do,' he assured her.

'No, you really don't,' Mielitta grated.

Declan looked from one to the other. 'Is something wrong, Mielitta?'

There was no point. 'No, nothing. I just wish I could find something interesting to do for the rest of my life as a child.' It came out as petulant but it was the truth. And just when she thought she'd found something, it had been stolen from her.

Declan's brow furrowed in concern. 'Maybe you'll reach maturity next year. If not, we could petition the Ten for a special role for you. There must be something you could do.'

'You think so?' Mielitta let the bitterness show.

'Yes, I do.' Declan answered the words not the sarcastic tone. 'And you know you're always welcome here. You can join in, the same way you always have.'

'I'd like that,' Kermon told her. His expression was as open as his words. He wiped smuts across his face and smeared it blacker as he smiled, teeth whitened by their dark setting. Toned muscles were a smith's stock-in-trade and the firelight outlined his to advantage but Mielitta was in no mood to appreciate her usurper's attractions.

'I can't stay,' she lied. 'Just dropped in to see what you were working on.' She turned and fled, before she cried in front of Declan and his new apprentice.

Might as well prove what a complete fool I am, she told herself, brushing tears roughly from her cheek. They had no business to fall without her say-so. She didn't like crying.

The day won't be any worse for me finding that a hole in a wall is just a hole in a wall, she decided. She marched along the passageways between the north and east towers until she reached the section she could see in her mind's eye. In that, at least, she was not mistaken, and it was easy for her to identify the stone in front of the cachette. It was just as easy to roll the stone out, feel in the dark for an invisible bag.

Seriously, Mielitta! she mocked herself. She shut her eyes, the better to squeeze back those uncontrollable tears and then she felt it, a soft oddness at first that became firmer, became unmistakeably a drawstring bag. Still with her eyes shut in case it should disappear if she opened them, she loosened the strings, let the contents escape.

Her head pounded as the memories flooded back. She remembered every word, every action of the Council meeting. Traitor, tests, history in walls, war… all the treasonous detail returned to her mind. Two words hammered at her as if six brawny men were working her into forged steel: *Forest* and *password*. The Councillors had discussed the unmentionable as if asking for a biscuit. And she knew the password to the water gate, to get to the Forest!

'Freak,' yelled a voice by her ear, laughing as she jumped. Bastien. She'd been so deep in her memory of the night before that she hadn't noticed them coming, and now she was surrounded. Behind Bastien, Jannlou blocked the passage in one direction and the rest of the gang blocked even the light in the other direction.

As if a mage had read her thoughts, a light-sphere flared on the wall behind her. The walls had kept her memory: maybe they would help? But she sensed nothing in the stone. She was on her own.

The light-sphere showed up her escape routes but it also sent mad, dark shadows gleeful on Bastien's face. Spite personified. As he leaned towards her, Mielitta folded her arms across her breast in instinctive protection, her hands gripping her own shoulders. He was so close, she could see a terrified Mielitta doll reflected in each dilated pupil and smell his excitement. Dark, vicious, sweat and sewage.

'This should be fun, boys. Just what you were hoping for, Jannlou.'

As if she were a prize, being presented to the shiny black-haired double of his powerful father. Mielitta shuddered as she recalled Crimvert's death. Jannlou's teeth gleamed between bared lips.

'Perfect,' he growled.

Bastien's moment of crowing was long enough for Mielitta to grab the only weapon she had. She stretched over her shoulder and took an arrow from the quiver. Bastien had leaned so far over to intimidate her, that his weight was supported by his hands against the wall, either side of where she was standing.

In one fluid stoop, she jabbed the tip of the arrow into his thigh. He lost his balance and screamed at the pain as she jerked the arrow back and pushed past him. She had no time to wonder how much louder Bastien could have screamed if she'd misjudged the stab. If it had gone in below the skin, she'd have had to leave her precious arrow or maim him seriously with the barb. Tempting though the thought was, she hadn't misjudged and the flesh would heal as soon as Jannlou applied magecraft.

Jannlou. There he was, black in her path, her only escape route. She kept up her momentum, relying on the shock of the moment to spur her past him – and on the arrow in her hand, ready for a second strike. She jabbed – and nothing happened. Jannlou's blue eyes danced with devil-light. She felt his mage's power as she side-charged his body, unable to use her hands at all.

'*Aiee*,' he shrieked, hopping on one leg.

'Bastard!' she muttered.

'You have no idea,' he whispered, bending as if in pain. She paused, met his eyes as he straightened. Sad, not triumphant. And she hadn't touched him with her arrow, however hard he rubbed his leg.

She rushed onwards down the passage, the scent of Jannlou filling her head. Earth, night, peaty darkness, trees, the Forest. Why did the Forest come to mind?

They would be after her as soon as Jannlou had healed himself and Bastien, mere minutes for one with his powers, so Mielitta must run. Not just run *from* but run *to*. Her feet were taking her inexorably to the water gate and she knew the password. Her life was endless humiliation and she couldn't bear one more day. The Forest was out there. What did she have to lose?

Down and ever dampwards, she ran. Footsteps echoed behind her. Gaining? Or was that a trick of the walls, whichever side they might be on today. They glistened, leaving a wet trace on her hand in a narrow passage. She stumbled on the uneven slippery stone. Historic stone, not mage-crafted cobblette. *Why don't the mages smooth the footing, if not the walls themselves? No time to wonder. Run!*

A prick of light and the sound of gushing water told her she was nearly there. She slowed along the treacherous path between the wall on her right and a water conduit gurgling on her left. Jannlou and Bastien would have to follow in single file if they came this far and, though faster and stronger in any race, they were clumsier than she was on difficult terrain.

She trailed her hand along the wall as she walked. It shimmered where water trickled down, glittered where mineral traces teased the light. She could see the path end now, in solid wall.

'There's no way out! We've got her!' came a triumphant shout, bounced by the walls into a dozen fiendish versions of Bastien's words.

'Agh!' Someone must have slipped.

'Careful!' Jannlou cautioned, after the event.

Careful! The word rebounded, softened in its travels, a whispered warning to Mielitta. She shook her head to clear the strange thought. She wouldn't put it past Jannlou to use glamour in tracking her. She'd seen his power put to that use with many a new woman, flirting her skirts at the Chief Mage's son. Mielitta believed herself immune but then, perhaps all Jannlou's conquests believed likewise.

She'd reached the curtain wall. She could feel the boundary wards that kept everyone in the Citadel protected. Beside her, water rushed in under the iron gate, a bright rectangle behind it. And behind that, the unknown.

Mielitta had only to say the password and – and what? And

the wards would allow her through, obviously. But how? Could she pass through a wall? She reached out, touched the stone in front of her and felt its solid denial. Through the water gate? It was a gate after all. But what if she was thrown into the water? She couldn't swim.

'I think I see her!' She hadn't been imagining the ring of boots and metal clanking, closing in on her. There was no choice any more.

She stepped out as far as she could onto a horizontal strut of the gate and clung to the slippery metal, while water poured beneath her, spraying upwards. She swallowed a mouthful, the tasteless liquid of her humdrum life. *Protected,* she thought. *Here, I am protected*.

'Radium,' she pronounced and the gate shimmered from solid black metal to a wavering rainbow. She stepped through.

CHAPTER FIVE

S he stepped through the rainbow gate onto a flat stone in the middle of a stream. The water split spray into a million rainbows, blinding her so that she had to squint to see the stepping stones that took her to the bank and dry land.

Once out of danger from the rushing water, Mielitta was attacked by heat and light, blazing at her from a fireball in the blue overhead. *Sun,* she thought. *Sky.* Trying not to panic, she recited book-words to match the world beyond the Citadel. Then she was attacked from the ground, green spikes prickling her legs. Tiny things with legs. *Grass. Insects.*

The words could not protect her from the assault on all her senses and the instinct to run took over. It was too much. She ran away from the dazzle, towards shade, towards things that made shade. *Trees.*

Beneath a tree, Mielitta took her quiver from her shoulder and doubled up, panting, her heart racing as after a training bout. As soon as the stitch had passed, she hooked the quiver to her belt, nocked an arrow, waited. If Jannlou and the others came through the gate, she would be ready. No doubt he'd have the password or could get it from his father, if he wanted.

Reassured by the familiar feel of her bow, she watched, tracing the route taken by the stream. The water burbled across a pebble bed through the grassland she had crossed, to the Citadel wall, where it seemed to disappear. No gate was apparent but it was a relief to Mielitta that the Citadel was visible from this side of the wall. As was the bubble above it. The canopy that the rebel Councillor, Crimvert, spoke of, no doubt, protecting the Citadel inhabitants from sun. Or from any other wildness in the sky. Mielitta racked her book memories. *Snow. Rain. Hail. Desert dust.*

She shivered despite the heat. It had been folly to leave the Citadel. She must get back inside and cover up her transgression. A stripe of sunshine reached her arm through the canopy of trees. *A different, less effective canopy.* The shadows were moving, growing shorter, which must mean that time had passed, with no sign of her aggressors. She should go back.

She unnocked her bow, slung it over her shoulder, braced herself and stepped into the fierce heat again. This time, she was ready for the uncontrolled warmth playing on her skin, tickling. She laughed. She need not fear the sun.

She made her way back to the stream, listening to the music of water on pebbles, a song she had never heard. She sat down to listen better, on a comfortably rounded rock, safely above the prickle of grass blades. This was a song like book poetry, not like the schoolroom songs which praised the Citadel and promoted good citizenship, with a side-nod to hygiene and reproduction.

Her exertions in the heat had made her thirsty and, in defiance of the schoolroom songs, she scooped up a handful of unpurified water, losing trickles between her fingers as she drank.

As she sipped, she paused to marvel and drank again. Bubbles burst on her tongue like a liquid giggle. Then the water told its history, from snow-capped mountains through forests and meandering pasture, to this small diversion from a mighty river.

The water told its geology, from glacial tarns through limestone pavements and hard bedrock, picking up a tang of calcite or magnesium, a glitter of gold, en route.

Then the water told its wildlife. Silver-scaled fish, seething jellies of tadpoles and slithers of eels. This and more, Mielitta could taste in her scoop of water, as she watched a turquoise glitter of tiny wings over the water. *Dragonfly.*

She wanted these pleasures again but when she scooped and tasted a second time, the story was different. How could that be? Did one change of pebble, one shadow over the sun, change the taste of water? It must be so. The sadness of change, of death, and the glory of a new adventure, in two scoops of water. She should go back.

But she was already outside the Citadel. The sun was not to be feared, the stream was shallower than she'd thought, grass blades did not pierce her skin. The Forest could be named and it was just – trees. She'd stood beside one and felt no harm. She should at least explore a little while she was here. She could go back later, when she could be sure it was safe. Maybe Jannlou and Bastien were just inside the gate, waiting for her as she had waited for them. Let them wait!

Mielitta marched back across the grass to her first tree. She studied the bark, its vertical furrows. She knew this wood from the Citadel fires but now she saw it alive for the first time. In the Citadel it burned fast and erratic. Did it live that way too? The leaves all followed the same form, edged with tiny teeth, curving to a curly point. The same type but each one different. Mage-made objects were not like this. She ran her tongue along a leaf. She didn't like the taste. She tore a tiny strip of bark in her fingernail, chewed on its bitterness and felt her mouth frothy. How did you know what you could eat in the Forest?

The next tree was different in kind. The Forest offered Mielitta as many different trees as the stream had offered scoops of water. She felt dizzy with infinite opportunities. *Too much* she told herself again.

If she were not to spend her lifetime studying three trees, she must block her senses, gain a broader impression of life outside the Citadel. She forced herself to walk more quickly, deeper into the Forest, ignoring the distraction of trees.

Eyes were more difficult to ignore. Blinking, flashing, hiding, gone before she could say *bird, fox, rabbit.* Knowing only words and pictures, she could only guess that strong stink was *fox* and the branch rustling was *bird.* What if something wanted to eat her? Even if she moved quietly, as she had learned, her banana scent must be alien to Forest creatures. And she'd drenched herself in it.

She shrugged. Human scent would be as alien as bananas, or worse. The parties of men who'd chopped firewood here must have smelled human and their acts would not have endeared men to the Forest.

The shadows seemed to grow darker, the trees taller, the canopy thicker. *Too dark.* She turned towards a part of the Forest where more light broke through the branches above and was relieved to reach a clearing.

Filtered by the high leaves, the sun striped the glade with green and gold, patterning bark with shadows and limning branches in haloes. Mielitta felt the ground vibrating gently, like a giant's snore, a sense of rightness.

She sniffed the air but found only the scents of composting earth, resin and roots, to which the Forest had already accustomed her. No eyes. Or at least, none she noticed.

On the opposite side of the clearing, a covered box was attached to a tree, the lid at Mielitta's shoulder-height. Its shape was fuzzy in an ever-changing black cloud and for a moment Mielitta felt her Citadel-bred fears return. *Pff.* She wouldn't have felt the sun, tasted the water or met her first tree if she believed all she'd been told as a child. There were many ways to become Mature and this would be her Ceremony, in the Forest. Even if nobody else knew, from today onwards she would be an adult, a new woman.

She tucked a strand of hair back under its snood. *Breeze,* she thought. The air smacked her cheek. *No, wind!* she corrected, as her banana scent was whipped into her nostrils.

She stepped into the clearing and heard the box hum. A happy, wordless worksong that matched the vibration underfoot. Like the thrum of an arrow shot true but sustained, no beginning and no end. She approached the box and could see now that the black cloud was made up of insects. So many! Flying into and out of the box, humming.

Was the humming inside the box louder? She thought it might be. What did they do inside the box that gave them this sense of purpose? She could feel it in the air, in the ground, in the trees. Purposeful humming.

She would just open the lid and peek inside. Then she must go back to Citadel before she was too late for the evening meal. She reached out and lifted the lid off the box.

She had time to see wax patterns and insects rushing upwards in the box before the insects' rage hit her in a roar that hurt her ears. Then the arrows hit her from below as the insects swarmed and flew at her, rank on rank. From above too, as the black cloud outside the box fired at her through the snood.

She started to run but the cloud stayed with her, surrounded her as her tired legs swelled, her head caught fire and she sank to the ground under a tree in the darkest part of the Forest, burning. She shook, sweated, felt the fire spread throughout her body like poison. *Bees,* she thought. And she died.

CHAPTER SIX

M ielitta didn't want to open her eyes. She could lie here forever, vibrating, vital, breathing the green scents of sap, moss; gold sacks of pollen; and – joy on the breeze – flower hearts ringed in colours she'd never seen before. *Ultraviolet*. Shades of ultraviolet, from yellowish to purple, opened nectar to her tongue. Then brown of fur hit her nose and her eyes snapped open, seeking the intruder. No furred beast. She raised herself onto her elbows, shaking a dense clump of dead insects from her thigh onto the Forest floor as she turned her head to check behind her. No threat.

She stood up, slowly, dizzy, and hundreds more tiny striped insects joined the piles on the ground, outlining the form where her body had lain. Dead bees. Their tiny darts were a cluster of black on her thigh and when she ran her fingers through her hair, she swept a shower of dark points onto the ground.

She repeated the sweeping motion over her hair and head until she no felt no prickles. She remembered the box, the bees' anger, pain from their stings; then she must have lost consciousness. Now, her body thrummed with barely-contained energy.

There must have been thousands of dead insects around her. They'd left their stings in her and died, fatally maimed. Poor bees.

They must have been terrified to be so angry. She began to hum gently, a dirge for the dead. The ground beneath her vibrated with her wordless song and, as she watched, first one bee, then dozens, began to change.

From striped amber and black to iridescence, each tiny corpse was transformed. Then it wavered into transparency and a final ultraviolet sweetness engulfed Mielitta's senses as the bees vanished. She touched a leaf where dead bees had been, the faintest trace of ultraviolet still lingering. *Passed,* she thought. *They have passed. But where to?*

She shook her head to clear the effects of bee venom but, apart from some strangeness in vision, which was clearing already, she felt normal. Better than normal, in fact. Any aches from archery practice and running into the Forest had disappeared, along with the scratches she'd accumulated. As had the visible effect of the bee-stings. Her skin had been covered with red, raised bumps and was now its usual smooth gold. Except on her thigh, where a dark patch remained. She shrugged. If that was the only harm from her adventure, she could count herself lucky.

The shadows had lengthened and changed direction. She must get home to the Citadel before the evening meal, so nobody would know what she'd done, guess where she'd been. But she'd run from the bees heedless of direction. Where was home? Around her each tree flaunted its difference and was no help. She had not marked her way and there were no paths in the Forest. She was going to die after all.

No, she was not. She had known and faced down panic many times over the years and she was not some Maturity-tested woman prone to hysterics. She breathed deeply, shut her eyes again, forced panic into an imaginary jar in her deep thinking and stoppered it so she couldn't hear panic-man shouting.

She'd decided in a very boring lesson on table service that the Citadel Steward was the personification of panic. Running around, shouting, 'We're all going to die!' was only a slight step up from 'Somebody's forgotten the goblets!' It always made her smile to see his gangling arms being folded into her mind-jar and to hear his last shriek of 'I knew this would happen!' before she shut him up. A smile conquered panic every time.

Where was home? She had to retrace her steps somehow. She conjured up the Citadel, the rainbow water gate, the stream, her first tree, the darkness of the deep Forest, the clearing and the bee box, her flight. Patterns shifted in her mind, like a geometric dance, lining up all the route markers she'd named in her thoughts and moving them until they settled into place. A map. Clear as ultraviolet arrows on trees.

Mielitta opened her eyes and saw only the same blank-faced trees. But this time she noticed the pattern of where they stood.

She shut her eyes again, saw the route she must take, and took a few steps forward. Opened and shut her eyes to confirm the shape and placement of the trees she must pass between. And she walked on.

In this manner, she followed an invisible path through the Forest, trusting her instincts. She moved more quickly as she gained confidence and could see the pattern of grasses, stones and trees with her eyes open.

'Beech,' she said, as she reached her first tree and the edge of the grassland, where blue harebells and pink campion commanded, *Look at me, drink my nectar, here.* They fluttered their invitations but she ignored the temptation. The sun had lost its heat but was still warm, edging the grass-blades with amber. She did stop for one last scoop of water, despite a flurry of foolish warning voices in her head.

Don't drown, don't drown!

As if she could drown in water as shallow as this! She'd have to be the size of a bee to worry about such a stream.

At the iron gate, she had to put panic-man firmly back in his jar. She'd traversed the gate once and she could do it again. She just had to think for a moment about what she would do when she reached the other side. Carefully, she walked across the stepping-stones to stand in front of the gate, the stream rushing around her and through the wards to the Citadel.

She reached out, held the gate firmly, pronounced, 'Radium.' When the gate shimmered to rainbow, she stepped through, without letting go, and swung her legs to the left to land firmly on the path. Everything was as she had left it, bar her pursuers, who must have long gone.

She retraced her steps up into the dry and into the Citadel. Grey was deepening through the windows so she still had time to change out of her bedraggled clothes before going to the Great Hall. If she cut across the courtyard, she could get to her chamber without going past Jannlou's usual haunts.

She unlatched a door, walked out onto the odourless green ground, which she scuffed deliberately. It mended itself immediately.

Fake grass. Grassette.

There were no shadows anywhere, just the optimum light for pre-evening, diffused through the canopy.

Fake light. Greylight. Mielitta scuffed the ground again.

She passed the empty practice-yard, without pausing. She kept her weapons in her chamber, close to hand, although, of course, she couldn't take them into the Great Hall, nor carry them during her servant's duties. In theory.

She couldn't help humming. If there had been words, the lyrics would have sung of the Forest, its cornucopia; of her fear and achievement. One of Tansies' sayings: without fear, where is the achievement? The Archery Mage would have been proud of her today. She sang of her maturity, for she was a woman now and had known her own testing; of her escape from the enemy. Her heart sang. And then she heard the unmistakable sound of a girl crying. And stammering.

Mielitta knew exactly where they would be. She knew all the

places where they cornered a victim. If she could hear them, then they were behind the practice-yard, in the barn where the equipment was kept. They'd have their choice of weapons, should their prey choose to fight, so running was usually the best escape option. But a twelve-year-old had no chance against a group of young men, at the peak of their fitness, with a mage for leader and an overdose of male hormones. Mielitta could smell the brash red testosterone and it offended her nose in its brutality.

Drianne cried out again but Mielitta knew that the Citadel was deaf to such an everyday occurrence. She crept up to the wooden side of the barn and listened, shutting her eyes to visualise where each person stood.

'You know where she is,' Bastien was saying, with pauses, as if he was prodding the girl. 'You follow her everywhere. You always know where she is.'

'I saw her g-g-go d-d-down, to the cellars, I think. But I cou-cou-couldn't follow because you d-d-did.' An involuntary cry of pain. The note of defiance had earned a blow.

'But you went down later, didn't you.'

'Yes.'

'And?'

'And I t-t-told you. She wasn't there and she didn't come up how she went d-d-down. She must have f-f-found a secret p-p-passage.'

A long pause.

'Maybe that's it.' Jannlou's voice. 'We've wasted long enough on all this. I'm bored. It's nearly time to go and eat.'

'Not yet.' Bastien's voice reeked unhealthy fervour. 'A worm to catch a fish, that's what we've got, like my father says. Now, girl, this is what you're going to do. You're going to ask the bitch nicely about her day and find out where that secret passage is, for the sake of our beloved Citadel. We can't have somebody spying, can we? Somebody knowing about a secret passage that even Jannlou here doesn't know.'

Drianne's reply was unintelligible but presumably vulgar

because one of the others stifled a laugh and Bastien's voice broke with rage. Mielitta heard steel unsheathed as he shouted, 'By the time you've f-f-finished spluttering, you'll find out exactly what I can do! What use is a tongue on a girl who can't speak and won't f–f–.'

Mielitta didn't wait for his last words but rushed to Drianne's defence, covering the final yards in a burst of superhuman speed. If it crossed her mind that an eighteen-year-old had little more chance than a twelve-year-old against this gang, she placed the thought firmly in a stoppered jar that was likely to become very crowded in the next few minutes.

Arrow in hand, she used the advantage of surprise to jab Bastien in the thigh but her assault merely increased the fury in his eyes. He did drop the girl, but from choice, so he could focus on Mielitta as Drianne crumpled to the ground.

'Padding,' he sneered. 'You don't get me that way a second time. Get her,' he ordered the others.

Then Mielitta smelled black, a throbbing cloud of fury that turned all the unfairness in her life to murderous intent. Enough hiding, enough running. An arrow in each hand, she moved as fast as a thousand bees, stinging Bastien everywhere he was not padded, starting with his poisonous mouth. Stabbing black darts into every pore of his skin until his fear hit her nostrils, acrid yellow, driving her berserk.

Then she turned on his friends.

She whirled and somersaulted as if flying, loosing her rage as a weapon in itself. Somewhere in that black cloud, a voice urged caution.

Defence, she was reminded.

'Don't kill them,' she muttered. 'Mustn't kill them.' Shaking with the internal struggle to control her darts, she stabbed just the skin surface, moving so fast they couldn't even see her coming. She mustn't jab too deep, mustn't kill but the urge was so strong she wanted to feel the barb catch and rip their enemy bodies apart.

'Run!' they screamed at each other and their fear turned the air acid green, bilious, feeding Mielitta's black cloud.

Only Bastien and Jannlou were left, standing over the girl who still cowered on the ground, hands over her head.

'Run, Jannlou,' Bastien yelled, distancing himself. 'She's insane. And she's using magecraft. It's forbidden! We can tell your father! We have witnesses!'

'No! We sort this ourselves,' Jannlou yelled back. 'How we've always done things.'

Bastien hesitated, arms flailing as if he fought off imagined bees. Then he shook his head and was gone.

Only Jannlou was left, hands by his side, no weapon drawn. Mielitta circled him, shifting her balance from one foot to the other, ready, humming a throaty battle song.

He just looked at her. Blue eyes with silver flecks, purple rings, like a pansy. His sweat strengthened the brown solidity exuded by his warrior's trained body. *Mage glamour,* she reminded herself.

She should finish this. Kill him. Why not? No witnesses now. Except Drianne and she would support anything Mielitta said. She deserved this death, sweet little soul. Drianne looked up at her, eyes pleading.

'Don't hurt me,' she said. And she was pleading with Mielitta. The knowledge was a bucket of cold water over Mielitta's fury but Drianne was just a child and this fight was between adults.

Shaking, still shifting in readiness, Mielitta was between battle-blaze and conscience, waiting for Jannlou to force her next move.

He stood stock still. 'You said, *Don't kill them,*' he reminded her.

She held his gaze. Blue, silver, purple. 'Go,' she told him.

'Truce?' he asked.

'You could call it that.' He nodded, turned his back on her and walked slowly away. She was suddenly very tired. She sat on the ground beside Drianne, took her in a hug, ignored the instinctive flinch.

'I would never hurt you,' she said.

Drianne gave way to a child's sobs against her shoulder, mumbling, 'I l-l-love you.' A child indeed.

Mielitta sighed and squeezed the girl. 'Love you too.' She threw the expected response back, staccato, embarrassed, not meaning it. It was just something you said, wasn't it.

'And I wouldn't kill them,' she told Drianne. This reassurance came out with more conviction but, in the heat of battle, she hadn't meant the men. She'd meant she mustn't kill the bees, who were now part of her, who could not leave their stings beneath the surface and live. So neither could she. *It wasn't you, I cared about,* she told an imaginary Jannlou. *It was my bees.*

CHAPTER SEVEN

Mielitta sat on her bed with her eyes shut, replaying the fight. Just recalling Bastien's attack on Drianne made her body vibrate with the rage of a thousand bees, the power of a thousand darts. Bastien had accused her of unlicensed magecraft and she knew it must be true. She could never have moved so quickly, stabbed with such skill and judgement, without powers she didn't have. Or rather didn't have this morning, when she'd escaped Bastien and Jannlou with two all-too human jabs. She shook off her doubts that she'd touched Jannlou at all – she must have done for him to squeal.

What if the magecraft in her fight had been somebody else's? What if she'd been a channel for a seam of raw power, Drianne maybe? Too young to realise what was in her blood and completely untrained? She would certainly have helped Mielitta if she could. Untrained herself, Mielitta could only guess how magecraft worked from observations of the Councillors, and they worked mostly in secret. Maybe Drianne could only support someone else, not act to her own advantage.

If Mielitta had been a channel for magecraft, there was another possibility. There *had* been an acknowledged mage present. Jannlou was behaving strangely these days. But why would he expend power, against the law, to defend her and Drianne against himself and his own gang? That made no sense.

She briefly considered some random spill of magecraft from a Councillor or lesser mage, that had coincidentally affected her, but her head buzzed with annoyance at this train of thought. She scratched at her thigh.

You know the truth. Own it.

She opened her eyes, looked at the chest to the left of the bed, at the arrow-slit window to her right, in front of her where a small sampler with her name in faded cross-stitch hung on the wall. She had to turn her head to see in each different direction. But immediately after the bees' attack, she'd seen differently. Her peripheral vision had doubled, colours had changed. The effects had faded but she could remember the flowers by the stream, blue and purple instead of yellow, with ultraviolet rings. There was no ultraviolet in the Citadel and she missed it. She found the Citadel drab and lacklustre. Since she'd visited the Forest, she saw differently.

She sniffed and felt a vestige of rage at a lingering trace of banana coming from the empty bottle. Using her discarded shirt to protect her hand from the repellent odour, she placed the phial back in its box and closed the lid. Her heartbeat settled as she smelled only cut balsam wood, from the box itself.

The scroll had fallen onto the floor and she sniffed, cautious, but it smelled neutral, of green ink and rag-paper. Natural pine wood, and paper, she noted, not paperette.

When the bottle is empty, you will be full.
No life ends while The One lives.
In the year of the prophecy, choose well.

She crumpled up the meaningless words. The bottle was certainly empty now and she couldn't believe she had ever put such a vile scent on her body. No doubt that's what had provoked the bees to attack her. She reached up to feel her head but the snood was long gone and her hair was loose. She remembered the way the bees targeted her hair and she felt reluctant to replace the snood with another like it. Her old one must be somewhere in the Forest, an anomaly, a Citadel fabrication among the mossy tree-trunks. Metal threads, she remembered, standard servant wear. From now on, she'd braid her hair with simple ribbons, keep her appearance understated, but it was going to take more than that to avoid drawing attention to herself.

Bastien would not rest until he exposed her latest freak show to the Council, whatever Jannlou said about settling matters among themselves. Mielitta plaited her long red hair and ferreted in the chest for clean clothes while her thoughts raced. And buzzed. She shook her head but the buzzing only increased as she fought to breathe.

Through the panic, she sensed a whiff of lavender, took a breath, calmed. This was too big, too crazy to fit in her panic jar but she did her best. Fear made bad decisions and she had much to consider.

It's only us, soothed the voices.

'Yes,' she said. 'That's the problem.'

What would Magaram do to her if she was right? If he knew she'd not only been to the Forest but brought thousands of spirit bees back inside her, with wild powers?

She drew hose on, tied her bootlaces, analysed events as if this impossible idea was a mere fact, like having two feet, not a reason to shut her eyes and scream. If the bees were dead, why did she have to be careful not to kill them when fighting? Why should she not let darts penetrate below the skin?

You know why, the voices in her head told her, a gentle hum that she was already getting used to.

'Hive mind,' Mielitta said aloud. This was not the solution to her loneliness she'd ever imagined would come along, but she undoubtedly had company. Bees in her bonnet.

She laughed, a bitter taste. Then she stowed her bow and arrows under the bed, grateful for the wards on her chamber door which meant only she could enter. Designed to prevent unautho-rised fertilisation, the magical barrier incidentally offered a safe place to the occupant – and her hidden belongings.

In her chamber, Mielitta could think, without looking over her shoulder for the next threat. Her bonnetful of bees stayed respect-fully quiet while she considered her immediate problems and her options. They all boiled down to one imperative. She must become ordinary, draw no attention, hold no interest. In the Citadel, there could only be one path to this goal. After all, she had become Mature today, so this was a logical consequence. Drianne would be bitterly disappointed in her but then, Drianne would become ordinary in her turn – and stay safe. She would find somebody else to l… l… Mielitta forced herself to use mockery as cruel as Bastien's. She knew it wasn't possible to care about little ones. They grew up.

The Council of Ten – of Nine, Mielitta corrected herself – sat on their dais at the High Table. Off-duty servants sat together on what could be called a lowly table at the end of the Great Hall near the draughts from the door. Almost a breeze, Mielitta thought as she sipped her insipid water, ate her sustenance and smelled only humans, overlaid with the tarry pong of the soap they all used. At least none of these scents aroused the rage of bees. She wasn't sure she could control the black waves of fury in a fight that was theirs, not hers.

She was taller by a head than any others at her table, all of them pre-maturity. Adults did not serve, unless you counted the Stewards and Cook, who managed all service activities, from waiting at table to cleaning. Mielitta ran through a mental list of the people she must speak to the next day, and in which order. Then she would return to the Forest. She spiked a clump of moist-ened white crumbs on her fork, raised it and swallowed, as did everybody else on her table, everybody else in the Hall. *Raise, swallow, breathe, eat, drink, live. No, not live. Exist. This is merely existence.*

Drianne was at the far end of the table, alternately flushed and white-faced, avoiding Mielitta's eye, silent. *Good. The distance begins. All the better for us both.*

The Council members had finished their meals at the High Table, served first as always, and stood up, as if to leave. *No speeches today then. Thank the stones.*

But they didn't leave. They changed places, leaving the empty seat beside Magaram unfilled. Mielitta shivered as she remembered why the seat was empty. *Beware, the mage who fills Crimvert's place.* And unfortunately there *were* going to be speeches.

'Sad loss… esteemed colleague… Crimvert.' If you hadn't watched Magaram reduce his esteemed colleague to a heap of ash and blow the remains into the fireplace, the eulogy would have been quite touching. Mielitta tried to concentrate but it had been a long day and she drifted into a half-doze.

'Cheer!' she was told, the instruction accompanied by a fierce elbow in her ribs. She'd survived in the Citadel long enough to get the message and join in, jumping to her feet and cheering with the rest of her table, all good citizens, while trying to figure out what in the stones' name they were all celebrating.

Waving her arms with joy, she looked at the High Table. Ten, she counted. The seat had been filled by somebody clasping Magaram's hands, pumping them up and down. The Council was ten again, which was of little interest to her, however much she joined in the shouting.

A Councillor for each seat and some rearrangement so that the new man was promoted from outside Council directly to Shenagra's right hand. Very nice for him. Ah – this was new. Two men hovered on the edge of the dais, also pumping hands and being congratulated. They turned to face the Hall, hands clasped modestly in front of their grey apprentice mage robes, and Mielitta suddenly felt that her arms were waving too much, high above the younger servants around her. She dropped her arms, crouched a little but the two men's gazes seemed to find her, to linger.

'Our Apprentice Mages,' announced the mage tasked with speaking above the noise, using speechcraft to be heard.

Mielitta didn't need to be told the names of the two Apprentice Mages. 'Bastien and Jannlou,' she breathed.

'Do you know them?' A little one beside her beamed up. 'They're so cool!'

'Yes,' sufficed. Then Mielitta added, 'I didn't think Bastien had much magecraft?'

'Oh yes. He's been training with Jannlou for ages now and he is a,' the little one grew round-eyed as he reported the gossip he barely understood. 'A Late Starter. I might be a late starter too,' he confided.

'Probably,' Mielitta replied absent-mindedly. 'And the new Councillor? Do you know him?' she asked, unable to identify the man who swirled his dark cloak amid a tableful of congratulations.

Shocked at her ignorance, her neighbour enlightened her. 'Mage Rinduran.'

She must have looked blank.

He sighed. 'Bastien's father.'

Of course. She looked at father and son, clasping hands in congratulations. 'Another late starter,' she murmured. 'But I have a feeling they're both going to catch up very quickly.'

Bastien's gaze searched the hall again, stopping once more at the back, near the door. He had no need now to report her to Jannlou's father. He had his own ear in the Council.

'I don't feel well,' Mielitta whispered and, crouching to be less conspicuous, she slipped out of the door. But she felt Bastien's gaze follow her all the way to her chamber.

CHAPTER EIGHT

Mielitta woke with a sense of purpose for the first time in her eighteen years. Today she would lay the trail and tomorrow she would become invisible. For years she had carried messages and observed the children as they were selected for the Maturity Ceremony. Now she would use that knowledge.

She would have to miss archery practice in the yard, not only today but from now on. That would be one of many activities she could only continue outside the Citadel, in her other life. But all that Tannlei had taught her of mental discipline was part of her deep thinking and nobody could take that away from her.

What was that story Tannlei had told her, about going into battle? 'Imagine you need a companion on a difficult mission. Who do you choose?' Of course, Mielitta had chosen the wrong ones from the options Tannlei described. She'd been very keen on the one willing to wrestle a tiger with his bare hands and found it hard to understand that someone who would go to his death without hesitation was not the best choice. Instead she should value someone who was fearful, planned well and would achieve what he or she set out to do. Today, she felt she could fit that description exactly, so she hoped Tannlei had been right.

First, the clothes. She slipped her underthings on automatically and noticed that there was still a dark patch on her thigh from the cluster of bee-stings. Strange. Her head didn't feel different – on the outside at least – and she'd taken far more venom in her head. Some allergic reaction on her thigh, she guessed. She scratched and raised a small weal before she realised what she was doing. It would never heal if she kept picking at it. She sighed. At least it didn't show beneath her clothes.

She donned britches and shirt, reluctantly left her weapons in place – her enemies were rarely out of the mages' tower before the afternoon. Whether they practised magecraft or slept in a stupor, she neither knew nor cared. What mattered was that she could traverse most of the Citadel without looking over her shoulder or carrying her bow. Today, she must change her ways.

She left the security of her chamber, assumed the servant's stoop she used to disguise her age and to avoid eye contact. She didn't need ultraviolet maps to find her way round the Citadel and she was glad of peace in her head. The day would be tricky enough without contributions from the hive mind.

She turned left, right, climbed a set of spiral stairs, took the passage towards the eastern tower, where the domestic artisans worked fabric craft: carpenter, shoemaker and seamstress. Some were mages, like Declan, using a combination of traditional skill and magecraft, and among these was the seamstress.

The door to Mage Fabrisse's atelier was open and at first Mielitta thought the designer was elsewhere. All she could see were two piles of material: unrolled bales of pastel dress satinette and of dun leatherette.

'What? What?' The sharp query came from underneath some pink fabric. With a heave and scrabble, Fabrisse's head popped up in a swathe of gown-to-be.

Mielitta looked at the ground, practising humility, which she knew would mean life or death later on. This was the easy part.

'May the stones be with you, Mage Fabrisse,' she began. 'Mage Puggy has need of one maturity dress for a ceremony tomorrow and she apologises for the short notice.' Fabrisse's eyebrows had drawn together in a thundercloud so Mielitta added hastily, 'She said only an artisan of your talents could respond to this exceptional situation.'

'Exceptional?' Fabrisse cocked her head to one side, like a tiny wren Mielitta had seen in the Forest, curious.

'My mistress said you must tell nobody but...' Fabrisse leaned greedily towards the pause, no doubt savouring the prospect of gossip.

Mielitta whispered, 'There will be only one child in a special ceremony, to be kept secret because she is such a *late starter*.' The words were breathed rather than spoken. 'And there must be no suggestion that starting late is *inferior* so this Maturity Ceremony should be done without any fuss. Just one more new adult, appropriately dressed, behaving as she should, as quickly as possible.'

Mielitta resumed her usual robotic messenger's tones. 'Mage Puggy said I was to wait until the gown is ready. And that she would deny this conversation if you were foolish enough to speak of it. End of message.'

Fabrisse's mouth was as round as her eyes. She stood up, leaning on a silver-handled cane to do so. She pushed the waves of fabric away from her feet until she stood in an empty circle of cobblette flooring.

'Size?' she asked.

'Extra extra large,' Mielitta replied steadily. Compared with the children, she should probably add another 'extra'. If she'd been younger, normal, this would have been a sweet moment. She was watching her ceremonial dress being made, a little girl's dream in satinette, her future expressed in a swish and a flounce. But the last of her little girl's dreams had been dashed years ago and this was merely part of the pretence that would keep her alive. Mage Fabrisse could pirouette and twirl but however pretty her magecraft, she was the enemy.

The Seamstress Mage ran the cane in a circle round her body, faster and faster, picking up some lavender fabric as it swirled, shaping a gown with bodice and loose sleeves, using herself as a tailor's dummy. As the dress gained form, Fabrisse lost hers, until she was no longer in the circle but following her bright cane in a swirl outside the new garment. She prodded with her cane, a dart here, a tuck there, laces, and the dress grew taller, cinched tighter than the Fabrisse-shape had been.

'That should do.' Fabrisse had beads of sweat on her forehead, was leaning heavily on a cane dull and immobile as its mistress. 'Take it and go now.'

Mielitta felt a pang of guilt as the seamstress hobbled to a seat by the window but she folded the gown over her arm. *Lavender. Flower-coloured. If only it had the scent too.*

'Thank you,' she said but the profile could have been stone in the misty window-light as Fabrisse looked down on the archery courtyard, her knuckles white on the cane.

Next, the Maturity Mages, Puggy and Yacinthe.

With the gown still draped over her arm as validation, Mielitta retraced her steps and headed for the mages' quarters near the schoolroom. She knocked politely on the fourth door, half expecting another 'What? What?' response but the door merely swung open.

'Enter,' she was told and she felt a frisson as the barrier ward on the sill allowed her to stretch it for three paces into the chamber before she was held fast. Mage Puggy was sitting in front of a three-sided mirror, stroking her beautiful face smooth and creamy. She didn't turn around, merely looked at Mielitta's reflection in the mirror, assessed her visitor's importance and returned her attention to her own face.

'You may speak,' she instructed.

'May the stones be with you, Mage Puggy.' Mielitta studied the floor. 'Mage Yacinthe wishes you to know of a Maturity Ceremony she is holding tomorrow but prefers to go unnoticed and unmentioned because the new adult is a late starter.' This time she delivered the message with no innuendoes, just a subtle shifting of the gown on her arm, to ensure it was noticed. The Maturity

Mages were sharp enough politically to understand all that was not said.

Puggy applied rouge to her parted lips then nodded. 'Tell her she is wise.' She turned to look briefly at Mielitta and immediately took on her everyday misglamour, looking as she had during the Council meeting: bad skin, dull eyes and lank hair.

Mielitta sniffed. The mage still emitted her unique bouquet. Scarlet, roses, danger and a drop of blood. Why would she hide her sensuality behind such a frumpy appearance? Or was it the beauty that was mage glamour, to be indulged only in privacy? There was no understanding mages or their craft but she was never going to fall for mere glamour. Never.

The door wards pressed Mielitta backwards, which she understood to mean she was dismissed. She had barely whisked every scrap of the gown's bulk into the passageway when the door swung closed behind her.

'And thank you too,' she murmured to the blank solidity of the door, then she resumed her humble expression and knocked on the second door along the passage.

This occupant opened the door herself, peered at Mielitta, then into the gloom either side of her, then pulled her into the chamber, stretching the door wards a good five paces.

'I'm so glad you've come,' gushed Mage Yacinthe. 'I don't know what to do. What to do.' Her round face wrinkled under its tight black curls. 'It's an honour, of course. I suppose. But I don't even like books and Mage Crimvert had a gift for that sort of thing… that is, not that I want to justify… not that anything could excuse… and, well, here I am babbling away when you've brought me the advice I asked from Shenagra.'

'Ah, yes.' Mielitta cleared her throat. Did she dare involve Shenagra in her web of lies? There seemed to be no choice but she tried to buy some time to think. 'Mage Puggy also has a message for you that offers a solution to your dilemma.' She rushed on. 'Mage Puggy wants you to know she's holding an emergency

Maturity Ceremony tomorrow but wants it to go unnoticed and unmentioned because the new adult is a late starter.'

Mage Yacinthe frowned even harder, clearly so troubled by her own dilemma that she was deaf to the finer nuances of Mielitta's news. 'I don't understand,' she said slowly, and Mielitta's heart sank. She couldn't suddenly seem wise regarding the Citadel politics, after her staccato delivery of the message. Should she just repeat it, hope the words sank in? And how was she going to think up a message from Shenagra regarding the unknown problem with hated books? She shook out the dress in front of her and settled it on her other arm.

'That's a big dress,' commented Mage Yacinthe. Mielitta said nothing, watched the cogs turn and prayed to all the stone gods she had ever heard of.

'Big dress, late starter...' Then the penny dropped. 'Oh my my, celebrating late starters won't do at the moment, no indeed. That would be taken as satirical. And we must all be so careful now. He came from nowhere, just a minor mage, but so strong in magecraft. He must have been hiding it, which isn't good, not good at all. And to put his son in my place! Well! No, we don't want to make a thing about late starters, indeed we don't. Such bad timing. Mage Puggy is very wise, very wise.' She nodded enough to set her chins wobbling, then stopped abruptly.

'But how does Shenagra think this will help me find a librarian and avoid me giving offence to Mage Rinduran by refusing this wonderful promotion?'

Mielitta felt as if she were on a high wire over the archery yard, doomed if she mis-stepped. 'Mage Shenagra said this new adult loves books,' she tested.

Yacinthe brightened, then gloomed again. 'But they're all so stupid after the Ceremony.'

Yes, I've noticed. 'Ah but this one's a late starter. That makes things different.' Softly, softly, so as not to put a foot wrong.

'I see! So she'll still have enough wits about her to catalogue the books, care for them, check who visits the library, all that boring stuff, even though she's suitably docile?'

'Exactly,' Mielitta replied, striving to keep the neutral tones of a mere messenger and not to grit her teeth. *Docile!*

'But what about me? I can't refuse the new mage. What does Shenagra suggest?'

This was a bit trickier and Mielitta spoke slowly, as if recalling the words entrusted to her. 'Of course, Mage Shenagra cannot speak of this directly, ever…'

'I understand completely!'

'But if you accept your new role with suitable gratitude…'

'Oh.'

That was a dangerous step but Mielitta saw no option. She'd be revealed if she promised the impossible. 'For now, Mage Shenagra said. For now.'

'Ah.'

'And let the Maturity Ceremony be directed by–' Mielitta left enough of a pause for Yacinthe to fill the gap.

'That little shit Bastien!'

That wasn't the answer Mielitta had expected but she swallowed her agreement in silence. So, Bastien was the son taking Yacinthe's place, as his father moved into prominence from obscurity. Quite a family coup. Not good news for her, either. Her plan *had* to succeed.

She continued, 'Your new adult will ensure the smooth running of the library under the title of Assistant Librarian. No mage could object to that and none bar Mage Shenagra and Mage Puggy will realise that she is competent to do all that is required. You will be free to continue your work with Mage Puggy *unofficially* and to keep an eye on Apprentice Mage Bastien.'

Yacinthe worked it all out in her mind, tried to think of a better alternative but couldn't. Acceptance smoothed her face again.

'It might be best.' She sighed. 'For now. With things as they are. What's the new adult's name?'

Mielitta didn't miss a beat. 'Assistant Librarian,' she told the mage.

'Good, good. Thank Mage Shenagra for sending her messenger, and Mage Puggy. You may go.' Yacinthe was watching her with sudden cunning, the same watchfulness she'd shown after opening the door. What was she watching for? Mielitta was supposed to be Shenagra's messenger.

Then she remembered what Shenagra did to servants who knew too much.

She did not go. She allowed her face to go blank for a long minute.

'Did you want something, Mage Yacinthe?' she asked brightly. 'I was passing after receiving instructions from Mage Puggy, when I heard your summons.'

Yacinthe beamed. 'So precise when she cleans,' she murmured. 'Yes, would you bring me a large pot of tea and some biscuits after you've delivered the gown.'

'At once, Mage.' Mielitta closed the door behind her, walked a few doors further along and waited for Shenagra's messenger at the only access to the mages' quarters.

It was easy enough to identify as the chosen one the lad who'd escorted her to the Council Chamber. He detached himself from the school-going little ones, his self-importance as puffed as his britches, and continued along the passage, towards Mielitta, and Mage Yacinthe's chamber.

'Mage Shenagra told me to intercept you,' Mielitta said to him, then remembered how young he was. All this politics was hard to keep straight! 'To stop you,' she explained. 'She added something to your message and sent me instead.'

He looked dubious – and disappointed.

'The message about the librarian,' she prompted.

'About accepting it for now but the time will come for upstart Rinduran and his Bastien son you mark my words,' he rattled off, then put his hand over his mouth. 'I probably shouldn't have said all that except to Mage Yacinthe.

'No,' agreed Mielitta, 'you probably shouldn't but it doesn't matter because I already knew.' And guessed close enough, she thought smugly, with the small addition of an Assistant Librarian. And now some more guessing was required.

'Please say thank you to Mage Shenagra,' she told the boy but his face stayed bright and open.

Of course, no mage would say please to a servant! 'Thank Mage Shenagra,' she ordered and his eyes shuttered, his little face frozen, not long enough to notice unless you knew what to look for. Then, it was unmistakeable. His memory had been cleaned.

'I'm off to get tea for Mage Yacinthe,' Mielitta told the boy brightly.

'I have to do schoolwork now,' he replied. 'May Perfection guide our footsteps.'

'In Perfection we trust,' replied Mielitta.

The boy trotted back to the schoolroom, not questioning why he had gone right past it in the first place.

No more schoolroom. No more service with the other children. The Assistant Librarian was going to spend her last day of childhood in the forge, relaxing after a hard morning's deceit.

CHAPTER NINE

Smoke! Fire! Hide!

Mielitta stood petrified on the threshold of the forge, her head fluttering with panic as the familiar white swirls caught at her throat. Dust motes whirled in the intermittent light of sparks as Declan heated and folded metal, heated and folded. She'd been coming here since she could toddle and nothing would keep her out of the one place she felt at home. Especially not this wave of alien panic, however strongly it flooded her with the need to dive down, deep and dark, protect the one who mattered most.

Stop it! she told herself as much as the bees. Her crisis in the Forest had left her mentally troubled, dealing with too many new experiences and her imagination had resorted to metaphor, imaginary bees. They were like panic-man, a useful visualisation, but they were still imaginary. They'd enabled her to draw on extra reserves of fighting prowess, which was amazing, but she needed to keep such mental aids firmly in their place. Which did not include panic about smoke in a forge!

They wanted deep and dark? That was fine by her! *Deep, dark and calm, get in the jar,* she told them.

Keep the One safe, keep the One safe, they buzzed as they scuttled into deepest darkness, where the noise calmed. They seemed almost torpid as Mielitta firmly stoppered the metaphorical jar containing the metaphorical bees, and entered the forge, her home.

Smithcraft had its own rhythm. First, sourcing the material in cold choice. Then, feeding the insatiable fire until it sucked on the raw metal thrust into its maw, transforming the steel under Declan's watchful eye. Solitary, his face glowing red in the forge-light, he would stand, for a moment outside time, his gloved hand on the lance piercing the fire.

Mielitta had learned weaponcraft from watching Declan's relationship with the fire-god who lived in the forge. She could sense the slip from conscious skill to instinct. One moment, a man was sticking a metal rod into a fire; the next, a master smith touched the spirits of fire and metal in partnership, in alchemy. As when Mielitta stopped thinking, nocked an arrow and let fly, knew whether it was true. She could have touched fire and metal this way too!

The rhythm changed. Now came the frenzy of folding, hammering, while the metal was hot. Sparks arced fiery light in the darkness, tracing the hardened muscles of a man's arms, the glimmer of sweat on dusty skin. Leatherette aprons sizzled and blackened. Once they'd been pristine bales on the stone floor of Mage Fabrisse's atelier, waiting for their life to begin.

Reminded of the news she bore, Mielitta jigged impatiently, knowing she could not interrupt yet. Not when Kermon was carrying the bucket of oil outside. She stepped out after him to watch. How could you tire of oil craft?

Speed was all-important now. Declan burst through the door with a super-heated metal rod, ready for its final transformation. He dipped the steel into the oil and the cauldron bubbled into flame. Even through human vision, with no ultraviolet, the colours flared in extraordinary combinations. Mielitta saw maroon edges to the white bubbles bursting on the surface, deep purple and indigo, a hundred shades of yellow and reds that danced into a wordless pattern that only she could read.

The One she read in the flames as they blazed and, too soon, died.

Pff. Their obsessions were leaking through the jar. She must work harder at how she lived with the damage from the Forest incident. She scratched absent-mindedly at her thigh, which still itched.

'Mielitta,' Kermon greeted her with a smile, his face no less friendly for being smeared with grease.

'I see you've been promoted to bucket-carrier,' she told him.

His smile faded, uncertain, and she was ashamed at her own spite.

'It took me years to reach that level and I never got any further,' she added, placatory.

Her intention rather than her words was enough to bring the smile back. He wiped his mouth, smearing the black over his cheek, and she couldn't help smiling with him.

Declan was watching them closely, too closely. He grunted approval, and Mielitta's stomach clenched. He needn't think she'd forgiven either of them.

'I'll just put this on the anvil to cool,' he told them.

She followed him back into the forge, where they could speak more privately. She sat on a table, swinging her legs over the edge as if she were a child again. The forge was briefly the dirtiest place in the Citadel but quickly became the cleanest. Every speck of dust was removed within minutes. 'If dust gets into the fabric it will destroy steel, sure as fire burns,' he'd told her. She knew that the forge cleaned itself by magecraft but she'd never known what else the Mage-Smith did that way. He was just Declan to her and he worked like any master smith would.

'There's something I want to talk to you about,' Mielitta began, then looked pointedly at Kermon and changed the subject.

'Would you make me a Damascene steel arrowhead?'

Declan looked up at her from under bushy brows and was blunt. 'Why?'

Two people could be direct. 'Because Kermon took the job that should have been mine and you owe me severance for my apprentice-work.' She couldn't keep up the cold tone. Her voice cracked a little though she still swung her legs, defiant as a five-year-old who refuses to come off the swing.

'Think of it as a parting gift, for luck in my life. You have been like a father to me.' She couldn't say more so she stopped, aware of Kermon, who couldn't help but listen, however much he busied himself with arranging pieces of wood and metal on shelves.

Eyes like green pools in the darkest part of the Forest, Declan growled. 'I am a father to you and will take none of your nonsense. You're a girl and that's that. I should have been firmer with you but what's tempered can't be put in the flame again and you're not as well-tempered as I'd like.'

Mielitta bit her lip and her legs stilled. When she spoke, her voice quavered. 'That's the trouble – I'm not a girl and I'm not a woman. So if I'm different, you should let me do what I'm good at!'

'You'll lead a Perfect life, girl, whether you like it or not! You must wait until Shanagra finds you ready for the Maturity Test. Maybe there's a reason she hasn't, with the mouth you have on you for answering back!'

Was he going to hit her? She'd not been chastised so since she was little. But no. He stepped back, calmed, came to some decision.

'Kermon,' Declan called, in a voice that brooked no refusal. 'Are you ready to make your smith-piece?' It was not truly a question and would not be asked twice.

Mielitta drew up her legs onto the table, hugged her knees. It should have been her. She knew the pattern she would have made, folding just so, to make an army of interlaced waves that moved like wings when the light caught them. Everyone would have marvelled, asked who he was, this new smith. And Declan would have said with pride, 'Not he, but she. My daughter, Mielitta.'

Instead, Kermon glowed, made no hesitation. 'I am ready, Forge-Mage Declan.'

I am ready. I am open. Mielitta silently mocked the courtesies. *Well, I am ready and I am open but only for what I choose. And I have been to the Forest, and survived, and* you *haven't.* If she was going to be treated like a child, then she would behave like one.

'Then treat Mielitta as your client and you shall make her an arrowhead. Note your client's requirements, then go to the archery yard to collect an example for a template.' Declan went over to the assistants to rearrange their work, leaving Mielitta more red-faced than any fire could have made her.

Kermon looked down at the floor. In the V-neck of his grubby workshirt she could see the hair on his chest. The silence grew. Then they both spoke at once.

'I want–' Mielitta began.

'I know I'm second-best–'

'Yes,' she told the honest hazel eyes raised to hers. 'but neither of us has a choice so there's no point arguing. Let's just get this over with.'

'You might be surprised,' Kermon told her. 'Don't judge my work before you see it.'

'I've seen the best Damascene steel in the world,' she said. It was just a fact, not an insult.

The apprentice took no notice of her words or her tone. Declan had taught him well. She was a client.

'You know what's possible,' he observed, 'so is there a design you would like?'

'Yes, I want–' She saw again the beauty of an arrowhead, a flight of wings in steel, aerodynamic and streamlined. And she let it go. Why would she punish Kermon? It wasn't his fault.

He was studying her face as if he could read it, as she had studied the cauldron of oil. Afraid no doubt that she would condemn him to failure, or at least to admitting his lack of skill.

'No,' she said. 'it's your smith-piece.' She gave him a weak smile. 'So, surprise me.'

He nodded, his face composed, serious, older than she'd thought. 'It will be my best work.' He gave a rigid little bow, left, and Mielitta realised she was alone with Declan. Her face flamed again. How was it that one person could reduce you to childish ways with just one word? Well, she would show him and he would be proud of her! She opened her mouth to tell him about the Forest and not one word came out. *Stoppered,* she thought. *Shit!*

'Well?' Declan's deep voice was comfortable, reassuring as a blanket. 'What did you really want to talk to me about?'

'My Maturity Ceremony is tomorrow,' she announced. She couldn't help sounding like a child who'd hit a nail with a hammer for the first time. However, the impact was everything she could have wished.

Declan looked stunned. 'B-but,' he stammered, 'I thought you weren't going to…'

She'd certainly practised the next line. 'I'm a late starter,' she told him. And then for good measure, 'Mage Yacinthe said so. And that the Ceremony was to go unremarked because it's just me, and the circumstances are exceptional. So as not to make a fuss over me being a late starter.'

'But nobody told me,' Declan said, looking at her strangely.

Just like nobody told me Kermon was taking my place as your apprentice. She knew it was wrong to enjoy such a petty revenge but it made her feel less child, more equal. Anyway, why should Declan have been told?

'I expect the children usually tell their parents, and that's what I'm doing. The Maturity Mages have more important things to do.'

'You want this? To be an adult. You're sure?' What was the matter with the man? One minute he wanted her to fit in like a good girl and the next he wanted to sow doubts about the joys of adulthood?

'Of course,' she told him. 'Why wouldn't I?'

He licked his lips before replying. 'No reason.'

'And,' she'd saved the best until last. 'I'm to assist Mage Yacinthe in the library.'

'That's nice,' he said, his tone listless.

'I'll be busy,' she said airily. *What with doing all the work in the library and visiting the Forest.* 'But I'll try to visit now and then.'

'That would be nice. But you know you can't use weapons when you're a woman. The arrowhead you asked for – you can never use it.'

'I know.' She smiled sweetly, pure woman. 'It's just for luck, for the memories,' she lied.

'For the memories.' Suddenly he looked so old, his face crushed.

She jumped off the table and hugged him, seeking shelter one last time in the blackened apron and hard-muscled arms. She was nearly as tall as he was now.

'Children grow up,' he murmured. 'Become forged, become adults. It is the way of the Citadel. I didn't think... but of course you must have your place here too.'

Trust Declan to think of people in steelworking terms. 'I don't mind being forged,' she told him and again, he looked at her strangely. Was that fear in his eyes? He blinked and the strangeness was gone.

This wasn't what she wanted for her last afternoon as a child with her parent. 'Tell me about my finding,' she demanded. She'd heard the story a thousand times but it was their story, their bond, and she needed to hear it once more, now.

'I'm fetching knives from the kitchen,' he began, 'minding my own business and I'm walking along the passage, when I hear this noise.'

'Where?' she interrupted, struck by a sudden thought. 'Where was the baby?'

'We haven't got to that part yet,' he objected. 'But it was – you were – on the way to the west courtyard door, I think, by the inside wall. Yes, definitely the inside wall.'

'I thought so.' *Where I hid my memories. A wall with history, indeed!* She didn't explain herself. 'Sorry, I won't interrupt again.'

'So I head towards the noise, which starts as a little cough then turns into a full-size baby's cry. And sure enough, when I turn the corner, the baby noise is loud and clear but there's nothing to be seen but stone walls and stone floor, same as always. Then the wall sort of shimmers and forces out this little basket, as if hands are pushing it through the wall into the passage. The wall goes solid and there you are, screaming. I put a finger to your mouth, say *sh* but you latch onto that finger, suckling away, and I know you're hungry.

'So I put the knives in my pockets, pick up the basket and take you to the nursery. And you know the rest. Same as all babies in the Citadel, you're shared out with the mothers so none of them gets tired of mothering or stuck with a tricky baby all the time. And I get to do a share of fathering, seeing as you're my Foundling, in a manner of speaking.'

He looked at her then, with all the pride she'd hoped for. 'A special father. And you go to school with all the children…'

'And I watch the other children become adults while I'm passed over,' she finished for him. 'But it's my turn now. You understand that, don't you.'

'Better than you do,' he told her and kissed her forehead.

'Tell me about the name,' she ordered. 'You missed that bit.'

'In that basket, you were all wrapped in white and I could see some writing pinned to you. I thought it was going to say something about where you were from but it was just one word. Mielitta. And when I said the word aloud, the writing faded and disappeared so nobody else ever saw it. But I spelled it out to the Nursery Mage and she said it had no meaning so it must be your name. And that's what you're called.'

'She was wrong.' Mielitta was fierce. 'My name does have a meaning – it's who I am.'

Declan shook his head. 'Still shouting after eighteen year-cycles,' he teased her. 'I should have known to walk on by when I heard that screaming. Still, I'm glad I didn't.'

The tension between them vanished like bubbles from oil and they spent the last moments of Mielitta's childhood choosing wood for handles.

Dead, piped the voices in her head as she debated the virtues of yew – beautiful patterns, the *spalting* so prized by craftsmen – versus walnut – plain but less prone to crack in cutting.

Dead, they told her again and she wished she could tell Declan about the living beauty that was wood in the Forest. But the words stuck in her throat and she settled for the affection between them as parent and child. More was not possible for they already lived in different worlds.

CHAPTER TEN

The High Table was empty for the evening meal, Mielitta's last as a child among the servants. If Jannlou and Bastien were too busy to harass her, so much the better. No doubt the Council and favoured mages were eating in the Council Chamber while they debated the threat posed by the Forest. Mielitta smiled. Little did they know.

'M-Mielitta?' Drianne queried the smile. She was still behaving oddly since the attack, flushing at nothing, avoiding Mielitta's eyes but watching her covertly. She'd get over it. Especially after the Maturity Ceremony. No doubt Drianne would have her own soon enough and Mielitta was only pre-empting the ending of a one-sided friendship.

'Just thinking,' Mielitta told her, still smiling, 'about the new apprentice in the forge, Kermon.' All young girls wanted gossip about attractive young men, didn't they? But Drianne's eyes flicked away.

Her problem. Mielitta shrugged, reminded herself of all the children she'd befriended, only to lose them to maturity. They'd turned into all those adults who made her squeeze against the wall as they gossiped past her, without even noticing her, let alone remembering her name. Well, it was her turn now.

She looked at the freckled young face opposite her, mouth tight against an unfair world, a world that mocked stammers and difference. What last message could Mielitta give? She leaned across the table, so only Drianne would hear, and the words came out before she could weigh their wisdom.

'Drianne,' she said. 'You are a beautiful person. Changes are coming, good changes.' The girl flushed crimson but didn't look up.

Damn. Mielitta had said too much already. The whole point of her plan was to fit in. She continued, 'You should make the most of your archery until your Maturity Ceremony and then you'll have adult matters to occupy you.'

Drianne flashed a look of contempt at her, well-deserved. She sounded like a lesson on citizenship!

'There is more than this,' Mielitta finished lamely, knowing all too well how it felt to be alone. But this was for the best. Drianne had already suffered from this impossible relationship. In a different world she could have been a sister. But Mielitta could never say so.

She instinctively reached out across the table towards the girl and then realised how odd it looked so she picked up a ball of grey sustenance from the plate in the middle of the table, to hide the gesture. *Don't believe the words,* she pleaded with Drianne. *Watch the hands.* Another of Tannlei's sayings. But Drianne didn't look up once, lost in her own misery, and Mielitta could only leave the Hall as if this were a normal evening at the end of a normal day.

In her chamber, Mielitta prepared for the next day. She rolled her discarded clothing into a tight ball and tied it with a spare bowstring. It would be more practical for visits to the Forest than would her lavender gown, which was shaken out over her chair. Inside the gown, Mage Fabrisse had tucked two cream modesty scarves, one for her bodice and one for her head. There was also a garment Mielitta had never seen before. She'd never seen a woman's undergarment but she was sure that was what she was looking at now, silky and stretchy. She'd grown used to binding her breasts with a shirt ripped into strips but she knew that from now on, she'd have to look the part she was going to play.

Her stomach fluttered with nerves but at least her head was quiet, empty of voices. She lay in bed, waiting for the greylight to dip to black at its customary time. Looking at the lavender colour of the dress soothed her and she thought of all the Forest colours she would see the next day. As the last light faded, she banged her head deliberately against the pillow six times, schoolgirl magic to wake her at a given time. Then she drifted into dreams of flight and flowers.

The pale greylight of morning turned the gown grey too, dove grey, thought Mielitta, excited at the thought of the life ahead, words turned into reality. She would see doves in the Forest. And hear them coo softly as they snuggled up to their mates. Mate. She savoured the word as she slipped into the stretchy silk, adjusted the elastic support, wriggled a bit. It fitted and was comfortable. Why then did she feel so exposed?

She had a hand mirror so she held it at arm's length to view her new silhouette. Pointy. Curvy. And embarrassing. But there was no alternative so she covered the undergarment as quickly as she could with yards of lavender, tucking the cream scarf down her front. That helped a bit but the shape was so different from what she usually wore. She'd rather have her legs on show and be free to run than display this bare expanse of neck and be cinched into a curved, waisted shape. It felt like an invitation. *Mate*, she thought. Why had she not thought about that aspect of her adulthood?

She braided her long red hair, tucked it under the second cream scarf and looked at her face in the mirror. Black, slanted eyes stared back at her, unblinking. Tawny skin looked darker and escaping wisps of hair redder against the cream scarves. Whatever she might be, she was no child, but she didn't need a mirror to tell her so. And if any man, attractive or not, had mating on his mind, an arrow would be within her reach!

She didn't need hose under the long dress so she'd cut some to make ankle-length socks. They were comfortable with her boots, which she saw no reason to part with. Maybe fresh air out in the Forest would heal that irritating patch on her thigh. Then she realised that her thigh no longer itched. Good! Healed, finally.

She hitched up her skirt to see what the patch looked like now, turning towards the window's growing light. And she gasped as a thousand buzzing voices woke in her head. *The One. Yes, yes, the One. At last.*

Outlined on her thigh, a huge bee was pricked on her skin in a thousand dark points, rippling its wings when Mielitta moved.

Beautiful Queen, the voices chorused.

Unnerved, Mielitta threw her skirt back down to hide the bee design. No time for that now. Nor to listen to voices in her head that weren't there. They quietened. She must live out the lie she'd constructed the day before and her first task was to get to her own secret Maturity Ceremony too early for anybody to know what hadn't happened.

She rushed across the empty courtyard. She unlatched the familiar door to the forge, ignored a weak clamour in her mind, warning her *Smoke! Fire! Fly!* and sped through the silent interior to the small door at the back. She had no idea why Maturity Ceremonies were held in a barn behind the forge but she'd often peeked through a spyhole in this same door as a little girl and witnessed the gatherings, longing for the day she too could be an adult.

Today was that day. She was not going to draw the wooden slat sideways and peek through the hole. She was going to go through the door, find a way into the Barn and come back as the fully-forged adult she'd been for some time. The Maturity Barn was forbidden except by invitation but so was the Forest and she'd survived that. No, she'd *enjoyed* it and she was going to return.

Once, she'd had to stand on a stool to see through the spyhole. Now, she had to stoop to go through the forge's back door and shut it behind her. She crossed the yard where new adults usually trod a circular procession, keeping step with each other to symbolise their citizenship. She was already trespassing and yet the ground felt no different from the archery yard. She scuffed some of the greenery underfoot and it mended itself. Ordinary maintenance magecraft.

The Maturity Barn was not stone, unlike the rest of the Citadel, but woodette, in rough vertical slats. Doorless and windowless. Probably password protected. Mielitta paused. She didn't have to get into the place, just look as if she was coming from there. But it would be nice if she could get in, more convincing if she was questioned. Especially as her only way back to the Citadel lay through the forge and she didn't want Declan becoming suspicious. He'd only worry.

'Radium,' she tried, without much hope. Nothing happened.

The two Maturity Mages would have set the password, she reasoned.

'Yacinthe,' she tried. Then, 'Puggy'. Nothing.

Maybe the password had already been reset for Bastien's use. Maybe it was mage-contact, not a word at all. Or set by voice. There was no chance of her getting in by magecraft or impersonation. What about more human means?

She studied the construction. The woodette slats were ill-fitted, part of the rustic appearance presumably fashionable when it was built. The Citadel had no logic to much of its construction. It just existed, as it had always done. Nobody knew when 'always' had begun, unless the walls told the mages.

Mielitta took the arrowhead she'd pinned to her bodice 'for luck' if anyone should ask. She slipped it between two slats and worked the space but the effort was futile. If she worked for several weeks, she could loosen enough slats to slip inside but she didn't have several weeks. And there was only enough space for bees to get through.

Bees could *get through*, they were quick to tell her.

What if she *could* communicate with them? Not that they were real. But if she pretended they were, and could send them into the Barn, as if it were a kind of magecraft, nobody would know she'd tried something so crazy. And if she succeeded?

For the first time, instead of using her willpower to quell the voices in her head, she sought them out. 'Hmmm,' she called to them. What did they respond to? What did they respect?

'The One,' she hummed, 'help the One.' She felt a ripple of wings on her thigh, a glow of power. They were awake.

'In,' she told them, felt their confusion – and their willingness.

Where? Where?

'In' meant nothing to them, nor did 'barn'.

How had they helped her return through the Forest to the water gate? She closed her eyes, pictured the place where they were, in bee-sight colours, aquamarine grassette, dark grey barn. There were no scents to help but she pointed like the bees had, a dance of compass directions, going through the grey crack in the slats into the dark barn. She highlighted the route in ultraviolet arrows.

'In.' she said again and felt the buzz of understanding.

Then the bee sigil on her thigh heated to burning, ripped itself from her body, filled her head with an imperial buzz until she had only one purpose. She must lead the colony into that dark place, be the One. She felt the rush of air, the company of her body-guards as she followed the dance moves and slipped through the crack into darkness.

Mielitta buzzed on the floor, enjoying the dark but not the space around her. *Too empty, too empty. Too big to build a home,* her people cried anxiously, seeking a corner to hide in. As she separated her body and mind from the bees, she observed that she was now inside the Barn, with no sign of any cracks bigger than a bee-space in the woodette slats. They filtered some light into the Barn but that made little difference as there was nothing to see. Even from a human viewpoint, the Barn was indeed too empty.

Mielitta stood up, a little shaky on legs that suddenly seemed very long and surprisingly few in number. She could feel the heat of her thigh, even through the lavender dress, and as she rested her hand on where the bee head must be, pointing downwards as if flying off her thigh, she felt it vibrate.

'Thank you,' she hummed, then just left her hand where it was. The contact was strangely reassuring and she could feel her own heartbeat steady, as the thrumming of bees settled.

One, the vibrations sang. *One world, our world.*

Now what? Mielitta was in the Maturity Barn, where there was nothing but herself and a thousand bees. She walked around inside the building but all she saw was a pile of ashes in one corner. No clue as to what usually happened here. However, she *was* inside, which gave her all the credibility she needed – if she could get out. If not, she'd have to yell for help and her lies would be discovered.

She felt the bees' exhaustion and she was afraid to ask their help to try a reverse journey. Her thigh burned and she felt in no fit state to experiment again with whatever had happened. If she appeared through a bee-space in woodette slats and collapsed on the greensward, her credibility would not benefit.

There must be another way. She looked at the walls, the pattern of light through the cracks and suddenly saw the outline of a rectangle – a doorway. Surely getting out of the barn must be easier than getting in, needed no wards? She reached out, traced the line of light from the ground up to the right-hand corner, along its top edge, down the left side to the ground again, waited. Nothing.

What did you say when you wanted a door to open? If you were a new adult and not the most sparkling wit in the school-room? It was worth trying.

'Open,' she said. *Come,* she told her bees, sheltering them in her cosy darkness, where there were no empty spaces. She stepped out of the Maturity Barn through the doorway, in all her lavender finery and posed so anybody looking could see her. Did she imagine a slat of wood drawn quickly across a spy-hole in the forge's back door?

Even though there was not a speck of dirt on the grassette greensward, she picked up her long skirt in one hand and sashayed towards the forge. The door opened before she reached it and when she entered, seven men bowed respectfully, as was proper to a lady. The assistants were irrelevant but she inclined her head towards them, mindful of her new status.

Declan held out an elbow, already too dusty for a handshake, and she touched his arm with dainty reserve.

Kermon was bursting to speak and she acknowledged him last with another graceful bend of the neck. This was easy.

'Lady Mielitta,' he began, 'I have your commission ready, to celebrate your maturity.'

She fingered the chain around her throat. 'Good. Please fetch it.' *Please* was a nice touch, a sign that she'd retained more manners than most adults.

'Where's Maturity Mage Puggy?' Declan asked, suspicion knitting his brows.

He'd not catch her out so easily. 'Mage Yacinthe,' she corrected. 'As I told you, she wanted my ceremony to go unremarked. She left as soon as I was – how did you put it? Forged. Yes, forged. Do you like my gown? I think it becoming. And I might rearrange my hair, perhaps one plait across the brow and two knotted behind. What do you think?' If he wanted a lady's conversation then he would have it. She had heard enough prattling to emulate it.

His scowl deepened. 'It's not the way things should be done.'

'No,' she agreed. 'Two braids usually suffice. But I do have such thick, long hair...'

Kermon returned, presented her with a blue velvet cushion, the setting on which to display her lucky arrowhead, his smithpiece.

'I wanted you to see it first,' he told her. 'Before the Forge Mage's judgement.' His voice shook. Pride? Fear of failure? Hope?

Mielitta picked up the arrowhead, felt its weight and balance in her hand. Forge-light caught its fine point and honed edges. Perfect. And deadly, in the right hands. Then she looked at the patterning and her breath caught.

'What made you think such a pattern would please me?' she trilled.

Fire danced in his eyes as he answered. 'I'm a soul-reader,' he told her. An assistant laughed nervously but Kermon showed no sense of his own foolishness. 'Does it please you?' he asked her.

Mielitta looked at the pattern of Damascene waves, like translucent bee-wings, natural forces folded into steel. Her pattern, the one she'd imagined making for herself. He'd stolen her pattern! And given it back to her, a thousand times more beautiful than she'd imagined. It was hers, beautiful and deadly. She ached to see it in flight.

'It's very pretty,' she fluted, adding a vapid smile for good measure. 'But I'm just a woman.' Which was probably even worse than being just a girl, if you didn't have another life in another world. 'What the Forge Mage thinks is what matters, for your smith-piece to be accepted.' She passed it to Declan.

The smith weighed it as she had, checked the evenness of the metal, tapped to detect flaws, ran his finger at ninety degrees to the honed edge to check its sharpness. Mielitta had learned at five years old that a knife edge cut along its edge but not across, and that you could hear a sharp edge. She knew every test Declan was carrying out and she knew the verdict before he gave it but she kept a bored expression throughout.

'It's good work,' he declared. 'You've earned the right to your own clients, under my supervision.'

'Thank you, Forge Master.' Kermon showed only quiet satisfaction, as would anyone capable of such a masterpiece. He knew his worth, as did Mielitta. That made two of them who'd achieved new status today.

'We can both celebrate this day as the start of a new life,' Kermon said. Was he really a soul-reader? 'And if my smith-piece pleases my lady, that is all I ask.'

Declan had finished with them and was collecting from the shelves what he needed for his day's work. Without even turning around, he ordered Kermon, 'Blunt it. A lady doesn't want edges on her lucky piece.'

Mielitta saw the raw pain in the apprentice's eyes, reflecting her own. Mar such work! But he swallowed and set to work, sanding the arrowhead blunt. He tested the blade, filed it, sanded it again, an agony of malwork. Mielitta had crept up behind him to watch but she dared not intervene. She dashed one rebellious tear from her cheek and watched it fall onto the beautiful Damascene wings, blending with a second teardrop, not hers.

Without looking up, Kermon whispered, naming the arrowhead in magecraft, an act he was strictly forbidden. 'Steelwing, know one master, Mielitta; one aim, to protect her; one revenge, reverse all harm.'

She put a hand on his shoulder, too choked to speak as he kissed the arrowhead, stood up to present it to her once more. Instinctively, she stepped back to avoid him touching her as he reached for the chain around her neck.

'I'll do it,' she said hastily, and saw his hurt. Whatever a soul-searcher was, he was also a man with *those* feelings towards her. She shouldn't have joked about him to Drianne. She undid the catch on her chain, with one-handed ease. She attached her new acquisition to the chain and dropped it out of sight beneath the cream scarf of her bodice, conscious that the artefact had been followed closely by at least one intense gaze.

'Have you finished?' Declan's voice made her jump. 'I need you to use the bellows.'

'It is done,' Kermon replied but his eyes still held Mielitta's, hazel turned to warm gold in the forge-light.

'I cannot linger,' she told the men brightly. 'And I'm sure you have men's work to do.' Was she over-doing it? Sounding as sarcastic as she felt? She searched their faces but no, they both accepted her new adult voice as real. More fool them.

'I shall be too busy to visit often but we must stay in touch,' she told Declan. He turned away, picked up a hammer.

'Ay, we'll stay in touch.' His gruff voice brought tears to her eyes and if he'd spoken then, person to person, asked her if she was all right, told her he loved her, she'd have confessed about the Maturity Ceremony, the Forest, the bees – or tried to.

'You have woman's work to do,' he said. 'You'd best be getting on with it.'

She stumbled on the threshold. *Smoke. Fire. Fly.* Stupid bees who didn't know the difference between going into the forge and leaving! Then she left her childhood behind.

She sashayed up the passageways, forcing servants out of her way. Was that Drianne she passed? No matter. She was a lady now and she must act the damned part. When she reached the second door down the passageway after the schoolroom, she knocked and waited.

The door opened slowly, Mage Yacinthe looked quickly up and down the passageway, then asked, 'Who are you?'

'Assistant Librarian, reporting for work,' answered Mielitta firmly.

'Thank the stones! Follow me,' was the reply and the Assistant Librarian dutifully followed in the Mage's wake until they reached the library.

CHAPTER ELEVEN

M age Yacinthe's instructions and subsequent absence had left Mielitta all the autonomy she hoped for. 'Keep the books clean and organised.' As a job description, it lacked detail, but no matter. When in service, Mielitta had frequently cleaned the library and sneaked some reading time so she felt at home among the book stacks.

Cleaning was a familiar task so that's where she would begin, from the top down among the natural history books. She perched on the top step of the ladder that slid along a stack and she ran an antistatic duster along *Trees and their Fruit*. Why, she wondered for the umpteenth time, did the mages not eliminate such menial tasks? Their governance and use of magecraft seemed without logic and they were never the ones to do the chores. Why should she have to? She might as well be a servant again.

This was not how she'd imagined womanhood when she was growing up. She'd seen the ladies laughing with each other, escorted by their knights, and she'd wanted the respect they were given, the desire in men's eyes, marriage and children.

Instead here she was, cleaning again.

Her head buzzed and she felt the bee sigil glow warm.

Why should you have to? repeated the voices. *You don't. Let us out. Help.*

Nobody else was in the library. Where would be the harm in an experiment? She was wary after the bee break-in at the Maturity Barn but already curiosity was dimming the memory of how ill she'd felt. Whether the bees were a product of her imagination or not, she was channelling some force and she must learn to control it. She could hardly ask a mage to teach her. So, what better way to begin than with a small domestic task?

Shutting her eyes helped her visualise the bees better, use their language. Communication seemed to work from intention, translating between her words and their vibrations, her mental pictures of places and their waggle-dance maps.

Place was easy. She pictured the ladder, the bookshelves, felt the happy buzz of understanding. Explaining the work puzzled her. She pictured one book, blew the dust off its top, spine, the surrounding shelf. She pictured the next book, followed the same sequence, and then she waited for the sad hum of incomprehension.

Instead, the buzz grew happier.

To work, girls.

Instead of the library stacks, Mielitta saw wax frames of hexagonal cells. Instead of books, there was a variety of contents, pollen, brood, capped honey, all needing to be cleaned. She could feel the bees' need to do hive housework, their vast experience of shifting dust and debris.

'To work, girls,' she agreed, and opened her eyes.

One book at a time and row by row, a thousand bees stirred the air by fluttering their wings, flicked the dust ever downwards to the woodette floor where the Citadel magecraft operated and not a speck remained.

At first, Mielitta could only watch in fascination. The bees at work were beautiful, as they hovered and dived, singing a worksong. Never had she felt such unison, such joy in diligence, in

86

completing a task within their competence. They filled her with resolution to do her own work and to do it well.

She read along the titles, where the bees had finished cleaning, and she rearranged the books, keeping some on the ladder to be placed elsewhere. A book on wilderness survival caught her attention and she skimmed its pages, wondering what she would eat on her next visit to the Forest. She could pack sustenance to take with her but surely there must be something tastier than Citadel food? Bark and leaves had not tasted good but her mouth watered as she recalled the flavours of Forest water and the scents all around her, edible scents.

There. A chapter on food in the wild. She flicked pages quickly. Berries, fruit, different times of year... her stomach flipped. Insects. Killing and eating animals. Her hand shook as she put the book to one side, to take to her room and read at leisure. Sustenance was without taste but at least nothing died so she could eat. She had much to think about.

The bees' song was diminishing and their contented vibrations filled Mielitta with satisfaction as she welcomed the workers back into her consciousness. She felt in tune with them and they with her and they worked together in simple harmony. How amazing that such tiny creatures could do so much work and with such pleasure.

Mielitta backed down the ladder, hugging her book and her feeling of well-being. She would make a plan of how the library should be reorganised. Then she heard the door open, male voices, and she climbed back up to the top of the ladder where she was invisible, unless somebody looked up.

'We can talk in here.'

'Thank the stones for that! How do you manage, when every word you say is analysed for treachery? I can't even ask for the water jug without worrying I've stressed the word *water* in a sarcastic way that could be taken as criticism of the Provisions Mage. If I could even remember who the Provisions Mage is! I can remember the names of the Councillors but all the minor mages – too much!'

'You'll get used to it, son. That's why I wanted time for us both with nobody watching us. We need to hide our full strength until the time is right.'

'When will that be?'

'Soon. The Council is already split into factions. Many have lost touch with the history in the walls, don't accept our way of life, are open to approaches by the enemy without.'

'I have felt it.'

'Magaram dealt with the water gate breach – and caused bigger rifts because of *how* he dealt with it. The fool thinks that a show of public loyalty reflects private belief. When bullied, weak men will always swear one thing and do another. Magaram has opened them to our suggestions of a middle way.'

'But I thought we were against compromise? That we must protect what can be sustained?'

'Of course. But first we must fly different colours from Magaram. Not that he understands what he professes to protect. We will pull the Citadel back to strict observance of Perfection, from the tolerance I see creeping in, everywhere.'

'But we'll speak of the middle way?'

'Now you see it. Everyone will support us and we will turn them to our ends by pressing on the pulse points of each man's wishes, fears and prejudices. Each man has such points and if we appeal to them separately, we tailor our arguments to what they want to hear and win them all. You could learn much from listening to the walls and their tales of the past.'

'But when we win? We can't please them all.'

'And we won't try. We'll be in power and we'll do what we've been planning all these years. They'll forget soon enough what we said beforehand – and we can deal with any who don't face reality.'

A pause. 'About my feelings, about the breach, the enemy. I

didn't just mean the water gate. I could sense the enemy, the enemy without, not the enemy within, in the Maturity Barn.'

'When?' The tone was sharp.

'Yesterday afternoon. I went there to place my wards, to prepare for the next Ceremony and I sensed something, I can't explain, some mockery around me.'

Bastien, for sure, thought Mielitta. With his father, the new Councillor. Her heart thumped as she realised what Bastien had sensed in the Maturity Barn yesterday afternoon.

'Like I felt with that servant,' Bastien continued. 'The old child.'

'You're obsessed with her.' Rinduran's voice was full of disapproval. 'You and Jannlou. And you've spent too much time with Jannlou. He is not at your level. And he is his father's son as you are mine. He has served his purpose. It's time to distance yourself.'

'But he's my friend. And he feels it too, the strangeness in that servant. Only he says she has a purpose and can be useful to the Citadel one day. If that's his magecraft speaking, we should listen.'

Oh stones! Jannlou's not another soul-reader, is he? wondered Mielitta in exasperation. Did all these men know her fate better than she did?

'You did my bidding, harried her, tried to force her into the Citadel's ways?'

'I did, father. So did Jannlou and the others.'

'And did it work?'

'No. She's more defiant than ever.'

Mielitta stayed very still. Maybe her new guise would hide her identity and maybe it wouldn't but neither mage would look kindly on an eavesdropper.'

'Then learn this: a rotten citizen is rotten to the core and cannot be changed, only suppressed for the good of others. Don't waste your time again.'

'She behaved oddly around the water gate. I think she's corrupting a younger servant. I tried to correct the younger one–'

'–and that didn't work either.'

Mielitta wished she could jab an arrowhead into each of them. Their arrogance in speaking of correction and suppression! Her 'corruption' of Drianne! These men didn't even know the names of the women whose lives they dismissed as inferior! Her head began to buzz in anger and she controlled herself. The last thing she wanted was a thousand enraged bees making her point, painfully.

'No,' admitted Bastien.

Huh! No mention of him being defeated by a mere girl and running away.

'This is what you will do. You will invite both these females to the next Maturity Ceremony. You're familiar with the ritual now? You can lead it?'

'Yes. Mage Puggy has instructed me and I've spoken to the Mage-Smith.'

'Then you can issue invitations and set the date. Mage Puggy is weak. She has 'interpreted' the Mage-Smith's tests and saddled us with new adults who are weakening the quality of our society. Weak people are the result of weak tests. You won't make that mistake.'

'No, father.'

'Also, it is time you chose a mate. My advice is that you use the Maturity Test to choose well.'

'I could select the younger servant, the less difficult one? Of course, if it's down to me, I'll suppress the older girl, the freak. But the younger one will be pretty. Her stammer is ugly though.'

'Who'd want to listen to a woman anyway?' Rinduran followed his own thought. 'Your kind heart will be the death of you, son. My advice is to suppress her too. But I remember the hot blood of youth. I could mute her and you could try to make her a good woman. How old is she?'

'Twelve.'

'A good age for a female mate, malleable. The consummation can wait a year if necessary. You'll find ways to satisfy yourself. If her test shows suitable qualities, I won't forbid it, but I think you're taking a risk. Suppression is the wiser course but you must make your own decision. And if you detect latent magecraft in any of the female candidates, suppress them. The growing number of women mages – Councillors even! – these last few decades has upset the balance, upset the men. You can feel the discontent that they must sit quiet while women speak. This situation cannot be sustained so we will return to what we know works best.'

'Yes, father. We could use that as our manifesto. What we know works best.'

'Tried and tested. Perfection based on the wisdom of the walls – we need to get back to basics.' Rinduran lectured his son. 'Sovereignty is a good word to use, and references to the way the Citadel used to be, in the old days, before well-meaning liberals weakened our values. We have the walls' truth on our side.'

'What if mages, or even ordinary adults, wish to hear what the walls say?' asked Bastien.

An unpleasant laugh. 'It takes years to hear all the walls say and make appropriate selections. I think we can choose suitable extracts to project, if needed.'

'Out of context?'

'Of course, my boy. You have so much to learn but you've made a good start. I'm proud of you.'

'Why bother keeping all these books? Most people can't even read and the mages get their history from the walls. Who needs any more than that? Why don't we just burn them all?'

'I thought the same at your age but I have spent years exploring the walls. They are very instructive and one message often repeated is that suppressing books is counter-productive. There are many theories as to the cause but no clear rationale, only the overwhelming consensus that this is so. Whereas suppressing people has often proved effective. We'll talk more of this another time. Let's get back to our public selves now.'

The voices moved towards the door, increasing in volume so any passers-by could hear them.

'Please pay my compliments on the state of the library to Mage Yacinthe when you visit her. I can see the results of her work already and we will all profit.'

'I will, father. I have an appointment this afternoon to pay her my respects. I only hope I can do half the job she has done as Maturity Mage and I am very conscious of the honour given me, so young. I will seek her help and support to continue her work in such a prestigious job.'

The voices tailed off as the door closed, leaving Mielitta on the ladder, shaking with rage. How dare they threaten Drianne with suppression or with Bastien as a mate – she wasn't sure which option was worse. Well, they'd missed their chance of suppressing *her* so easily. And as for plotting against Magaram to carry out their vile plans! They were more guilty of treason than she was but nobody would ever believe her if she accused them.

Underneath her outrage ran a darker unease. Declan was consulted by Maturity Mages, was responsible for their test? She didn't like the link between the forge and the Ceremony being any closer than a path from the back door to the Barn but she saw no reason to doubt what she'd heard. She knew Declan worked on commissions but she'd never seen or heard this kind of discussion, nor any such test, in all the years she'd peeked in every corner of the smithy. And she'd seen no sign of smith-work in the Barn.

She shrugged off the unworthy suspicions. It was a mystery, as was much of what mages did. She could ask Declan about it next time she saw him, pretending she'd felt his work in her own testing. They would laugh about it together.

Help! Help! buzzed the voices in her head.

'Not now,' she told them. 'Thank you but I don't need help. I was just angry at what I heard. Nothing for you to worry about.'

Not us helping you. You help us. Needed, they buzzed wildly, more agitated than she'd felt them even when panicked by smoke and fire. *The One has died and we are not prepared. You must take her place or we will all die. Until we are ready. Come now.*

Her thigh throbbed and their need made the word 'No' impossible. Hadn't they shown her what unity meant? As she was their responsibility, they were hers, indivisible. She barely had time to think *indivisible* when the bee on her thigh raised her head, rippled her wings and ripped Mielitta into the whirl of time and space that landed her in the Forest. In a dark box, crowded with miserable bees.

Home her voices told her in despair. *Help us.*

CHAPTER TWELVE

A bodyguard of her bees protected Mielitta, fluttering their wings in agitation. *Respect for the Queen,* they told her. *For you.*

Clumsy on six legs, adjusting to her enlarged, blue vision, she stumbled forward, in more of a crawl than a walk.

Her bees rubbed against her, crowding her so closely she was almost being carried.

They'll kill you if you smell wrong. You have to smell like us, like home hive.

She was in a narrow crevasse between vertical honeycomb cliffs and forward had many options; up, down, sideways. Her bodyguard directed her downwards and her instinct impelled her away from the lighter region of the heights, so she let herself be guided.

She could smell the misery in the hive. Beyond the bodies of her bees, she glimpsed others, drooping in apathy, idle. As she made her progress towards deepest darkness, she sensed a change in her wake: some activity and wary hope. Her bees clustered less tightly, allowed some brave scouts to investigate the intruder. To kill her if she didn't fit in. The story of her life.

She could see their poison darts, big as the top part of her body, her thorax. It wouldn't take many stings to end her little life but she was no longer afraid. She could feel the confidence of her bodyguard as they escorted her deeper into the hive, their pride in her.

You are our Queen, they told her, dancing respect with their wings, signalling to the other bees that she had come.

Their antennae tickled Mielitta as the scouts scented her. Bees had no sense of personal space. She could feel the brush of hairs, see the yellow trace of pollen on the empty sacks attached to their legs. The hexagonal cells of their huge eyes looked like a children's board game but she didn't know the rules and stared back at them, at risk of provoking an injection of the venom that pulsed in those huge darts.

Her body burned at the memory of the attack in the Forest, the thousand darts left in her body. Her queen bee's body had no room for a thousand darts but one would no doubt suffice. Below her armour-plated thorax, the bee-skin of her abdomen felt so much thinner than human skin that the bee who killed her would keep her sting and her own life.

Maybe Mielitta could sting them instead. What equipment did she have on this body? Who could tell her what she needed to know to be queen? Her voices? They were all females, warriors and workers, cleaners and nursemaids, and so were these scouts, probing her. As if she hadn't been tested enough these last few days!

I can tell you. A new voice spoke in her head, a voice she knew as a brand on her thigh, a connection to the hive, the queen who lived inside her.

Mielitta recalled the design, compared it to the worker bees surrounding her. The body was longer, the wings stubby and impractical. That was a disappointment. She'd hoped that she'd at least get to fly before she was killed as an imposter.

Look.

One of the scouts moved away from her, making the same wing-flutter as her bodyguard.

Respect for the Queen.

She'd passed the test. She held up one of her six legs to give a regal wave and made her cumbersome way past empty cells, downwards. The flutter dance surrounded her as she moved, taken up by all the bees who crowded to see her. She could get used to this.

Her coterie paused at the bottom of the vertical cliffs, where a passageway ran horizontally, just tall enough for her to walk along.

Your home. Explore. Fill them with hope.

She walked the length of the bottom, alongside a wooden wall, until she was stopped by another wall. Of course. She was in a box. She waddled back the way she'd come, counted ten vertical cliffs of double-sided wax comb, towering above her. She'd come down a cliff in the middle so she would explore one near the side wall. She could spread well-being amongst her people as she progressed, with pauses to observe and to listen to her inner queen.

Most of the comb in the middle cliffs had been empty but she had seen a thin scattering of covered cells.

Brood, bee babies. Females. Not enough.

Before she'd reached the bottom, there had been bigger, bumpy lids to a cluster of filled cells.

Brood. Male.

That was interesting. She'd only seen females and she wondered what the males did and where they were.

As she walked across the bottom to reach an end cliff, she had to duck and detour to avoid rocky outcrops dangling below the comb, shaped like peanuts

'Brood. Male,' she declared with satisfaction at how quickly she was catching on.

No, corrected her inner queen, quivering. *Queen cells. Your rivals. Kill them!*

'I don't think so!' Mielitta had only just been accepted into the hive and she was not going to rush into killing anybody. She *did* want to understand what was going on and then she'd make her own mind up about what to do.

She climbed up the cliff nearest the wall.

'No brood.' Silence meant that she was right this time. Some cells were filled but again the pattern was patchy. Clusters of fluffy blue balls confused her for a minute as she adjusted to her bee vision, which showed no red and many violets. So the ball would be yellow and orange to a human.

'Pollen.' She poked her sticky tongue into a ball just for a taste. Better than Citadel sustenance. Like eating clouds. Unfortunately, she'd signalled that she was hungry and immediately she had courtiers offering pollen-balls and poking their proboscses out at her, long bendy cones that dripped sticky stuff.

Open your mouth. She was no keener to be killed for improper behaviour than to kill, so she opened her mouth. Immediately there was a bee's tongue in her mouth and she gagged instinctively. Then the nectar flowed down her throat and she no longer cared about the feeding method. This was what she wanted to drink for the rest of her life. Another bee was waiting anxiously and so she just opened her mouth to see what would come next.

The bee regurgitated a gelatinous substance and passed it on to Mielitta, who rolled the oily cream in her mouth and swallowed. The bitter aftertaste felt medicinal, like bark and leaves, food that was good for her rather than a treat.

Royal jelly. All brood begins life fed on royal jelly but those females chosen to be queens are surrounded by it in their cells, made royal by its magic.

Mielitta saw other filled, wax-capped cells on the furthest cliff. 'Not brood?' she queried but she didn't wait for the answer. She could smell the dark amber sweetness and she had to taste it. She scraped away some wax and immediately the liquid trickled down, to the consternation of all the neighbouring workers. She lapped as much as she could before her courtiers cleaned up the mess she'd made.

You should not feed yourself. It is a criticism of your courtiers.

Their feelers gesturing anxiously, her courtiers brought her more royal jelly, pollen and nectar. At this rate, she'd be too big to move through the bee spaces! However, a queen had her duties to perform so Mielitta opened her mouth and added another stock of food to the delicacies in her stomach. Honey distilled the flavours of nectar and she'd only tasted one mix of flowers so far. This was the life.

Not flowers. That is forest honey made from sugared tree sap, honeydew. Aphids chew the sap, take what they need, give the rest back to the tree. And our people harvest the honeydew. You will taste many honeys in your lifetime.

Satiated and buoyed up by the love of her people, Mielitta was ready to find out what the hive's problems were, or rather, had been. The coming of the Chosen Queen would no doubt solve everything. She waved a foreleg in regal benediction.

'Why was there no queen here?' she demanded.

There was a swarm. The old queen took a third of the colony, sought a new home. As was proper, the new queen hatched, took her mating flight and then disaster struck. A crow killed her.

'But there are new queens growing. Couldn't the hive manage on its own for a bit?'

It was weak, struggling. The old queen did not lay well. Not enough brood, no new babies for too long. We need brood or the new queen will have no people. You must be the Queen.

'Well, if I kill the queens in their cells – and I have no idea how to do that – then there won't be a new queen, will there. And I have to go back.' Mielitta couldn't remember why but she knew she was needed back at the Citadel, just as much as she was needed here. She couldn't stay here too long.

'Let's get this over with, then. What do I have to do?'

You have a stinger but it is of no use except to kill rivals. So that is what you must do. There can only be one queen and you are preparing her way. You must kill all those I showed you. The queen we have chosen to replace you is in a cell apart, safe.

'How did you choose her?'

She is the only one we are keeping alive.

Mielitta gulped at the brutal logic of bees. What if she became surplus to requirement? She didn't ask because she knew the answer.

She needs you to give her the best start. The hive is too weak for battles. Use your dart on each cell and inject the queen inside with venom. Otherwise they will all seek you out when they hatch and mortal combat will follow. You will weaken with each challenge and your chance of survival is poor unless you kill the queens in their cells.

'Apart from the killing and poisoning, eating too much and being inspirational, is there anything else I must do, while I'm the Queen?'

You must take your mating flight as soon as possible and lay brood. Our population is low, the nurseries are bare and once the last grubs hatch, our number will drop below what can be sustained.

'Mating flight. Explain.' Mielitta liked the idea of flight but there must be ways to avoid both murder and mating.

This is what you were born for. Once in a lifetime, now, you must fly where the drones, the males, congregate and the fastest, bravest of them will put a lifetime's seed in you so you can lay our colony back to health.

'And how exactly does the seed get into me?' Mielitta kept her tone as neutral as she could – otherwise she'd scream.

A successful drone will insert his endophallus –

'Penis,' realised Mielitta, feeling queasy.

–into your sting chamber and, if it is a good flight, maybe fifteen drones will succeed. One glorious flight will result in five years of laying eggs for your people.

Mielitta's stomach heaved again. 'I can't do that,' she said. 'I'm a virgin.'

Of course you are. The inner queen was astonished. *This is your maiden flight. It is very rare that a queen would make a second such flight… only if no males are found the first time, or there is some weather catastrophe.*

Mielitta tried again. 'I can't. It's sort of – personal. And the first time should be special, with somebody you care about.'

'Personal' drew a bee blank. There was no such concept. 'Somebody you care about' drew a response, though not what Mielitta had hoped for.

Yes yes. We care about each other, about the hive. This is our purpose, that we live and die for each other. That is caring for each other. You care for us and we would die for you. You will do this for us so that we all live.

Put like that, how could she refuse? Mielitta felt trapped in her human viewpoint. Her bee body and her inner queen made her see how foolish her qualms were. What was one mating flight compared with the fate of tens of thousands of bees? She wasn't even being asked to die for them. Just behave as a queen bee.

'Will it hurt me?' she asked.

Bee laughter sounded like little shivers. *Oh no. You won't be hurt, at all.*

CHAPTER THIRTEEN

The hive was atingle with the news. *Maiden flight,* was all the buzz. Mielitta would have found it exciting if it she hadn't been the topic of the buzz. It was bad enough that she had to lose her virginity to save thousands of bees and their future.

If only it wasn't so public. All this celebration was so mortifying. She didn't feel like giving even one benevolent wave as she tottered onto the landing platform of the hive, adjusting to the bright light of day.

Calm, no wind. Dry, no rain. Warm, sunny, perfect, noted her inner bee with enthusiasm.

'Just perfect,' Mielitta echoed, without the enthusiasm. 'So, I fly. Where to? I don't see any drones.' Perhaps there were none and she could return safely to hide in the dark centre of the hive, after a few swoops and turns in the air.

Scent the air with your antennae and you'll smell them, their maleness, their invitation to play. Let your instincts guide you.

Mielitta had already realised that her antennae acted as her nostrils and were a thousand times more sensitive than her human nose. She vibrated them, separated out the familiar smells of her bodyguard, her worker bees, all female. Then she caught a waft of something different, musky, irresistible, and her little wings responded, lifting her up and away from the hive.

'How will the males know why I'm there? Who I am?'

More bee-laughter. *As you scent them, so they are waiting for you. They have been waiting for you and this moment all their lives.*

That sounded romantic enough to cheer her up. Mielitta just hoped she didn't smell of bananas as that had not gone down too well in her first encounter with bee-strangers.

I'll be with you, reassured her inner bee, but Mielitta needed no help in flight. How many times had she loosed an arrow, felt its trajectory, felt it fly true and hit home? Now she *was* the arrow but one who could draw loops and arabesques in flight.

She wrote *Maiden Flight by Mielitta* in invisible letters as she wove an intricate path between the trees. Why fly in a straight line when you could have fun?

She noted the colours of her bee vision: blue tree bark, purple leaves and flowers, white and ultraviolet concentric circles, targets to attract her bees. But she was a queen, above such distractions.

As the scent of male pheromones grew stronger, Mielitta could hear buzzing, see a black cloud hovering in a glade. She panicked, tried to fly back, but her inner queen pushed her relentlessly towards the attendant mass.

She could feel their excitement throbbing in the air, anticipation building to fever pitch. She couldn't help responding. Once in a lifetime, she told herself. And nobody in the Citadel need know.

'What do I do?' she asked but her wings already knew.

High, fast, dart around. Make them chase and try not to get caught. You will be, but only by the fastest, strongest, best!

Mielitta zoomed right through the cloud of drones, faltered as the male scent hit full strength. A leg lunged at her and she twisted away, down, sideways, up into the clear air, with the whole cloud in pursuit. She was not going to be caught so easily.

She felt like the ball in a children's game, escaping one set of clutching hands only to narrowly escape another, as she made the most of all the directions available to her. Humans were so limited by gravity.

Just as she was enjoying a side twist downwards, two legs grabbed her abdomen and dug in. She felt the weight of the drone on her back but she was helpless to dislodge him. She felt the thrust of his body, then something broke and he was gone, falling.

Oh stones, she thought, her heart thumping madly.

Keep flying, her inner queen insisted. *They are closing on you.*

Thank goodness she was so fit from training. Up she soared again, frustrating the drone nearest her and causing the mass to change direction yet again. And again.

Twelve times she was caught, bore the drone on her back, concentrated on maintaining her flight. Twelve times a male lost his grip, fell to the ground.

She was tiring now and she wanted to go home. The route to the beehive was clearly mapped in her mind and she felt no desire to zigzag or draw word patterns in her flight. Wearily, she made a beeline for home.

And a large group of drones flew with her.

'Why are they still here?' She'd had more than enough now and was nervous at the thought of being caught again.

To join your hive. You have won their respect and that of worker bees from further afield too, so they are all joining us.

So it was that Mielitta returned to her hive tired and triumphant, accompanied by hundreds of bees who'd acquired her scent and sought permission to join her hive.

Mated queen returning, her new companions buzzed as they submitted to the scout bees' investigations.

Mated queen returning, her bees buzzed as Mielitta alighted clumsily on the landing platform, crawled towards an open door in the metal gateway.

Before she could reach the guard bee in the doorway, she was surrounded by a welcome party, who half-carried her to the doorway and through to the celebrations inside. Several fussed around her body, cleaning her.

See, the mating sign. Mated queen returned.

She felt a prickle as they completed their work around her tail and then she felt no different than she had before her flight.

She had gone out alone, done what was asked of her, returned with enough bees to swell the diminishing ranks of the hive until a new brood could be laid and hatched.

Mated queen returned.

There were just two questions to which she wanted answers before she glutted on royal jelly and nectar, then she would sleep.

'What happened to the drones who mated with me?' she asked her inner queen.

What happens to all successful fathers. They died. They were ripped apart in mating and died a glorious death.

Mielitta swallowed. *Oh.* 'And what's a mating sign?'

The penis of the last drone who mated with you. Each drone knocks out the sign of his predecessor and the last one remains as a sign of success to your people. They have cleaned it from you now.

Oh. 'Perfect.' Mielitta obediently opened her mouth and allowed the first of many tongues to feed her nectar and the regurgitated cream that was royal jelly.

You must kill the other queens.

'Tomorrow,' she promised. 'I'm tired now.'

But the next day passed and two more. She still felt tired and she wanted to enjoy the new atmosphere in the hive, where bees had set to work again, each pursuing her own designated duties: cleaning, harvesting, feeding the hatched grubs. Even the drones contributed, fanning the hive with cool air as the heat outside increased during the day.

Then, five days after her maiden flight, Mielitta felt a new imperative. Ponderous, she waddled to the middle of a central comb cliff, flicked her long tail and laid fertilised egg after fertilised egg. She made a neat pattern in the comb, filling every cell as she spiralled outwards. Never had work felt so satisfying.

After laying a thousand baby workers, she held back the fertilised eggs and laid a cluster of infertile ones at the bottom of the cliff. Drones, she thought with satisfaction. Without drones, no hive was complete. Any more than it could survive without a queen.

She was resting after a satisfying day's work when the hairs on her antennae screamed *Danger!*

CHAPTER FOURTEEN

A body equal to her own in size hurled itself at her and she was knocked off all her feet. Pinned in a wrestling hold by her assailant, Mielitta rolled downwards, the claws on her back legs clutching at the comb in an effort to slow her descent.

'Drone?' she thought, confused. Worker bees were smaller than she was and would have no cause to hurt her, now she was accepted and laying well.

Bite your head off, impostor! screeched the mass of hate that gripped her and squeezed ever tighter.

'Help!' Where were her courtiers? Her bodyguard? Mielitta could feel the presence of her bees but they merely watched, impassive, awaiting the outcome.

Told you so. A queen has hatched from one of the cells you ignored. Her inner queen's smugness provided the jolt of extra strength needed to break free and Mielitta had a microsecond to take stock before the rival queen's sting jabbed towards her abdomen.

To the death! The new-hatched queen hurled her battle-cry. She was still shiny and golden from the royal jelly in the cell, fresh and full of purpose. Mielitta had been laying eggs all day and was tired. She was still clumsy, still discovering the potential of her bee's body. But she had years of training on her side and this newcomer had no more knowledge of her own body than did Mielitta, however strong her instincts might be.

'To the death,' agreed Mielitta, arching her back to jab with her own sting at her foe. While the other was off guard, she clamped down on a leg, chewed it off and spat it out. Hardly classic tactics but she must use the weapons she had. Strong mandibles, stronger than those of her workers; amazing range of vision, above and to the sides, so she would always know the position of her attacker; and her poison dart. Their initial clinch had shown Mielitta that she was physically weaker and must avoid being crushed.

Her opponent had clearly come to the same conclusion and threw herself once more at Mielitta. This time she was prepared. She lowered her head to bite, curling down below the grasping forelegs. At the same time she curved her back and kicked at the other queen's exposed abdomen. Kicking with six legs was complicated. The soft pads on her back legs did little damage so she concentrated on hooking skin with her forelegs.

Losing a leg seemed if anything to have increased her enemy's fury and Mielitta took a bite to her neck. Having her head bitten off suddenly seemed an all too probable result and she felt her strength waning as she clambered around the space cleared by her people.

She was going to lose. A killer glare fragmented a hundred times in the hexagons of her huge front eyes told her she was doomed. A drop of venom had already dripped from the sting-tip, aimed at her, approaching – and she was alone, as always. With only one arrow.

Mielitta was not merely bee but also a trained archer and she had to get back to the Citadel. She had not been through all this, the mating flight and egg-laying, to lose her life to some petulant adolescent! Mielitta appraised her surroundings. 'Make the ground your friend,' she reminded herself. They had wrestled and rolled their way to the floor of the hive, cutting off one potential direction of movement.

She timed the moment carefully, dropped onto her back so her rival's sting embedded itself harmlessly in a pollen ball, stored neatly in the cell wall. Then Mielitta curved upwards to her maximum, jabbed again and again.

The other queen had already withdrawn her sting since there were no barbs on their weapons but she could not change position quickly enough and the poison took hold as Mielitta continued to use her dart. She was still stabbing when the body dropped on top of her.

Still nobody came to help. 'What's new?' she thought as she heaved and rolled, a little at a time until she could crawl out and proclaim her victory.

As she piped her sovereignty in her shrill queen bee voice, her people rejoiced with frantic wing flutters and celebration. Then they all went back to work. Long live the Queen.

Mielitta also went back to work, her heart hard and determined. She crawled along the base of the hive and she could hear their cries as they sensed her approach, the rival queens waiting to emerge from their cells.

Murderess! Poisoner! Save us! they called. Every bee in the hive felt their cries and carried on working cheerfully. All was as it should be. The Queen was strong. *Long live the Queen.*

Mielitta felt nothing but her duty. She stopped first at a peanut-shaped cell where crunching sounds told her that the new queen was eating her way out, about to emerge. All sounds stopped while Mielitta stood close to the cell. A pretence of sleep, of absence, of invisibility: ploys with which Mielitta was all too familiar. Nobody used Mielitta's own tricks against her. She crawled on the cell wall, stabbed it with her poison dart, felt the point enter the bee inside. She stabbed again to make sure and moved on.

Systematically, she used her stinger on every queen cell she passed until there was no longer any cry of *Bite your head off.*

She stood still, shaking, and was immediately surrounded by bees, expressing their concern by grooming and feeding her. She felt the reassurance of their antennae combing debris off her body. She refused to think about what kind of dirt her body might have accumulated. She opened her mouth obediently, accepted the mash they regurgitated for her. She might be queen but she was helpless in so many ways compared with these capable worker bees.

Well done, her inner queen told her. *Now you do understand.*

Mielitta did understand. Without her, a strong queen, laying well, the hive died. But if she wasn't strong enough, or laying well enough, a challenger could replace her and her people would be just as happy. She was the most important bee within the hive but not as an individual. She, Mielitta, was replaceable. The community needed one queen, hundreds of drones, fifty thousand worker bees, all of them replaceable.

'What happens to the drones who don't mate?' she asked.

They are expelled from the hive in the autumn so as not to use up winter provisions when we don't need them. The queen lays new drones in the spring.

'They die outside.'

Yes.

'But don't they try to get back into the hive, to live?

They try. But the guard bees defend the entry, prevent them.

'Poor drones.'

They live purposeful lives. Is that not what matters? Longer lives than worker bees, not as long as the queen.

Mielitta slept all night and recovered to lay another thousand eggs the next day. And another thousand the day after that.

'Six hundred and seventy-two,' she was saying, on duty for the third day, when a shadow above her head alerted her to a new presence, lumbering towards her. She steeled herself for another fight.

No, not this time. This is the chosen one. She knows you, her inner queen assured her.

It was indeed a newly emerged queen and Mielitta curved her back, suspicious, ready to sting.

Thank you, said the other. This was more promising than *Bite your head off* but Mielitta was still wary.

The Young Queen continued, *Your scent is everywhere and I have grown in the shelter of your strength. You have saved my people.*

Mielitta felt her sting rise in a little stab of jealousy and she controlled herself with difficulty.

I know, the other acknowledged. *It goes against instinct to hold back your weapon against a rival. But we are not rivals. There are even hives in which two queens live together, in which one hands over peacefully. It is known so it is possible. And we are a new breed of queen. You must return to your other world and I must take on my duties with the added burden of our link.*

'Your maiden flight?'

Yes, when my outside shell has hardened enough to leave the hive. What is it like?

Girl talk in a beehive! Mielitta considered her answer. 'A wild ride,' she answered. 'You will know what to do. Fly high, fly fast and make them work to catch you.'

How many caught you?

'Twelve. Which is good enough but you should try for fifteen of the best drones. Keep flying until then. That should guarantee you respect and a long life.' One mating flight and a lifetime's worth of fertilised eggs. When the eggs ran out, the queen's life would become worthless.

Why does a long life matter?

'Because...' Mielitta couldn't find an answer that could be communicated to a bee. In fact, she was no longer sure that she had an answer. She'd often heard the phrase 'good, long life' and never questioned what was good about 'long'.

'Because you and I have a special bond,' she said. 'Because my people need *you*, not just any queen.'

This caused much puzzlement. *Special* made no sense and was dismissed. *Me* was considered longer. Finally, the queen concluded. *Yes, the Queen of my people, here in this hive, has this bond. No need to worry about how long I live. Our bees will dance all that is*

*needed to the next queen when she comes. Thank you for all you have
done. I will call you when I need you and you will call me when you
need me. My people will come to you.*

'And I will come to you when you need me.' How could
Mielitta not give her word when she felt their connection in her
guts?

'The Forest is in danger,' she blurted out, remembering
Rinduran and Bastien, the Councillors, the wards on the water
gate. 'And our people, our bees.'

*I know. That knowledge has come to me because of you. We will
protect our people and the Forest together. And my people will help you
in your other world. It must be hard to be queen there.*

Mielitta laughed, bitter. 'Yes, it's very hard to be queen there.'

Go then, to your other world.

'Mielitta's stomach heaved and her body blurred from six legs
to two, five eyes to two, two mid-sections to one and she whirled
in nausea. She would far rather travel in her own physical body
through the Forest to the water gate and Citadel but that required
inhabiting her own human form, which was where, exactly?

She remembered being in the library, feeling her bee sigil burn
and summon her, but she had no idea when that had been. She'd
been away long enough to mate, murder, lay eggs and discuss
apian manners – no word could cover how long that felt to her
but she thought she'd probably passed six or seven nights away
from the Citadel.

She opened her eyes. She was not in the library. She was lying
on her bed, fully dressed, and a man was staring at her. She
curved her back to stab him with her sting, while knowing full
well that she could only kill other queens.

'How did you get into my chamber?' she asked him. The
wards were supposed to be proof against all break-ins, by force or
even magecraft, the one place she could guarantee safety, and yet,
of all people, Jannlou was here. She would never have invited him
in, not even if he'd used glamour at full strength!

His blue eyes sparkled, as if she'd said something funny.

'It's my chamber,' he told her. With dawning horror she took in her surroundings. Of course all beds and their covers looked the same but the chest was black metal instead of woodette and there was no little mirror. The window was on the opposite side and a man's clothes were folded on a chair, beside a cushion embroidered with the Magaram monogram. She was a prisoner and her only weapon was missing.

CHAPTER FIFTEEN

Mielitta's bee sigil throbbed with power, offering her an escape route. If she could pass the wards of the Maturity Barn, then she could break out of Jannlou's chamber in bee form. But if she did so, Jannlou would alert his father and the whole Citadel would know she was a Forest traitor. Could she defy the Council of Ten, who would surely hunt her down?

And why in the stones' name was her human body lying on Jannlou's bed? What had it – *she* – been doing while Mielitta was also in the beehive? She needed to find out what had happened and she wouldn't do that if she shifted shape and tried to fly. She ran through a wild range of reasons why Jannlou might want her in his chamber. None of them helped her think, so she became the Assistant Librarian once more and blinked at the mage.

'Good. I see you're back in the land of the living.' Jannlou moved towards her, bulky, muscles shining brown under the skin of his bare arms. He had the lithe power of a big man who trained hard.

She flinched backwards, hand clutching her own neck as if scared, reaching for her arrowhead. Nothing. The chain had gone. Death and damnation!

'I-I-I don't know what you mean. Please don't hurt me. I

117

don't know what I've done wrong.' It was always safe to assume you'd done something wrong. She added for good measure, 'Or why I'm here. Or anything that happened.' Stones! That was a mistake. If he'd raped her, he was hardly going to admit it if she said she remembered nothing! But she didn't feel as if she'd been abused. Surely, even if there'd been something consensual between them, her body would feel different? She flushed at the thought, focused on the puzzle of what was going on. She felt a little spaced out, but only her head felt strange, nothing else.

'I feel woozy,' she told him, wondering if she'd been a victim of his magecraft. She watched his reaction closely but those startling blue eyes seemed as wary of her as she of him.

'What do you remember?'

Laying a thousand eggs a day after a successful maiden flight. Saving my people. It was easy to look dazed, as if she was struggling to get her memory back.

'I was in the library, organising the books.' *While the bees were cleaning.* 'I'd reached *Ancient Natural History* and survival stories and was just deciding whether to keep the survival stories together in a separate section or to categorise them by the survival environment…'

Did that sound too intelligent for a new adult? Jannlou was nodding encouragement, and at least he hadn't jumped on her with either a knife or amorous intent, so she sat up. He stood still, neither threatening nor relaxed.

She risked further movement, swinging her legs over the side of the bed. She felt less vulnerable sitting, with her bare feet firmly on the spotless woodette floor. She could see her boots, placed neatly side by side under the chair which held Jannlou's overclothes, but at least she seemed to be wearing all of her own garments.

She licked her dry lips and continued, '…when I must have blacked out. I don't remember anything until I woke up here.' Too late now to pretend she did. She'd just have to watch his face for lies or evasions. Fat chance of catching a mage in either – it was what they did for a living!

He nodded as if he'd come to some conclusion. 'That's where I found you. I was seeking some information in the library…'

Evasion, she thought. *I wonder what sort of book he wanted.*

'… and I saw you picking up books, walking round with them, putting them on shelves. You took the same books off the shelf, carried them back to the stool you'd taken them from and placed them there. Then you repeated the same sequence. I watched you do this several times before I spoke to you. You acted as if I didn't exist and I thought you were ignoring me, to provoke me.'

Wide-eyed and innocent, Mielitta asked, 'Why would I do such a thing, my Lord Mage? Surely I must have been ill to behave so?'

He looked away from her, studied the pile of clothing on the chair, the boots underneath. When his gaze returned, it was unveiled. No silver today, no clouds, no canopy, she thought. Sky blue with violet nuances. You can't hide from the sky. She looked down.

'Apprentice Mage,' he corrected her. 'And I know who you are, Mielitta.'

She giggled. 'That's who I *was*,' she corrected. 'Before my Maturity Ceremony. Before I became a new adult. Now,' she showed pride in her office, 'now I'm Assistant Librarian.' Her heart thumped, so loud he must surely hear it.

'You are – you were – the girl my friend Bastien thought was a threat to our society. A threat Bastien wanted to render harmless.' *To suppress,* she thought. Should she tell him what Bastien and his father were plotting? What Bastien really thought of Jannlou? He'd never believe her. But she *had* shaken his confidence in his previous judgement of her; perhaps enough, perhaps not.

'I don't understand why Mage Bastien, *Apprentice* Mage Bastien, would think such a thing.' She kept her voice gentle, soft, womanly. 'I was not selected, so I trained and became good at child's play because I had more years than most to do so. But when I was tested, I left childish ways behind.' She let her hand slip to her neck. 'I kept a lucky arrow as a souvenir but, now I am an adult, I have given up all the behaviour that might have annoyed your friend. And you,' she added, remembering all too well Jannlou's speed as he chased her, calling out to Bastien where she was.

Did she imagine it or was it his turn to grow hot-faced? Difficult to tell with his dark skin tone – he was lucky in that too!

'I'm surprised you passed the test after all this time,' was all he said.

'May Perfection continue to guide and protect me,' she smiled at him. A thought struck her. 'Maybe that is why I've been ill. The Maturity Test and Ceremony affected me because I was older. And you rescued me.' She batted her eyelashes and smiled. *Possibly*, she thought. *But I reserve judgement on your motives.* Something troubled her at the thought of the Maturity Test. Something she had to remember. Danger. But not to her. Danger to somebody else. She dismissed the half-memory. Once she was out of this trap, she would spend time recalling the days before her time in the beehive.

'I went back to the library at the end of the day and you were still repeating the same ritual.' He shrugged. 'So I took your arm and led you to my chamber. Nobody noticed your odd behaviour and nobody considered it strange that I should bring a lady here.' His eyes crinkled in laughter. 'I fed you and I took you back to the library each day so nobody would notice. And then today you came back to yourself.'

'You fed me?' Mielitta remembered opening her mouth, accepting nectar, regurgitated food, honey. She wanted to giggle at the thought of Jannlou's tongue down her throat. Then she flushed again.

He nodded. 'I brought you water and food. It would have been too difficult to take you to the Great Hall, too obvious that there was something seriously wrong with you. When you were here, after feeding, you slept. And nobody noticed you carrying the same books over and over, in the library.'

'No, they wouldn't.' She frowned. 'How long have I been here?'

'Two nights. This is the third day.'

Exploring the hive, fighting the queens, her maiden flight, her triumphant if short reign had taken far more than three days. Time behaved differently in the beehive – or perhaps in the Forest. Shelved under *to be revisited*. She had spent far longer than three days in the beehive. Then she registered all the implications of Jannlou's words. *Nights*. Where had he slept?

As if he'd read her mind, Jannlou shook his head. 'I slept on the floor, on a blanket. Good training.' His eyes sparkled.

She had to ask. 'Why did you look after me?'

'Because you're a lady.' *Lie*.

The thing she couldn't bring to mind teased her memory. She was getting closer to it. 'Bastien.' She frowned then remembered to look vacant, uncaring. 'I mean, Apprentice Mage Bastien, your friend; he has seen me too and knows I'm an adult now?'

'I don't think he's recognised you.' Hesitation. 'I will tell him that he need look no further.' So Bastien *had* been looking. There was something she should remember. She shook her head to clear it but the hint of a memory was gone.

'Then I may go now?' She stood up, half expecting him to reach out a hand, stop her.

Instead, he crossed to the chair, picked up her boots. 'You'll need these.'

While she was lacing her boots, she asked, 'You haven't seen my lucky pendant by any chance? My necklace?'

He moved so quietly that she almost bumped into him as she straightened. Before she recovered, he slipped the chain around her neck and let the arrow drop down her bodice to nestle in its accustomed place. Darkening, navy and purple, his eyes did not follow the pendant but held hers.

'I didn't want you to do me some mischief,' he told her

gravely but his eyes were alight with laughter. 'While you were not yourself.'

She remembered all too well the mischief she'd tried to do to both him and Bastien while she *was* herself and she couldn't help smiling.

'Oh no,' she spoke to herself as much as to him, backing away. 'I'm not falling for that mage glamour, so you can just keep your magecraft to yourself, thank you very much.'

He merely looked puzzled and she collected herself, blushing yet again. 'I mean, I'm much obliged but I shouldn't be here. I must go.'

He reached under the bed – they must all keep their treasures in the same place! – and he pulled out a book she recognised straight away. *Survival in the Forest.*

'You had this one tucked under your arm and wouldn't let go of it until you were asleep,' he told her.

Oh, stones. Now what must he think of her. After all that play-acting to hide her true nature. Her brow cleared. 'Thanks be to Perfection!' she said brightly. 'Mage Yacinthe asked me to find such a book and deliver it to her.'

He didn't challenge her explanation. No doubt Mage Yacinthe would come under suspicion for her reading tastes but it couldn't be helped.

'It's time you went to the library and shelved some books.' Jannlou opened the door and she fled through it, sure she could hear gusts of gruff laughter in the chamber behind her. The walls echoed her footsteps all the way to the library.

'Drone,' she muttered. 'He's just a drone.'

Stung into a rebuke, her inner bee pointed out, *Without drones, we have no people. Their strength and their deaths create our lives.*

'Bees,' replied Mielitta, 'do not see the full picture.'

CHAPTER SIXTEEN

With only books for company, Mielitta pursued her cataloguing as mechanically as if her spirit were still in the beehive. *Fungi Identification* took its place beside *Flora in Wetlands and Wolds* while she tried to catalogue her thoughts, a more difficult exercise.

Whenever a title made her hesitate between categories, she placed it in her *To be revisited* bookstack, cleared for that purpose. She did the same with the questions that led nowhere. *To be revisited.* Why had Jannlou helped her after years as gang leader, making her life hell? What was he hiding?

Her attempt to evaluate what she knew of her new powers was more fruitful. Whether it was a psychedelic experience, entirely in her own head, or not, made no difference subjectively. She felt connected to a community of bees, via the sigil on her thigh and voices in her head. She could summon their qualities to help her and sometimes they came unasked. That was a danger if she wished to remain invisible, innocuous among the Citadel adults.

If she was to believe Jannlou, she'd left her body like an empty shell for several days, while she experienced life as a queen bee. Yet, when she'd broken into the Maturity Barn as a bee, she'd regained consciousness in her own body, inside the Barn. So there must be some way of reuniting what she could only call her bee self with her human self, of moving the human body through barriers only a bee could cross. For a short distance at least. Whether she could travel to the beehive instantly in bee form and reunite there with her human body was a different matter. She remembered how sick she'd felt in the Maturity Barn and doubted the wisdom of such an experiment. If she wanted to go to the Forest as Mielitta – and oh, how she longed to go there! – she must take the long route through the water gate.

The optimal, safe greylight made her long for shafts of sunlight and pools of shade. 'There is more than this,' she murmured, carrying more books to a shelf.

What if she talked to someone? Showed them the bee sigil and told them what it meant, what she could do? Declan. She had always talked to Declan, of her finding, her lessons and archery, her smith-work. She had even told him of her pain in being passed over, of losing her childhood friends year on year. But he had chosen Kermon, told her what girls could not do, told her to be a lady, to accept that she was an adult now. She could hardly tell him that her maturity had been fabricated.

How would Declan react to her tales of bee powers? He was a mage, accustomed to magecraft and its appearance in those chosen. But she had never been chosen, had been the dullest of children, had worked hard for every small achievement in her ordinary world. At best, he would think she was attention-seeking, telling stories that made her seem important.

If he thought *she* believed what she was saying, he would think her mentally impaired. What excuse had she made to Jannlou? An adverse effect from the Maturity Test. Jannlou had accepted that easily and so would Declan. He'd seek medication for her and wait for the madness to pass. In the Citadel all madness passed – or the mad person did. She shivered.

And if Declan believed her tale as fact? Then he would know how many crimes she had committed. Lying about the Maturity

QUEEN OF THE WARRIOR BEES

Ceremony was insignificant compared with stealing a mage password, breaking out of the Citadel to trespass in the Forest. All were crimes too terrible for her even to know the customary sentence. Nobody had ever been accused of so much treason. Not even Crimvert, and look what his fate had been.

And she had no words, not even book-words, to describe what she was doing with the bees. She knew it was beyond forgiveness. If, that is, it was real and not just a figment of her imagination.

She started work on the Psychology section, removing the section Women's Mental Health problems and carefully putting *Delusional and Hysterical Phases in Women* next to *Delusional Psychosis in One Hundred Patients*. Surely, they had more in common than difference? She was the Assistant Librarian and she would make all such decisions. If she couldn't shape the world, she could shape the library according to how the world should be.

And why did the mages keep books on so many subjects nobody was allowed to talk about? Who read them? She opened the ledger showing which titles had been checked out and by whom. Very interesting. Rinduran's reading on wall history and safety in wall visits was unsurprising. But his forays into revolutions and propaganda in ancient times might be of interest to the Council.

Bastien's taste was for erotic romances. Mielitta's mouth screwed up in disgust at the thought as she skimmed names that meant little, noted Puggy's preferred mixture of philosophy, gender politics and make-up tips.

Jannlou's name caught her attention. She felt almost guilty, prying into someone's reading habits. But wasn't that part of a librarian's job? Perhaps she could start a conversation with mages who visited, recommend books to them, make use of her memory. If, of course, the Citadel calmed enough for simple activities like reading to be popular again. Meanwhile, she would learn what she could about the mages and their apprentices.

Her heart skipped a beat. *Forest Predators* was not what she'd expected to see checked out to Jannlou, along with *Heredity and*

Magecraft. The latter she could understand being of interest to the Chief Mage's son but the former was too close to her own secret. A Citadel predator, he was stalking her, and she must be wary. But the book had been checked out *before* she visited the Forest. Had his magecraft sensed something of the Forest in her before she had?

She shelved that question with the others waiting to be revisited. If Jannlou suspected her true nature, she was in even greater danger but she could not ask Declan for help. She had closed that door. She'd never told him that books and their words entered her mind as she cleaned in the library, so that she knew of life before the Citadel. Such knowledge was meant for mages and she did not want to be banned from the library.

And she had never told him of the harassment from the gang. His intervention would only harm both of them. It was just the same regarding her new powers.

The gang. Bastien, Jannlou, and their new roles. There was something she needed to remember. Another disadvantage of her bee life to be filed: her memory after shifting shape had gaps relating to the events just before it.

She checked the books were straight on the shelf.

Let us work, buzzed her voices.

Why not? There was nobody in the library.

'Dust the books,' Mielitta told the bees and soon the shelves were alive with a working hum and a whirr of wings. Her spirits lifted in such company and her own work became satisfying in its rhythm rather than boring. Bees had no concept of boredom and Mielitta had no urge to change their mindset.

Engrossed as she was in cataloguing the books on Macrobiology, Mielitta took a few seconds to notice a change in the working rhythm of some bees on an empty section of shelf. They were crawling round a bee-sized object, covering it in orange goo. When Mielitta looked more closely, she could see a dead bee being wrapped up in orange. She touched it. Sticky. Some of the orange stayed on her finger and she had to rub it off. She stroked a bee working with the orange substance, soothing it, as she looked more closely.

No, not a dead bee. A dead fly. Mielitta had seen flies in the Forest, their whine so different from the hum of bees, so irritating. There had never been a fly or any creature other than humans in the Citadel, dead or alive. Until now. *Dogs, cats, rats, mice, spiders, flies, fleas* – book words. Citadel society was safe, hygienic, Perfect. So how was there a dead fly in the library? Was it Crimvert who'd breached the Citadel's defences, guilty as charged of allowing Nature to infiltrate? Or was somebody else responsible. Somebody who'd defiled Perfection with thousands of bees.

The hairs rose on the back of her neck at this new evidence of her treason, even as she instructed the group of bees anxiously disposing of the dead body. 'Leave it, little ones. I will take care of it.' Carefully avoiding the bees, she swept the fly to the floor with one finger. Let the floor do its work.

The woodette around the dead fly rippled as it always did when absorbing a snag of fabric, crumb of sustenance or other accidental debris. But this time the ripple hit the fly and froze, forming a hard outline round the small corpse, an outline that grew larger as more ripples hit the previous ones. When the floor gave up its attempt at cleaning, there was a dark accusatory stain around the fly's orange-wrapped body.

'What's in that stuff?' Mielitta asked, stroking her bee sigil to calm her racing pulse.

Propolis, her inner queen answered. *It protects the hive from infection if we cover debris in it. We seal joints with it when we're build-ing, to keep out rain and secure the walls. It is both medicine and glue.*

'It's certainly sticky enough.' Mielitta still had specks of orange on her finger. 'And looks so weird!' Worse than weird. The fly's body was incontrovertible proof that the Forest was in the Citadel and Mielitta did not want the Council of Ten investigating the library.

She tried to pick up the dead fly but it was now firmly enmeshed in the fabric of the floor. A knife or an arrow-point

---

***

might cut it out, but what if the hole left in the floor caused damage to the magical structure of the Citadel itself? Unthinkable! Far worse than the flaw caused by the dead insect.

She moved a stool to stand over the stain but the dark patch was clearly visible, even from a distance. She took a pile of books and stacked them under the stool, then piled more around them and on top of the stool. There. Unless you knew what you were looking for, you wouldn't spot the faint shadows rippling through the woodette, outward beyond the stool. Just cataloguing in progress. Nothing unusual.

The subtle change in greylight was enough to alert one Citadel-born to the day's end. She breathed a sigh of relief and recalled her bees. At last, she could retreat to her own room. She picked up her book on survival in the Forest, to take with her. She wanted to ensure its words and pictures were fully memorised before returning it to its shelf and she should have an hour's guaranteed solitude, perfect for reading, before she must brave the evening meal in the Great Hall.

She would seek a table in the middle, be invisible among the other women in their gowns and gossip. If she'd fooled Jannlou, she could fool everyone in the Hall. Declan and the Maturity Mages would have sent the necessary messages, announcing her adulthood, to the stewards, archery tutor, teachers, in kitchen and schoolroom, so her absence in her old haunts be expected. Nobody would miss her.

Then she remembered. Drianne. Danger.

Everything came back to her, the whole conversation between Bastien and his father in the library. Now Bastien was Maturity Mage, he had power over Drianne. Mielitta might be safe in her Assistant Librarian disguise but Drianne would suffer twice over. Bastien had said, 'I could mute her and make her a good citizen.' And days had gone by since then. What had he done to Drianne?

CHAPTER SEVENTEEN

I n a float of pastel gowns, the ladies settled around Mielitta, who was just one more petal in their midst. The Hall was full to bursting, with barely space to move between tables or elbow room to eat. Squashed between a lemon gown and a rose pink one, she glanced at the back of the Hall, where she used to sit, at the servants' tables.

Thank the stones! Drianne was sitting there as always. In the first flood of relief, Mielitta wanted to rush to her friend and warn her but, luckily, the cramped seating prevented any spontaneous escape from the bench. Second thoughts reminded her why she could not renew contact with Drianne, for both their sakes. She turned resolutely away from the hunched shoulders of the youngster, the drooping misery, to face the blue gown opposite her. She would watch over Drianne from a distance. The best way to protect her was to keep a close eye on Bastien.

She turned to look at the High Table, which was as full as all the others. The whole of society was in attendance for tonight's meal and there was a buzz of anticipation. Or apprehension. What events and announcements had Mielitta missed during her evenings in Jannlou's chamber? It was too late to ask him now. There he was, solid, filling his Apprentice Mage's robe. Beside him, grey cloth billowed around Bastien's whip-thin figure, as they both took their places by the minor mages, furthest from the Council Table, furthest from their fathers.

No doubt their mothers were somewhere among the pinks and blues, ladies like herself. If they'd had any magecraft, they'd be mages. Mielitta had never thought about the process by which girls became mages. She had been so sure she lacked magecraft that she'd paid no attention to how those in power gained their positions.

There is no difference between baby workers and baby queens. You didn't know you were a queen, not a worker. We fed you royal jelly and made you a queen.

Mielitta shushed her voices. Did her bee powers make her a mage? Should she be at the table with Bastien and Jannlou? Their reactions would be quite a picture. But it was a foolish thought. If she had true powers and not a mental illness, the source of her powers was the forbidden Forest and it was treachery she carried, not magecraft.

But she couldn't help day-dreaming. If she were a mage, she would start off as an Apprentice Mage. She scanned the mage tables. Apart from Bastien and Jannlou, there were no apprentices and *they'd* been so elevated because of their fathers. She had no such pedigree. And she was a girl.

For the first time, she counted the number of female mages. Two among the Ten Councillors. Five among the thirty lesser mages. Surely, there used to be more? Female mages weren't allowed to marry, which of course meant they couldn't have children. If they did, would more girls have magecraft? If she had children, would they have bee powers?

You have thousands of children. They are bees.

Mielitta's stomach dipped. Mother to thousands. She must be mad but she saw no benefit in fighting her own rambling thoughts. Could you be insane if you knew you were? She drank her purified water, ate her sustenance and yearned for flavours. She wondered what evening light was like in the Forest, whether night was empty black. In the Citadel, the optimised evening light for the interior had a yellowy tinge which was more flattering than daytime grey.

Her morose thoughts were interrupted by a friendly introduction. 'I'm Hannah.' The rose-pink gown beside her at table was apparently worn by a person with a name and a smile. Artful brown curls, a complexion and voice to match her dress all contributed to an impression of womanly Perfection.

'Mielitta,' she offered, then she realised she'd been abrupt. 'I'm a new adult,' she added, then realised how many questions that would provoke, to which she wasn't keen to give answers. She beamed a *Let's be friends* smile, hoping that would divert curiosity.

'I'm Georgette,' Lemon gown, opposite Mielitta, introduced herself with a simper. Fuller in face and figure than Hannah, her arched brows suggested permanent surprise.

'Ninniana,' said the blue-clad lady sitting beside Georgette. 'How lovely to meet a newcomer. I'm sure you have lots of stories for us!' She pronounced each word carefully, as if offering the fruits of her wisdom from a mulberry-dark mouth.

Stones, thought Mielitta as she practised her smile on Georgette and Ninniana, names she shelved instantly under *Identical Moss-for-brains*.

Hannah's limpid grey eyes had narrowed and her mouth pursed as she inspected her table-mate. 'You're older than–' she began but her words were lost in the growing murmur around the hall.

There was a bustle of activity at the High Table and the general hubbub stilled as Magaram stood up to speak. This in itself was unusual as announcements were usually delegated to lesser mages.

'My people, I know you are worried. In your chamber at night, you wake and wonder whether you are still safe, whether the wards that protect you could be broken, whether something could break the floor spells and come from under the bed, like a strand of evil hair, seeking the heat of your body, circling your throat, tightening…'

Hannah shuddered and another instinctively put a hand to her throat, brushing away an invisible hair.

With the High Table's speechcraft, all mages could address the Hall without any effort, reaching the furthest corners, so everybody jumped when Magaram shouted, 'You are right! Evil is here among us!' He flung out one arm and the sleeve of his robe dropped back as he pointed, accusing.

Mielitta had jumped too and felt everyone's eyes on her. Did her guilt show on her face? A dead fly. Floor magecraft broken. And secret bees. She risked a glance across the table. Georgette was flushed, looking down and Ninniana was gazing wildly around, neither of them paying any particular attention to Mielitta.

Still she felt that finger pointing at her, those blue eyes piercing her buzzing black heart, condemning her. Her hands were clammy with sweat and she clenched them under the table, her heart pounding.

The stare was familiar and the last time she'd endured it, the Mage had been as close as the blue gown was now. Jannlou. *Glamour*, she reminded herself. If the son had the power to charm her, how much more power over people's feelings did the father have! Well, he'd picked the wrong citizen. She'd protected her feelings against Jannlou's charisma often enough and she could do likewise against Magaram.

The Chief Mage's voice regained its calm authority. 'We will keep you safe from the evil without but we need your help with the evil within.' In case the message wasn't clear enough, he continued softly, 'The evil inside you, inside the person sitting beside you, inside our community. The evil that comes from forgetting who we are.'

All the mages were standing, facing the hall, in a show of black-robed solidarity. Magaram waved a hand in their direction. 'We never forget. We endure hours, days, years in the walls' memories to preserve our society. We are the force of law and order against the forces of chaos. We dedicate our lives to you and some of you have forgotten why. We know who you are and you cannot hide from Shenagra.'

On hearing her name, Shenagra nodded as if receiving instructions and stepped down from the dais. As she walked between tables, seated diners shrank back to allow her to pass. Her hair writhed, as if sniffing out traitors. When she stopped beside a table, everybody sitting there froze, moving only when she'd moved on. As she followed her path round the room, then paced it again, so that none could think they were safe now, Magaram continued:

'Our blessed ancestors recorded their sufferings so that we may live safe, Perfect lives.' His voice blasted again. 'Will we shit on their wisdom?' The crudeness shocked as much as the volume. 'Some here think they know better.'

He'd said *they*. He didn't know it was her. He was bluffing. Mielitta tried to blank out her thoughts as Shenagra stalked between the tables, scenting.

Deliberately, Magaram repeated, 'Some here are shitting on our ancestors' wisdom. And I will tell you the suffering this has caused. Stand up if there is an empty place to your left at table.'

Reluctantly, afraid of what would happen to them, one person after another stood up in the Hall until there were eleven of them so exposed. The seats were so crammed, Mielitta wasn't sure she'd have noticed an empty place but she wasn't going to volunteer, regardless.

'One, two...' Magaram pointed at each quivering citizen in turn, counting aloud. 'Eleven. That's eleven of our people missing from the evening meal today. Did you wonder where they were? Some of you know all too well.' Stifled sobs could be heard from two of the tables with empty seats.

'Eleven people, who were loved, who had family and friends, *eleven* people have died in the last four days because of the traitors. Eleven people grew sick from the allergies we protect you from and they died! Nobody here need face the wildness of Nature and its deadly consequences. No cancer, no diseases, no stings, no bites, no food poisoning and no allergies! The Citadel is safe for all! But traitors want to murder us in our beds, spoil our happiness, end sustainability! *We* won't allow it! Will you? Will you allow it?'

Mechanically, Mielitta joined in the shout of 'We won't allow it!' while she waited for the questing hair to find her. Had Magaram's choice of nightmare imagery been deliberate? If she survived, Mielitta for one would be checking under her bed for any change in the floor. Another pang of guilt as she thought of what she'd done to the library floor.

'This one,' declared Shenagra, amplifying her voice as she sent tendrils of hair out to a brown-clad man at the table beside Mielitta.

'Have you harboured thoughts of discontent? That there must be more to life? That you would like to see outside the Citadel?

'Yes,' he whispered, while those around him shrank back in case his thoughts were contagious. 'Forgive me.' His voice shook.

'You are forgiven. And punished. May you serve as an example.' Shenagra's braids uncoiled, reached into the man, who stood stoically, accepting his sentence. Mielitta looked away but she could hear the gasps around her. The details she imagined were worse than if she'd watched. She'd seen what happened to Crimvert.

She slipped her arrowhead up from her bodice, smoothed it, let the patterns give her courage. *Steelwing.* And she waited her turn.

The next person accused tried to run. His screams were barely audible above the roar of the crowd. In the resultant mêlée it was unclear whether he was trampled to death by enthusiastic citizens or executed by Shenagra.

The five subsequent traitors learned that lesson and died peacefully, forgiven for their sins.

Mielitta felt sick. This was her fault. She'd introduced pestilence into the Citadel, killed eleven fragile souls who'd been safe before 'wild Nature' found them. She should confess, accept her fate and stop Shenagra executing more people.

No, the voices told her but they could only tell her she was the Queen, too important, and that was not enough for her conscience. As she opened her mouth to proclaim her guilt, she felt somebody staring at her. Blue eyes piercing her buzzing black heart. But not Magaram's eyes.

Jannlou had protected her before, was saying nothing now when it would be so easy to point a finger at her strange behaviour. Why? Already he'd looked away but merely asking the question made her resolve to confess falter, and led to other questions. Were the accused really traitors? If so, why did she feel no kinship with them? If not, why would Shenagra execute them?

As her brain whirred, Shenagra announced 'This one,' at the other side of the Hall. 'Have you thought our community prejudiced against women? Have you wanted more for your daughter than you have known?' Shenagra asked a mousy-haired lady in a lime gown. 'Have you spoken of such matters and raised discontent? Threatened sustainability?'

'I have,' was the quiet reply and the eleventh traitor met her end.

'Eleven,' announced Magaram. 'Eleven traitors for eleven deaths and we will know if there are more.'

That made no sense. The number of deaths would have been a result of allergic reactions, not one murder victim matched with a murderer. Far from looking like an organised group of traitors, the accused had seemed the most innocuous of citizens with the most trivial of qualms. And she should know what acts of real treachery were like! Crimvert had known too. His paean to Nature had made her own heart sing. Now *he* had been a traitor.

Was it possible these were ordinary citizens who'd just been killed for everyday thoughts? But why?

Then the answers came to her. Because they had no idea who had let in the forces of Nature. And because they wanted a display of strength that would strike fear into every ordinary citizen. Who in that Hall had not pondered such questions in private? Unless their Maturity Test had left them as brain-dead as she was pretending to be. She did not look towards Jannlou, nor to Declan where he and Kermon stood among the artisan mages. What had Kermon called himself? A soul-reader. No, she did not want to catch the eye of a soul-reader this day.

Magaram was speaking again. 'If you hear of such wickedness again, tell us. Even if it's your wife, husband, daughter, son, friend – better to lose one person and sustain society! Any strange words, any strange behaviour, tell us! May Perfection guide and protect us!'

So, that was how they planned to find her. By turning every other person in the Citadel into her enemy. If only they knew – they'd changed nothing. Her only friends were her bees and they would not betray her.

'But we too must beware of the evil within and we have come to a difficult decision. Mage Rinduran will explain it to you.'

Bastien's father took centre-stage, his aura of modesty so great it drew all eyes in curiosity.

'Mage Magaram does me too much honour. He wanted to spare you this burden but we feel there is no choice.'

So, Magaram had been outvoted on whatever this decision was and Rinduran was spokesman. Interesting.

'I have made special study of the walls, so I know better than most the toll that such an experience takes on a person. I will prepare those chosen, so as to keep you safe.'

The word 'chosen' chilled the Hall after the fate of those previously chosen.

Magaram responded to the silent apprehension. 'Fear not. Shenagra is choosing ten to represent you, to go into the walls and hear our history and report back to you on what Perfection truly means, why our society is sustained with our laws and practices, so you all understand what we mages know already.'

This time Shenagra's hair remained neatly braided as, once

more, she paced the Hall, selected one person here, another there. They were clearly of different backgrounds and types. *As the traitors had been*, thought Mielitta, not sure whether she was relieved or disappointed to be passed over again.

Then she saw the chosen ones file down towards the dais, among them Drianne, her thin arms hugged tightly around herself. Bastien exchanged a glance with his father and then his eyes never left the girl. Eleven dead and ten more chosen.

CHAPTER EIGHTEEN

For the third time the bees checked under Mielitta's bed.

There's nothing there, they told her again, returning to her mind, which was buzzing with more than bees.

She couldn't ask them again so, finally, she looked under the bed for herself, pulled out her bow and quiver, her book on survival. She lay on the floor peering into the shadows, thankful for the optimal room lighting as she scrutinised the surface. Only when she was sure that there was not one ripple there and certainly no hairs, did she turn her attention to her weapons.

She drew a short arrow from the quiver, threw it at the cork-board on her wall, enjoyed the ping and thud as it flew and hit home.

She repeated the exercise until there were no short arrows left. She sighed. If only the arrows would return of their own accord. Maybe she could enlist some retrievers.

'Work,' she suggested to the bees but they became still, feigning sleep.

We're not ants! Her inner queen was indignant. *We don't carry weights.*

'Sorry,' she told the bees. 'I'm still learning. Anyway, it keeps me fit. I was just being lazy.'

Checking her equipment, changing a flight, smoothing a splintered shaft, merely postponed the moment she had to face what she might have done. She'd destroyed the hermetic seal around their community, brought sickness in, killed people. However, listing the facts of the matter prevented her wallowing quite as deeply in guilt. The mages had been discussing a breach before Mielitta had been outside. Crimvert had not been innocent, unlike the eleven in the Hall. But those deaths had not been by her hand. Maybe the infection had not been caused by her either. All she knew for sure was that she could not trust the mages to tell the truth. Maybe there had been no casualties at all and Magaram's intention had been to spread fear, gain support for his rule.

As did Rinduran, with one tiny difference. He wanted Magaram out of the way. Mielitta was sure that Bastien's father was going to use this visit into the walls to his advantage but she had no idea how. When the volunteers – hostages? – reported back in the Great Hall tomorrow it might be too late to rescue Drianne from whatever that conspiratorial look between Rinduran and Bastien had meant. But what could she do? She had her bow, arrows and bees against all the magecraft in the Citadel. Not to mention being under surveillance by all its residents.

Work, the bees told her.

'How?' she asked.

Work, they insisted. *What if.*

Mielitta had not played 'what if' since the days when she had little friends to play with. The principle was that you could imagine anything you wanted to happen and then the team would each state a step to take on the way to making it happen. There was no winner but their stories had brought their dreams to life. A dangerous game to play beyond childhood, judging by what had happened to the eleven in the great Hall.

Defiant, Mielitta played *what if*, imagining Drianne and the others hosted – imprisoned – in the mages' quarters, then in 'preparation' with Rinduran tomorrow before going into the walls to experience history. What if she could be there during the preparation, go into the wall? She could check on what was happening to Drianne, know whether she should risk a daredevil strike or wait patiently. What if she too could go into the wall, experience history first hand, maybe – her pulse raced – maybe even experience her *own* history, find out where she had come from before the Finding?

She remembered book-words. What if she could be there like a fly on the wall?

Bee, the voices said. *Bee on the wall.*

'Bee,' she agreed. Maybe that would work. In the morning. Nothing would happen tonight. The volunteers would try to sleep and so would she. Rinduran was responsible for them and every citizen would witness them reporting back tomorrow so Drianne should be safe. And if she wasn't, Mielitta would know. If her plan worked.

Mielitta shelved the survival book in its alphabetical place. She didn't need the physical copy any longer, having memorised text and images. They made little sense to her at the moment but, as with bees and sunshine, when the experience reached her she would have the words and the understanding required. Living in the Forest would be very different from visiting it and she shied away from the prospect, unless she was forced to flee.

The library was a calm haven as usual and with such momentous events happening in the Citadel, Mielitta felt it highly unlikely that she would be disturbed. The mages had better things to do than seek out books and Rinduran was certainly occupied for the day.

'One bee,' she ordered and instantly one bee was hovering, investigating a book.

She remembered the dead bees surrounding her after the attack, the way they'd passed. Or so she'd thought. The way she'd died. Or so she'd thought. But second chances didn't mean immortality and she didn't believe them to be proof against magecraft.

'It is dangerous,' she told the bee. 'You might not come back.' Truth compelled her to change that to, 'You will probably die.'

She should have known bees better.

Why should this matter? buzzed not only the bee chosen but all her workmates. *Work*, they agreed. *It doesn't matter who does the work. Each has her turn to be nursemaid, to clean, to tend to the queen, to collect pollen, to die. We tend to you, our Queen. Next, you will want bees to have names. We are all worker bees.*

Work, buzzed the one bee selected, happy.

'I just hope it does!' muttered Mielitta. Whatever the bees' opinions, she felt a pang, sending this little friend on such a mission. *What if,* she reminded herself.

She shut her eyes, concentrated, made an image mapping the route to the Council Chamber, for that would surely be where Rinduran was preparing the volunteers. She shared the image with the bees and they danced it together, so they could reinforce the scout's mind map. She pictured the bee crawling on the wall, observing the humans, transmitting its impressions.

She danced the danger of getting close to the humans and she showed Drianne. Her mind linked with the bees, she could almost see Drianne through their eyes, as a blue human, with a lilac face. If only she could communicate Drianne's scent, that would make it easy for the scout.

Mielitta remembered holding the girl as she cried, recovering from her ordeal with Bastien. Her nostrils flared in recall and the girl's scent burst onto her senses and imprinted on the bees: salty tears and freshly soaped young skin, fear and dried sweat, with base notes of pure sweetness.

The bees were pleased with her and hummed approval. *Your Drianne flower, your sweetness, joy.*

What mattered was that they had the scent true, not what was lost in translation, so Mielitta just agreed.

Flying in small loops, the scout bee set off on her mission to find Mielitta's precious flower and report back. A little investigation found a bee space in the door frame and the scout was soon out of the library and out of sight.

What if? Mielitta closed her eyes, felt the bees' presence, imagined the scout's route and what the Citadel would look like from the bee's viewpoint. Dim at first, then more vivid, Mielitta saw the walls either side of her, far from her zigzag flight. Blues and purples, and a macro perspective changed the familiar landscape. The three eyes on top of her head were alert for danger from above as the scout followed her mind map, humming a worksong.

'Quietly,' Mielitta pleaded.

The scout was now close to the door of the Council Chamber but there was no detail in the bee's vision, just woodette, which blocked the way, and shadows, which were holes accessing the room beyond.

Mielitta felt dizzy from the shared flight and relieved when the scout followed her instructions and landed on a wall. The relief was short-lived as her view of the room turned through a full circle.

Glimpses of the room, along with her memory of the Council Meeting, showed Mielitta the volunteers sitting at the table while Rinduran paced about, talking to them. The human voices boomed along the bee's antennae and Mielitta could only interpret odd phrases.

'Overwhelming... millions of voices, sounds, pictures... say the search word clearly, focus... each his own search word... different tasks... or distraction... get lost,' Rinduran lectured them.

A volunteer's voice. '... help?'

Rinduran. 'Each one... word... get out.'

Then the scout found a match for the picture of Drianne in her mind and buzzed in excitement.

'Hush,' warned Mielitta but the bee was on her mission. She flew straight towards Drianne, alighted on her bare wrist. She unrolled her long tongue, sipped the tear-drop that had landed there unnoticed. Mielitta could taste the bitter-sweet tear, feel the human pulse connect with the vibration of the buzzing bee.

A gentle finger touched her striped back, stroked her, whispered something that sounded like, but couldn't have been, 'Wh-where are you from, honey g-g-girl?'

Then the bee's buzz seemed to grow, fill the room and Mielitta realised that the voices had stopped.

'Get out!' she yelled.

Get out! the bees echoed.

The scout sensed something, crawled underneath Drianne's hand to hide but it was too late. Mielitta felt a flash like midday sun knock her onto the table, pin her there on her back, helpless. Magecraft.

Then the voice rumbled, 'Forest filth. How dare you send your vermin here! I see you, turd.'

Mielitta had only just realised how clear his words were when she felt the mage's power sear into her. He was looking through the upper eyes of the scout but he wasn't looking at the bee. He was seeking her, tracing the link between her and the little scout, and she was pinned to the table.

Rinduran laughed. 'Come and join us. We want to see *you*, not these pathetic creatures you send. In the name of Perfection, I command you, show yourself.'

Mielitta was helpless to resist as she felt her body wavering, being dragged into the bee's, the same sickening jolt as she'd felt in the Maturity Barn but this time across a far greater distance and she would have no recovery time. She could hardly breathe, in the blast of magecraft that drew her inexorably to a fate worse than Crimvert's. If she could only reach her arrowhead, maybe she could make one effort and stab the mage as she fused with the bee on the table. She struggled but her arms were as firmly pinned by her side as the bee's wings.

Rinduran missed nothing. 'I can feel your feeble struggle. I can feel your panic. And soon I will see you, know who you are. Then we can have a proper traitor's death for our good citizens to enjoy.' His will was entirely focused on her, his eye closer and closer, magnified in hers.

Desperately, she named library books, trying to stay in human form. *Flora in Wetlands and Wolds, Delusional Psychosis in One Hundred bz bzz bzzz.* She was losing the battle.

Dart, her inner queen told her.

If Rinduran's attention was wholly on her, he would not be thinking about the pathetic little creature on the table. What if?

Mielitta stopped fighting, let herself whoosh into the oil-black void of nightmares, a whirlpool eye seen through thousands of hexagonal facets. That sucked her into the body of a bee.

For a micro-second, Mielitta and the bee were one. She breathed, 'Sorry,' as she bucked her abdomen, pierced the mage's glaring eye with her stinger and watched the venom drip off the jettisoned dart.

Rinduran screamed, flailed his arms in a blind attempt to hit the unseen enemy as one eye swelled like a balloon and the other watered, equally useless.

'Call me back!' Mielitta ordered and as her bees danced her back to the library, the last thing she heard was Drianne laughing hysterically. A reaction for which she would no doubt pay dearly.

CHAPTER NINETEEN

M ielitta stretched until she woke up enough to open her eyes and check that the light was paling to daytime grey. She threw off the covers, jumped out of bed and curved her back into an exercise routine. She hadn't been to the archery yard since becoming an adult and although working out would keep her body toned, she was worried about losing her speed of reaction without practice. She might need all her skills to rescue Drianne. If only she could figure out when and how to intervene, but she didn't know what the Maturity Test involved and she could hardly ask. Or maybe she could.

The terrifying events in the hall had put an end to casual conversation but now would be a good time to resume acquaintance with her table-mates. Her new friend Hannah enjoyed girlish conversation so it would be a kindness to encourage her. Mielitta shrugged her clothes on, combed the tangles out of her hair and braided it, then headed for breakfast. Servants flattened themselves against the walls as she swished past and she barely noticed.

She took her place by Hannah at what had become her table and smiled at Georgette and Ninniana. If they wanted to join in the conversation, they were welcome but she would work Hannah first.

'May the stones be with you,' she greeted the other girl, observing her more closely this time. The rose-pink gown bore an embroidered heart with the initials HG inside and space to add more. Uneven needlepoint stitches suggested that this was Hannah's work rather than that of any seamstress.

'Thanks be to Perfection,' replied Hannah, taking her seat and bestowing her smile on Georgette and Ninniana.

Once the greeting formalities and obligatory smiles had been exchanged, Mielitta began to dig. 'I'm so excited about the Maturity Celebration and you said there's going to be a Courtship Dance too!'

Hannah raised a delicate eyebrow, surprised. 'There always is after a Maturity Ceremony. Didn't you know?'

Mielitta looked down, suitably mortified, caught out. She stuttered a bit for effect and thought of Drianne. 'I-I my test was–' she whispered the word but projected it enough to be heard by all the girls. '–*different* because I was a late starter.' She wasn't sure whether 'late starter' was a permanent condition or one you could resign to the past. She could hardly ask Rinduran or Bastien for their judgement so she chose the past tense. With an appropriate expression of downcast shame at such a past.

'I was the only one,' she confessed, 'and the Maturity Mages kept everything very quiet so as not to embarrass Mage–' she broke off prettily, her hand to her mouth as if she had realised she should not speak so freely, '–other late starters.' All wide-eyed innocence, she continued, 'I don't know what usually happens. I was a child for eighteen years.'

The ladies were hanging on every word, shaking their heads, trying to imagine such an interminable childhood.

'Awful,' summed up Hannah. 'I was thirteen.'

'I was thirteen too,' Georgette said. 'But not at the same Ceremony as Hannah. I'm a year older than her.'

'Fourteen.'

'Eleven,' the others chimed in.

'And now we're ready for the Courtship Dance!' That brought the smiles out again but Mielitta wasn't ready to find out more about the Dance. That could wait. She should feel guilty about abusing their trust but she didn't. She found it difficult to tell the ladies apart in any deep way, so alike were their experiences and responses. Perfect responses. No wonder they were excited at meeting a newcomer and hearing her stories.

'I was tested in the Barn,' she gambled, 'Was that the same for you?'

'Of course,' Hannah replied and the others nodded agreement. 'Whichever Maturity Mage is leading the Ceremony unlocks the wards on the Barn and takes all the candidates inside.'

They'd obviously compared their experiences before as Georgette followed on smoothly from Violet. 'The boys are on one side and the girls on the other.' A thought struck her. 'If you were on your own, you didn't see what happened to the boys? You just took your drink?'

'Yes, I just took my own drink. There were no boys,' Mielitta improvised.

'Oh, well, as you know, we were given the pink cups, and the boys were given blue ones, so the tests were different.'

'We *think* the tests were different,' corrected Ninniana.

The other two looked at her with contempt. 'Well of course the tests were different. The cups were different colours,' pointed out Hannah.

'And,' Georgette gave the clinching argument, with indisputable logic, 'men and women are different so it's obvious the tests were different.'

'My test was in the drink,' Mielitta said, guessing.

'Yes, that's always how it's done and I felt all floaty, full of Perfection and so glad to be female, made for procreation and dresses and dancing.'

Ah. Mielitta could do this. 'It made me feel so gentle, wanting to be held by somebody strong.' *Drones* she thought. *Mating flight.*

'Exactly like that.' Georgette looked at her in approval.

'And then you feel the change, that you're an adult now. So good to forget all those childish things you did!'

'You forgot everything?' Mielitta wondered how Hannah could know they were childish things if she'd forgotten them all.

'Of course. Didn't you?' The ladies frowned at Mielitta.

She screwed up her face as if racking her memory, then giggled. 'I don't know. I can't remember.'

Hannah and Georgette giggled too.

'Of course, my mother has told me some stories about when I was little,' confessed Georgette.

'And mine. But that's not like remembering *being* a child.'

'I don't have a mother,' said Mielitta. The ensuing sympathy distracted the others from pondering any odd responses, or odd questions. She hesitated before asking but she had to find out, for Drianne's sake. 'I was worried, beforehand, in case I didn't pass the test.'

'But we did!' Hannah pointed out.

'And we're all here!' The ladies laughed as they chimed in at the same moment.

'What about the ones who didn't pass the test? What happened to them?' asked Mielitta and held her breath.

The ladies looked at each other, confused.

'We all passed,' Hannah repeated, shrugging, and the others just nodded agreement.

'Everyone who went into the Barn with you?' Mielitta knew she was pressing too hard but she had to find out. 'You all passed the test and came out as adults for the Ceremony. All the girls and all the boys who went into the Barn came out as women and men?'

Hannah considered the matter. 'Of course. Why wouldn't they? What a strange question.'

Georgette's expression cleared, her eyebrows lowering to their customary state of mere surprise. 'You wouldn't know that, if you were on your own but there were adult clothes ready for each one of us. There would have been spares if anybody had failed the test.'

'And everyone I know passed the test.' Ninniana enunciated each word as an absolute truth.

'So you don't need to worry about your children,' Hannah reassured Mielitta. 'They will all be fine, just like us.'

Mielitta smiled at this wonderful prospect and listened to the ladies describe their first dresses, which segued neatly into a discussion of what to wear to the Courtship Dance. With as many smiles as her face could manage without setting into rigor, and interjections of 'lace trim' or 'V-neck', Mielitta's unease grew.

Why was it called a test if everybody passed? Shenagra's tests in the schoolroom had contained a threat, created the same atmosphere as when she identified the eleven in the Hall and the traitor mage in the Council Chamber. Mielitta could still see Crimvert diminishing to a pile of ash, blown into the fireplace. She could still hear the discussion between Rinduran and Bastien in the library. *'Weak people are the result of weak tests. We won't make that mistake… use the Maturity Test to choose a mate… my advice is to suppress her.'*

Another picture came to mind: the interior of the Maturity Barn. She'd scoured the dark corners, seeking clues as to what happened there and she'd found nothing. Except for a pile of ashes. Her blood ran cold. *Suppression. Ashes.*

She excused herself as quickly as she dared and as soon as she was out of sight, she raced back to her chamber to collect her weapons. She would spend the day in the Forest, in target practice and preparation for Drianne's rescue. Tonight, the volunteers would report back and Mielitta would seize any chance to grab the girl and escape to the Forest.

She rolled her britches up in her servant's jerkin so she could change into more practical clothes once out of the Citadel. Then she strung her bow and shouldered her quiver. She could make up some story of taking it to the archery yard for a man. A beau. Enough fluffy giggles seemed to overcome most suspicions.

Help. We need you.

'Not now,' she told the bees. 'I'm coming to the Forest anyway so I can look at the hive, see if I can help. Just give me a little time.'

Now, was the inexorable response and Mielitta just had time to lie back down on her bed before the dizziness swirled her away, into her bee's body and the darkness of a teeming hive. Into the mother of all thunderstorms.

The bees' wooden home shook and Mielitta's antennae went numb from the crashes that detonated all round them. Between deafening blasts of thunder, the wind howled, forcing its way through any tiny holes in the hive walls, whistling ghastly threats. Trees groaned, creaked and splintered. One cracked completely and crashed to the ground, shaking the earth.

Still nauseous from the transition, Mielitta cowered in the dark centre of the hive, hiding from the noise and searing light that found the same pinholes as the wind to enter the hive. She sought comfort from the multitude of furry bodies surrounding her, in their protection.

Instead, she found worse horrors than the storm. The colony vibrated with panic, incapacitated with fear, spreading the scent of doom as quickly as they usually passed nectar. Mielitta was drowning, drenched in the bees' certainty that their community was dying, in the futility of action. The stench was overwhelming. There was no point fighting the weather, even if they could have routed the invaders.

Invaders? Just as Mielitta was informed of this other danger, she saw something black charging towards her, cutting a swathe through the bees as if they were mere pollen in its path. She held her ground but had no defence against its full body armour. The bees' attempts to sting bounced off its carapace, useless. Even though it was little bigger than a bee, it was more solid and carved its path through the colony, without hesitation. Hive beetle. And there were more of them.

Mielitta's eyes had adjusted enough to the darkness to make

out the comb either side of her and then she joined in the keening despair. Some of the brood had been damaged by the heedless tracks of beetles and in their place were maggots, breeding the next generation of destroyers. Compared with the murdered young, dribbled honey and stolen pollen were petty crimes. The trail of damage in the wake of hive beetles was highlighted in each flash from above.

Once more the hive shook in the earth-shattering rage of the skies. Then, after a pause, the unnatural light sought entry, its ultraviolet menacing, with no hint of flowers.

Every instinct screamed at Mielitta to crowd tightly, to die with her people, but part of her remained human, separate from the bees, and fought to survive.

There was a pause, she thought, remembering her survival book. That meant the storm was moving further away from the hive. Weather would not kill them, at least not this time.

'The storm is going,' she told her bees. 'It won't hurt us now.' There was a tiny relaxation in the tension but not for long. Some other force was contradicting her.

'Where's your other queen?' she asked but she already knew the answer. She could hear the high, frightened cries, like the song of the rival queens in their cells when they heard her coming for them.

I can't go on! Keep them away from me, please. So rough, so many of them. We're all going to die and I don't know what to do. I'm too young to be queen. You should have chosen another queen and let me die. I've let you down and it's all my fault. All for nothing, my babies dead, dying. They're all going to die.

Mielitta located the Young Queen's voice as being somewhere below her, between the same comb cliffs, further from storm light but subject to more contact with the invaders. No wonder the Young Queen was going crazy and the hive with her. Fear and its smell pulsed in waves, infecting all but the black beetles, leaving only debris and maggots in their wake as they scuttled wherever they wished to go, unhindered.

'I am your First Queen,' Mielitta told the bees. What would calm them and allow her to neutralise the damage the Young Queen was doing, while she figured out how to fight these armoured invaders? She mustn't think about the damage they were doing or she would go crazy too. What she had to do was stop them. The storm could be ignored. The sky grumbled at her resolution, then roared its anger once more. She ignored it.

'Work,' she informed them, 'You have work to do.' The mood lightened instantly and the Young Queen's lament was less insistent.

Mielitta sent a patrol to seal any chinks in the walls or roof with propolis, while the lightning was revealing where these tiny openings were. She insisted that cleaning and nursery duties be resumed, despite the beetles' vandalism, and that cleaning should include re-capping leaked honey.

'Let's feed on any spilled honey,' she told them. 'Consider it a bonus in compensation for your ordeal.' This caused confusion in bee thinking so she simplified the concept. 'Feeding on the spilled honey will be flowers for us, after the storm.'

Flowers. Their buzz was hopeful and the thought was passed around the hive. Flowers. Happy times.

'Drones, warm the hive. It's cold after the storm.'

'At once, Queen Mother,' a large black-furred bee told her, one of the more mature drones. She suddenly felt very old and not just because of her new title. How much time had passed in the beehive since she had last been here?

'Is he…?' she asked her inner queen.

Bee laughter tinkled. *Yes, he's one of yours.*

Mielitta felt faint and gulped, watching the drones cluster in the centre of the hive, thrumming as they created a warm, beating heart around the Young Queen. If the hive was too hot, they would cool it by fanning their wings. Now, they regulated their beats to create heat. How many of them were her offspring? How many of them had died during the Young Queen's maiden flight?

Everyone knew where babies come from but suddenly it felt personal to know too much about where the brood came from.

'When I laid eggs,' she said. 'I could decide whether they would be drones or workers. The drone eggs came from a different part of my body. Why was that?'

'They are unfertilised,' explained her inner queen. 'They are made by your body alone.'

How strange. Her sons, blood of her blood and wing of her wing, her descendants. But stingless. She laughed. She would think twice before calling Jannlou a drone in the future. The word was too good for him.

She made her way past the drones to the Young Queen, who still quivered and cried but more quietly. Mielitta used her right feeler in the traditional greeting, vibrated reassurance.

'I am here now. We will fight these beasts. I have a plan,' she lied, with as much confidence as she could muster. The Young Queen's shaking calmed a little but would no doubt return at the passage of the next marauder. Mielitta went looking for a plan.

She shut down her emotions and catalogued her observations. In the damaged comb, there were tunnels, random vandalism and a smell of decaying oranges from honey that frothed. Small maggots where there should have been young bees. The beetles were invincible with no chinks in their armour, they were unaffected by the bees' attempts to sting them, barging their way past any attempt to combine against them. However, they showed no sign of intelligence, no communication among themselves, no capacity to plan. Each beetle followed its own random path.

As she traversed the upper half of the hive, she noted that huge sections of comb were untouched, replete with brood, pollen and honey. There were enough provisions and more to allow the hive to recover and repair the damage. If they could get rid of the intruders.

Then she made her discovery. In between several of the comb cliffs, near the top, was a building like a miniature stable, a sort of shed behind a row of openings. Mielitta stuck her antennae through and sniffed. She didn't like the oily smell and clearly the other bees had felt likewise, as the stalls were all empty of bees. Man-made, like the beehive itself. Mielitta looked at the size of the openings, the enclosed nature of the buildings and she considered their use, if not for bees. Then she thumped her orders so they could be heard throughout the hive.

'Round them up! Drive them, herd them upwards and into the sheds.'

She waited, at the top of a cliff, where she could look down on the scene at the shed below and see if her plan worked. It relied on the beetles being docile enough to go in the easiest direction and stupid enough to fall into the traps.

The hive buzzed with a chorus of *Work! Push! Upwards!* as the bees united to herd the beetles into the sheds. Bees swarmed past Mielitta to ensure that the upward path was blocked beyond the shed as the first beetle was driven up and into an opening. There was a small liquid squelch and the beetle remained in the trap.

As more beetles followed and the bees became more efficient at herding, Mielitta vibrated her pride in her people. She extended her praise to the Young Queen, letting the whole colony know that their great courage and matchless work skills came from their leader, who had held the hive together until help came.

'May the stones be praised!' Oops. Mielitta felt the bees' puzzlement and tried, 'May the Queen be praised. All hail the One!' This was well-received and Mielitta thought it time to leave beetle clearance to the workers. There was only one bee left who had to be convinced of the Young Queen's worth.

'I let them down,' the Young Queen told Mielitta. 'You left our people in my care and I let you down too. After all your work repopulating the hive. I am too young and when anything goes wrong, I don't know what to do. You should stay here, be queen again. I will crawl into the trees and leave.'

Mielitta tapped the Young Queen with her right feeler, emitted positive vibrations, felt the bond between them, then told the truth. 'I'm young too, in my world. And I'm shit scared, most of the time. Correction – all of the time. I've been alone all my life.'

Alone aroused consternation from the Young Queen. 'Until our bees found me,' Mielitta added. 'And I don't want to be alone ever again. You don't want to be alone.'

Silence.

'Our bees cannot live without their queen and I must go back to my other people. Somebody there needs me too,' Mielitta said.

You have another people?

Drianne. 'Yes. And there is no queen who can take my place there. We have a duty to our people. Every queen is young at first and must learn.' A sudden thought struck her. 'Who called on me for help?'

We did. The Young Queen obviously considered the question silly.

'Then you are a good queen. You work together. And help came. You know what to do now.'

My work, said the Young Queen and the air filled with hope, then turned bitter again. *I stopped laying.*

'That is a queen's choice.' Mielitta was firm but she remembered fullness in her abdomen, the compulsion to lay eggs, and she knew that holding back was no light matter. 'And a queen's duty. Your mating flight was a success?'

Sixteen, was the response, vibrating with pride that she'd beaten Mielitta.

A bee's face did not smile but Mielitta's spirit did. 'Then you must fill the comb in honour of sixteen drones.'

Work, agreed the Young Queen. Then she raised her voice again but not to wail this time. *Let's work,* she exhorted her people and she waddled off to an undamaged, empty piece of comb, where she started laying eggs, in a neat outward spiral.

Heartened, the worker bees organised their duties: a watch over the beetle-sheds and parties to evict and clean the maggot-infested cells. The nursery cells were cleaned and more prepared for the new eggs.

The Young Queen took a break from laying to order nectar and good honey for herself and the Queen Mother. As the storm diminished to the patter of raindrops, Mielitta accepted nectar by tongue and savoured the moment. If only she could believe her own pep-talk. She was too young for what she faced at the Citadel. Everything was her fault and she feared for Drianne, felt guilty and responsible. But she knew one thing for certain. She would never give up her bees.

CHAPTER TWENTY

The ten volunteers were helped onto the dais, stumbling like sleepwalkers as they came to the front to address the Hall. Mielitta was relieved to see Drianne among them. The summons to the beehive could not have been worse-timed but what could she have done if she had been in the Citadel? Her attempt to use a scout bee for observation had been a near-disaster. But it had caused some damage, she thought with satisfaction.

Rinduran stood behind the volunteers and the black patch over his right eye was stark against his pale skin. She'd hoped he was allergic but no such luck. She had an idea how much the sting hurt, though. She could imagine the burning inflammation from bee venom in such a sensitive place, the blindness. Before she'd jerked free, she'd felt the sting splinter into two lancets, each saw edged needle impossible to withdraw. Underneath that black patch was a blind eye marred by a black dart. A fitting memorial to the little scout bee of whom he'd been so contemptuous. Let him think again before sneering at bees.

'In the name of all that is Perfect,' Magaram declaimed, 'the representatives of the people bear witness to the wisdom of the stones.' It was rare that speech-making began with such portentous formality and Mielitta's stomach lurched. What had happened to these citizens in only twenty-four hours, that made them look ten years older? Of course, they had seen ghosts, but was the past so painful to confront?

'Begin,' Magaram waved his black-clad arm at the woman on the extreme left of the line, her face as pale as her hair. Drianne was at the other end; due to speak last, Mielitta assumed.

'Thanks be to the stones, we don't suffer weather!' The woman's voice broke on the dreaded word and there was a gasp in the Hall. 'I was shown skin-burn and drought from the fiery sun, corpses as swollen as the rivers they'd drowned in, dwellings ripped from their foundations by gigantic windstorms, stones made of ice, water falling incessantly from the sky. Our ancestors had nowhere to go that was safe from weather. This horror was their daily life.'

There was a murmur around the Hall and people looked at each in the peaceful atmosphere and gentle greylight, trying to imagine weather.

Mielitta didn't have to imagine it.

Warm happy. Flutter of breeze wings, the bees suggested, tentative.

Winds breaking trees, she thought. *Sky crashing, breaking apart in blinding light like a sting in the eye. Huddling in the hive, while the wind wails and wants blood. It is all weather. You can't choose only what is gentle. You let all the wildness in or you keep it all out.*

She concentrated on the dais again, where the second volunteer was speaking, his voice enhanced by the speechcraft.

'Our people are many colours, none better or worse than another,' he said, 'thanks be to the stones. I saw people ill-treated because of their colour. I saw fear and hatred of difference. Their eyes did not see people but only colours of people. We see all people as people.'

Unless they're green, thought Mielitta. Nobody really believed that the experiment which produced Hamel was a good idea or they would have repeated it to produce more green people. So there were limits to this colour blindness. Acceptance based on what was usual. And what about mages? Weren't they seen as different? Or women?

As if in response to her last thought, the third volunteer said, 'Thanks to the stones, we have Perfect relationships between men and women.' She swallowed hard, shook her head as if to clear away the worst memories of her ordeal. 'Women denied their biology, used magecraft to choose times for mating and procreation. Their demands drained the mages so there was no magecraft left for healing because it was wasted on women's selfishness. They wished for dominance and,' she paused, 'some gained it.'

There was a shocked silence in the Hall.

'And men were forced into increasing violence against women, could only be restrained by magecraft. Everybody suffered and this could only end in our extinction. Thanks be to Perfection, we have men's ways and women's ways so we live together without violence.'

'Thanks be,' murmured Mielitta, along with a thousand others, but she wasn't thankful. She knew she should be but she wasn't. She was infected by bees and she knew that her life could be different, *should* be different.

With growing resentment, she listened to the other volunteers thanking the stones for their wisdom, confirming the Citadel as creation finished, in its Perfection. She did not doubt the truth of their horror stories but she could not accept the conclusions.

She heard how magecraft had taken people's employment.

No work, murmured the bees sadly.

Without employment, people had become angry and violent. In the Citadel, magecraft was controlled so as to leave appropriate occupations for all citizens.

She listened to more atrocities: people without rooms of their own, overcrowded even to the extent that they filled boats, villages, countries and died – or killed each other.

The bees puzzled over the concept of overcrowding and gave up on it as bizarrely human. However, they did understand starvation and buzzed sympathetically as a volunteer described empty-bellied children sucking stones as pretend food.

More than one volunteer spoke of food and thanked the stones for daily sustenance and water, for the lack of obesity or famine, for the absence of liquor that brought forgetfulness, violence and anger.

All the descriptions of past life were as painful to hear as for the volunteers to describe but when one spoke of what was in the food, she retched just at the memory of what she'd experienced. Killing-sheds for the animals, which were chopped up and served as food.

The greed and selfishness over food vied with extremes of hunger – unbelievable! People ate what they liked, poisoning not only their own bodies with dead creatures and substances such as salt and sugar, but also condemning their fellow-citizens to disease and death from allergies. As more and more people were diagnosed with lethal intolerances to foodstuffs, others defended their right to eat and drink as they chose. Thanks be to Perfection that every citizen in the Citadel was nourished in complete safety and optimal health. The many lived according to the needs of the minority, as was humane.

Finally, it was Drianne's turn and all eyes were on the slight figure of the youngest volunteer. Rinduran pushed his way in between the volunteers to stand beside her and he grabbed her hand, as if in reassurance.

There was some muttered curiosity about his damaged eye, which he quelled swiftly. 'I was injured yesterday in defence of the Citadel, may Perfection be preserved.'

Magaram chimed in, 'Mage Rinduran was subject to a vile attack from the enemy without, and thanks to his heroism not one citizen was harmed!'

If any of the volunteers saw events differently, none seemed anxious to speak, least of all Drianne, who stood passive and silent in the grip of Mage Rinduran, who continued, 'You have heard the testimony of your brave representatives and you can see how tough the ordeal was for them. I have endured immersion in the walls for years, to better serve you, and none knows better than I the dangers.

'I prepared these citizens as if they were my own children, made sure of their safety and exit routes but alas, this one was young and heedless...' He shook his head sadly as he looked at Drianne, never letting her hand drop.

He whispered something to her and she raised her other hand to point at her mouth while she also shook her head.

'She forgot her instructions and stayed too long in scenes so shocking that those of us who can still speak of them prefer not to. For this fragile girl, it was all too much. The trauma has taken her tongue and she can no longer speak.'

Drianne! screamed Mielitta in silence, remembering the words 'We can mute her', the shared glance between father and son.

Amid murmurs of sympathy, another robed mage, in grey, pushed through to stand on the other side of Drianne. Kermon.

He looked at her but he spoke to the Hall. 'I can speak for this lady.'

'She has lost her tongue, young man,' repeated Rinduran as if Kermon was deaf or daft, or both.

'I am a soul-reader,' said Kermon simply. 'I will read in her soul what she wishes to tell the Hall and I will speak her truth.'

'Poor girl,' whispered Hannah to Mielitta. 'I can't imagine what she must have been though. Barbaric it was back then, barbaric!'

'Barbaric!' agreed Mielitta, too loud and with too much vehemence, looking at Rinduran's hand gripping Drianne. Hannah looked at her oddly and she remembered that all citizens were on the alert for strange behaviour. She had to try to fit in.

'My heart goes out to that girl,' Mielitta said, quietly. And it did.

Hannah smiled her understanding.

'I need to be the only one in contact.' Kermon spoke quietly but with the authority of his gift and Rinduran dropped

Drianne's hand. She rubbed her wrist as she stood waiting, silent.

Bastard. Mielitta longed to hear Drianne's testimony, what the stones had shown somebody she trusted, but she was afraid for her friend. What if that testimony ran counter to Perfection? Eleven citizens had already demonstrated what that would mean.

Kermon put his hands gently either side of Drianne's face and looked at her in silent communion. Mielitta fingered her arrowhead, remembered creating the patterns in her mind's eye. She'd been the subject of just such a look but she'd felt no intruder in her mind, not like during Shenagra's infiltration. Nor had he touched her. Maybe that had been a ploy to remove Rinduran's physical constraint. Or maybe Drianne needed the reassurance of touch as she had not.

'Ooh, it's exciting isn't it?' Hannah squealed.

'Ooh, I know,' Mielitta squeaked back. 'I can't wait to hear what he says.' For good measure, she added, 'He's good-looking, isn't he?' She'd have to wash her mouth out later.

'Just what I was thinking,' Hannah agreed. 'I hope he's going to the Courtship Dance. Imagine, if he asked you...'

'Amazing,' Mielitta concurred, giggling. *Stones! There are so many stupid women.*

Kermon's voice stopped all gossip. 'These are the words of Drianne, chosen representative of the people, who went into the stones in her twelfth year, the five hundred and thirty fifth year of Perfection.

'I had only seen one living creature not human,' began Kermon, his mage's voice giving gravitas to the girl's words. And fluency. To hear Drianne's words in a male voice, without a stutter, changed their worth.

Mielitta knew what that one living creature had been, remembered Drianne stroking the bee, its trust and happy vibrations, its death.

'So I spoke the search words to find all living creatures, to know the world before we made the barrier between us and the Forest.'

If the previous testimonies had drawn gasps and horror, the mention of the Forest created turmoil. The mages turned to each other and their unease showed although they kept their comments off speechcraft and inaudible to the Hall.

Magaram spoke. 'Usually we do not name our enemy but these are special circumstances and this girl has suffered deeply on our behalf so we forgive the lapse.' The weight of his glare at Kermon was a clear enough warning to translate Drianne's thoughts in appropriate language.

Kermon bowed his head once in understanding but his hands stayed gently on Drianne's face, the connection unbroken.

Did soul-reading flow in both directions, like her contact with the bees? wondered Mielitta.

'I saw animals and fish being farmed. They were nourished and their products harvested. Some were killed and eaten.' This was less shocking a second time of hearing and the audience began to lose interest, especially as there were long silences, as if Kermon was listening to Drianne. The statements that followed were short, presumably summaries of longer descriptions – thanks be to Perfection. Nobody wanted details of more horrors but after the initial novelty of a mute girl speaking, the exercise had become tedious.

'People lived with animals as their friends,' Kermon announced, reviving interest – and disgust.

'Filthy!' Hannah's mouth pursed in distaste.

'Many people lived in separate buildings, not communities, and they preferred to live with animals, not people, as companions. They called such animals pets. And they liked to see wild creatures and plant life around them. Birds on trees, wolves, bears and squirrels in the F– countryside. Even though these animals ate each other. They thought this was natural and –'

Whatever Kermon had been about to say was interrupted by Magaram, whose voice carried over the growing noise in the Hall.

'I don't think we need any further examples of past depravity and insanitary conditions.' He spoke to Drianne. 'Thank you for your courage in enduring such terrible conditions and reporting here.'

Then he included the Hall again. 'We can all understand how such a horrific experience left this young volunteer traumatised and speechless! We thank her for bringing the truth back so all may know the origins of Perfection and be thankful.

'If any have doubted the need for a barrier, let him doubt no longer! You have heard what happens when people allow the enemy into their lives, seduced by some ideal of Nature. You have heard what Nature truly is – violence and disease, tempests and poison.' His voice rose to a climax. 'Eating each other!' He banged on the table and amplified each blow with speechcraft to emphasise his words. 'If the enemy brings war to us, then we shall retaliate, obliterate, annihilate! Perfection will win!'

Magaram allowed time for the cheers and shouts of 'Praise Perfection!' to die down, none more enthusiastic than Mielitta's, although, like Hannah and the other ladies she maintained womanly restraint even in her fervour.

'While the mages prepare for battle, every citizen can do his or her part. Stay vigilant! And stay true to the ways of our community! We will prepare for the next generation in our customary manner with a Maturity Test and Ceremony a week today. Mage Bastien and Mage Shenagra have chosen those for testing and it is with pleasure that I announce that this young lady – what was her name again?'

'Drianne,' said Kermon quietly.

'Drianne has been selected for the Maturity Test and I am sure she will grace our Hall again in a beautiful gown, blooming in her new womanhood.'

Kermon had no excuse for leaving his hands on her face, nor for preventing Rinduran from grabbing Drianne's wrist once more. Bastien came to the front, basking in the limelight and edged Kermon out of the way. He and his father sandwiched

Drianne between them and raised her arms in a victory salute. She was swaying so much she might have fallen otherwise.

'Poor girl,' Hannah said again. 'What an exhausting experience. She needs plenty of rest so that she can enjoy the Ceremony and put all this behind her. I remember my Ceremony like it was yesterday,' she giggled. 'Well it was only a few months ago but you know what it's like. Womanhood changes everything, opens your eyes.'

'Yes,' said Mielitta, wondering whether Hannah even remembered the conversation they'd had about the Maturity Test. 'That it does.' She watched Drianne being half-carried off the dais. 'Poor girl,' she echoed. She had to think of a way to help her.

Part of her mind was pondering the testimonies, cataloguing them as *To be revisited.*

Pets, she labelled her bees.

She felt what she had come to recognise as bee laughter.

Wild things, was their retort.

CHAPTER TWENTY-ONE

Mielitta trailed a hand along the walls as she walked the familiar passage from her chamber to the library. Newly conscious of the history contained in the stone, she reached out, seeking its wisdom. The witnesses' reports had only added to her longing to explore the past, especially her own past. However many times Declan told the story of her finding, she felt anew the mystery behind her emergence from the wall as a baby like a bee-grub from comb. If only she could go into the wall and find out more. But the stone was dead to her touch, shutting her out.

She turned inwards, seeking the solace of the bees, but they too were quiet. With a sigh, she entered the library and sought the one comfort that never let her down. *Work,* she told herself and sensed a sleepy echo. Shifting and cataloguing books took on its usual rhythm while her subconscious worked on the problem of rescuing Drianne.

She kept seeing Rinduran's hand gripping the young girl, the exchange of glances between him and Bastien. Drianne's words uttered in Kermon's voice had conveyed what the mages wanted to hear but was that really what Drianne felt? In spite of all the times they had used the archery yard together, Mielitta barely knew the girl.

What would Tannlei have said? If Drianne did have a crush on her, then Mielitta was in some sense her leader, however hard she'd tried to keep her distance. When she'd intervened to prevent Bastien bullying the girl or worse, she'd taken sides and declared her responsibility. For one follower. Tannlei's words came back to her. *Don't ask how many followers make a person a leader. Ask what a person does to earn that title.*

Facts. Drianne was mute. She was selected for the Maturity Test. Bastien wanted to 'cure' her and marry her. Rinduran thought it safer to suppress her. The Maturity Test would be in a week's time and meanwhile Drianne was with the other candidates in their hall.

Assumptions – a different shelf in Mielitta's mind. Drianne was in danger but probably not until the Maturity Test. Then she would either be forced to marry Bastien or she'd be suppressed: rape or ashes. Mielitta stopped her imagination pursuing either fate further and filed them both under *Impossible.* Her stutter had been 'cured' and her soul was no doubt next but for now, she was still Drianne.

If Mielitta could talk to her before the Maturity Ceremony, she could warn her, tell her of an escape plan. Drianne could nod, shake her head. Or Kermon could interpret her thoughts so Mielitta didn't mistake them. That would mean trusting Kermon. Did she? How could she know that his soul-reading was the truth?

What if Drianne wanted to be forged, to be an adult, to belong? The Test and Ceremony would change her as they changed all girls. What if she was prepared to marry Bastien? This was the way of the Citadel. Hannah would be ecstatic if she were chosen by Bastien and she was not the only one. He would be a powerful mage and Drianne would be under his protection. He might mature, become less radical under Drianne's influence, grow independent from his father. Bastien and Rinduran already disagreed.

She sighed. *To be revisited.* At least she had a few days to come up with a plan. Probably. She sighed again.

When the door creaked open, she was at the top of the stepladder, so she couldn't recognise the visitor until he spoke.

'The stones be with you, Mielitta.'

Jannlou.

'Thank you, Mage Jannlou, Apprentice Mage Jannlou. And with you,' she answered mechanically, concentrating hard on *Fossils of the Neoplastine Era.* 'Is there a book you seek?'

'No. I want to talk to you.'

She glanced down and immediately regretted doing so. Jannlou picked up the pile of books on the stool, put them on the floor and sat, immediately above the distortion in the woodette caused by the dead fly. What if the mage sensed the aberration? What if he moved that other pile of books, beneath the stool and saw the corpse and the ripple? He'd guess it was her doing.

Jannlou shifted restlessly.

She had to keep him distracted and looking up, so she stayed on the highest step, pretending to continue her work.

'What do you want to talk about?' seemed a simple enough question but apparently it wasn't.

Silence ensued.

As if dragging the words out of the walls themselves, Jannlou said, 'I know you don't trust me, that you remember running from me, from us. I want you to know that it wasn't like you thought.' He finished lamely, 'I never actually hurt you.'

She sparked. 'Never hurt me? You think living in fear is nothing? You think the words you all shouted are nothing? You think a gang bigger than you, stronger than you, laughing and crowding round, prodding you – you think that's nothing? And those so-funny practical jokes! You think humiliation is nothing? Pity you don't get a bit more of it then!' The moment she drew breath she realised how stupid she'd been. She should have been the one rendered mute, for her own safety.

'You don't need to bite my head off,' he told her, looking puzzled rather than outraged at her disrespect. 'I'm trying to say sorry. I'd like to explain–' He shook his head. 'But I can't. It's too dangerous.'

She'd already spoken too freely so she controlled her curiosity. 'I told you before. Childhood matters can be left behind in childhood,' she told him briskly and gave an inane smile for good measure. Blue eyes observed her steadily. Silver wriggling in the purple depths, like fish in the stream, like slippery thoughts. The male scent of sun-warmed earth rose to her flared nostrils.

'That's not the only thing,' he continued. 'You're different. I believe you when you say the forging didn't work properly with you. I feel like I can share my thoughts with you.'

She giggled nervously. The nerves were genuine. *Different* was not a word she wanted as a compliment. 'I'm just an ordinary woman, Mage Jannlou.' She allowed herself a touch of pride. 'Though I am Assistant Librarian.'

As if she hadn't spoken, he continued, 'You must wonder, like I do, why we do all that weapons training, to excel at something which has no use, us with swords, you with your bow – I saw how good you were. Yet there is no real combat here and conflicts are solved by mages, with craft.'

Mielitta didn't allow herself to think. She could do that later. 'Perfection requires that children and men keep fit and have a harmless outlet for their competitive hormones so training and sports are required.'

'But there is no point to them! We might as well run on a grassette treadmill for exercise.'

'I do not question the wisdom of the stones and the mages in their Perfect choices.' *And neither should you,* she thought, intrigued despite herself.

'It's not just weapons training. It's everything about the way we live. Activities are random and pointless, to give the illusion of purpose. Artisans create objects we don't need, that could be better made by magecraft anyway. We are told that such work exhausts mages, and yet the choice of what it's used for makes no sense.'

'It's Perfection.'

Jannlou looked down his nose at her. 'Perfection has become a creed that men follow blindly or manipulate to their own ends.'

Mielitta gasped. 'May the stones forgive you.'

'The stones.' His tone was bitter.

'You are a mage. You are so lucky to receive the wisdom of our ancestors directly. I wish I could!' In case he hadn't got the message, she added, 'Maybe one day, I'll be chosen as a representative and I could go into the stones. If a mage ever finds me worthy…' Now she would find out how deep his interest in her really was.

His bitterness increased. 'I can't even–' He shook his head and broke off, changed the subject to one just as shocking.

'I don't see why women can't carry on with weapons training or any other activity they want to.'

'Like smith-work.' The words were out before she could stop them. If he were setting traps to expose her as a traitor, she could at least try not to fall into them.

He was kicking the books under the stool as he swung his legs to and fro. Any minute now, he would realise, move the books and discover the mess she'd made in the fabric of the floor.

'Yes, like smith-work.' He showed no sign of finding her reply odd. His legs stopped swinging. 'And you shouldn't be forged differently from men.'

Sidestepping making a treasonous reply was tricky as Mielitta had no idea what really took place apart from the vague hints she'd picked up from Hannah and her friends. 'Perhaps your mother could explain Perfection from a woman's point of view,' she hedged.

His face darkened. She'd judged that wrong too. 'My mother's dead.'

'May she return to the stones,' Mielitta said automatically but then she was ashamed of giving him nothing but a platitude. 'I'm sorry,' she said. 'I don't know who my mother was. Or my father. I'm a foundling.'

The set lines of his face softened. 'I know. Everybody knows how Mage Declan found you.' He smiled at her weakly. 'It's a great story. I'm not surprised you love the walls.'

'When did your mother die?' she asked, not sure whether it was better to let him talk or change the subject again. There didn't seem to be any safe subjects.

'Years ago. From allergy. I was eleven.'

Her heart sank. The dead fly. She'd let the Forest in and other mothers would die. 'I-I-I'm sorry,' she stammered again.

'Don't be. She wasn't.' The silence dragged and presumably he felt it would be polite to explain such an extraordinary statement. 'She was allergic from babyhood and she told me–' he swallowed. 'She believed Perfection caused it, the Citadel, our way of life. She told me,' he lowered his voice although only the two of them were in the room, 'she told me the cure was in the Forest.'

Mielitta's heart pounded and her gasp came a little late, when she remembered that ought to be her reaction. As lightly as she could, she forced herself to reply, 'But the Council Mages told us there is a traitor here who has let the Forest in and more people have died of allergy. So your mother was–,' she searched for the tactful word, '–mistaken. I'm really sorry she was so ill – but maybe the illness affected her mind.' *Dead fly,* she thought.

'Maybe,' he conceded. 'She never had the chance to test her theory so I don't know. Maybe those dying now have had too big a dose of natural forces when they've lived too long in the Citadel. *Survived,* she called it. She said we weren't meant to live like this, that there must be another way. We won't know, will we, unless we try another way?'

Oh, stones. What should she say now? If he was trying to entrap her, he was doing a great job. She remembered Crimvert saying much the same as Jannlou's mother, about existing not living; look what had happened to him. She said nothing.

'I thought,' he said slowly, 'that you might be interested in what she thought.'

Hating herself, she replied, 'It must have been very hard for you, a mage, to listen to such treason from your own mother. She must have suffered to speak so against Perfection.'

Jannlou's expression closed down. 'Yes, she suffered,' he said shortly. 'All her stunted life.' He rose abruptly and left without any attempt to speak the formula of parting.

Mielitta backed down the steps, piled books on top of the stool again, and straightened the heap underneath so that the fly was well buried. She tried to focus on devising an escape plan for Drianne but Jannlou's words refused to stay on their *To be revisited* shelf and reverberated round her head like bees.

CHAPTER TWENTY-TWO

A lone in her chamber, Mielitta kicked herself for having missed the chance to visit Drianne. She should have asked Jannlou to take her. But maybe it was for the best. She wasn't sure such a request would have been wise. She didn't know what to make of Jannlou any more but she *did* know what to make of Bastien and it was all bad. Not that Jannlou would see it that way. He might well tell his long-time friend every word he exchanged with Mielitta, and she with Drianne, in all innocence.

Or Jannlou might be as deceitful as Bastien – more so, as he was better at setting verbal traps, which she kept falling into. At some stage, she'd run out of luck and would face the mages' righteous anger. It was more likely to be Magaram and Shenagra who'd punish her than Bastien. She shivered. She knew what that punishment was likely to be but whatever the risk, she had to reach Drianne somehow, and soon.

As a last resort, she would launch a surprise attack during the Ceremony, with the full force of arrows and bees. Maybe the power that had surged through her when she rescued Drianne from Bastien and Jannlou would be enough to extricate the girl from the Maturity Ceremony and give them time to flee.

She would need her weapons and skills in top condition, just in case. She pulled the quiver out from under the bed and inspected each arrow, one at a time. No splits in the wood, no crushed featherettes in the flights or dints in the arrowheads. No frayed loops on her bow.

She stroked the wooden bow, old-style yew, a gift from Tannlei for her fourteenth-year disappointment at still being a child. The bow was used to her draw and nobody else was allowed to touch it. However much they'd harassed her, even Bastien and Jannlou had never tried to steal her bow – and never would. As Apprentice Mages, they couldn't risk an accusation of theft or even the attempt. Such a crime against Perfection ranked with breaking into a bedchamber – unthinkable.

She nocked an arrow just to check the tension. *A drawn bow is seven-eighths broken so never test it empty.* She found a rough edge in the nock, which she sanded smooth with glasspaper. Then she tested it again. Perfect.

Perhaps that was part of the laxness in the Citadel that Rinduran had complained of, her archery teacher's love of historic materials. But Declan used wood and steel in the forge. It was as Jannlou had said – no logic in how Perfection was implemented.

She had some basic equipment in her pack: a knife, some glasspaper, two spare flights, one shaft. She pulled the neck-chain up from her bodice and fingered the steel of the arrowhead. Kermon's work was perfection, not only in the patterned steel, but even in its blunt edges, appropriate for its use, purely decorative. Mielitta knew that if she could only hone the edges of the arrowhead again, it would be as sharp as it was strong, her lucky, deadly arrow.

She could go to the forge early, before anyone was awake, don the smith's gauntlets. It would be child's play to oil and whet the arrowhead until it was sharp. Even easier to shave the end of a wooden shaft to fit into the tubular end of the steel arrowhead. But then she would need to light the forge, wait and, when it was hot enough, heat the steel tube to the exact shade of cherry red required. If it turned white, it was too hot and would set fire to the wood. If not hot enough, it wouldn't char the wood enough for the shaft to enter the tube and stay there. She knew every step, from hammering the pin into the tube on the stone anvil, the final reinforcement, right down to quenching the head in oil.

No, it wasn't any lack of technique that was her problem. It was the secrecy. It wasn't possible to light the forge, wait the time required, pursue all the stages, without Declan appearing during the process. She was under no illusions as to how angry he would be at anybody else using his forge without permission, let alone a lady. Worst of all, he would doubt that she *was* a lady. At best, he would swallow her story about a problem in her forging but she suspected he knew more than she did and would *smell a rat*. Another of those book sayings that expressed exactly what she meant. *She* was the rat. And he would smell her rattiness.

She fingered her arrowhead again, longing to give it the chance to fulfil its purpose. What a waste of such workmanship! Kermon's workmanship. Once more, her thoughts brought her back to the Apprentice Smith. He could complete his work on her arrow, put an edge back on, without Declan being suspicious. He'd been just as upset as she was when he was made to blunt the arrowhead. He could take her to Drianne, perform his soul-reader magecraft.

But she trusted Kermon even less than she trusted Jannlou. Kermon's ambitions were in the open but nevertheless he was getting everything he wanted, which was suspect in itself. He'd taken what should have been her place in the smithy. He'd appeared so conveniently to interpret for Drianne and win the mages' plaudits, and Mielitta would never know whether his words matched Drianne's thoughts.

Drones. You can't trust them.

She ignored the buzzing of bee disapproval at such poor community spirit but their longing for the Forest matched her own. She told herself that practising her archery was the best she could do for Drianne at the moment. Her heart leapt at the promise of water, sun and honey, storms forgotten.

The slow way, she admonished her bees. *No whooshing and nausea. I'm doing this as a human.*

She rolled her practical shirt and britches up into a ball and strapped her quiver round her waist. She put her bow over her shoulder and threw a cloak around herself to disguise her weaponry as much as possible. No doubt she looked hunchbacked and strange but if challenged, she would simper and use her planned excuse, that she was on an errand to a knight in the archery yard. Besides which, it was so early that nobody would be around. Perfect ways were predictable ways.

Mielitta glided at the quickest pace a lady could be expected to manage, along the familiar passages, down to the narrow path by the dripping rockface. She paused to touch the walls, for luck or a blessing from the ancestors, but she felt no connection. If they were indifferent to her fate, why had they sent her here? Why didn't they open to her as the Forest did, calling her with its wild colours and scents?

At least her hurry this time was only from her own sense of urgency, not from her enemies' pursuit. She remembered Jannlou and Bastien shouting behind her, imagined their faces when they reached the blank rock and she'd gone. She smiled. She recalled their chase so vividly she even thought she heard footsteps echoing behind her and she shook her head at her foolish imagination.

'Radium,' she called, rushing through the water gate, feeling the different tastes of the rainbow colours, allowing her bee senses to enjoy the blues and ultraviolet.

She stooped by the stream, cupped and drank the water of the day in her hands, today's flavours of ochre, granite and lightning. The storm had left its taste in the water and she quenched a thirst that had not left her since her last visit to the Forest. The purified drink that sustained the Citadel kept her from dying but this water made her feel alive. She remembered Jannlou's treasonous quote, his mother's words: 'I am surviving, not living.'

The meadow grass looked so soft and springy that Mielitta

threw off her shoes and swirled her skirts in a dance, humming softly to her own tune. Her bees joined in, a chorus of thrums that made the earth itself seem to vibrate. The grass was spongy and sun-warmed under her feet and when she had skipped and whirled herself dizzy, the water sparkled, inviting. She took another drink, wondered if she was allowed to stand in the stream.

Allowed. What did *allowed* mean in the Forest?

She took off her cloak and carefully laid her clothes parcel and weaponry on it. Then she hitched up her skirts and stepped into the running water, gasping at its unexpected chill. What was pleasant to the mouth was startling on her feet but after the initial shock, the tickle of cold water over her toes made her giggle.

She stepped boldly out into the stream and slipped on a large pebble that was slick with moss. Waving her arms to keep her balance just made her giggle more and she landed with a thump on her bottom, the icy freshness striking her through her lavender gown and Mage Fabrisse's best embroidery.

She stood up with some difficulty and watched rivulets run down the clinging fabric of her dress, dancing into the stream to continue on their way. She preferred not to think about the flavours she might have added to today's water. She allowed herself a moment to enjoy being a human-shaped waterfall, then she waded to dry ground, clumsy with the weight of her soaked gown.

She quickly stripped, spread out her wet clothes on some large rocks and donned her britches. Her fancy underwear was soaked through so she bound her breasts with a scarf as she had all the long years of her puberty. Her woman's clothes would soon dry in the sunshine and she had work to do. She could pick them up on the way back. She laced up her boots, grabbed bow and quiver, and raced into the woods, not looking behind her.

She stopped at the beech tree but not, this time, to marvel at each separate leaf. Instead she slipped an arrow into the notched rest of her bow and looked around for a target. She could hear Tannlei's voice. 'What is your target today, Mielitta?'

The day she was told Tannlei had gone, she'd hated her teacher for abandoning her. Hated her in angry tears and blurred shots until she disciplined herself to shoot in Tannlei's honour, in memoriam. Until the day she heard that voice again, preserved in her deep thinking, saying 'What is your target today, Mielitta?'

And she'd replied, 'To honour the best teacher, ever.' She'd tried so hard to centre herself, loose her arrows with skill but she'd been blinded by tears. When she went to collect her arrows, she couldn't believe that one was right in the heart of the bull's-eye.

As if Tannlei had been watching her, she'd answered the unspoken question. 'Today I learned that a lucky hit is still a hit. And that the archer cannot control all events.' And she'd wept again, for the events she could not control.

Today, in the forbidden Forest, surrounded by the difference of each tree, each rustling leaf, she asked herself, 'What is your target, Mielitta?' and she let the answer come from her deepest thoughts, unforced.

'To be worthy of my teacher. To rise to any challenge to rescue Drianne.' As she relaxed, felt her body in tune with the bow, felt the vibration, she saw a formation like a cross in the bark patterns of a tree. A tricky shot between the trees. She felt the invisible line between herself, her bow and its landing point, the arc of motion and she loosed an arrow, smiled.

Darts. Stingers, murmured the bees in approval.

Then she held four arrows and turned so her target tree was behind her. She whirled and loosed one after the other, forming a neat five-pointed letter M, with the middle dip at the heart of the cross she'd first noticed. She stepped forward to recover her arrows and was nearly bowled over by a solid brown creature with fey eyes. *Deer*.

The doe froze, fixing Mielitta in its liquid brown gaze, then bounded off, weaving skittishly between the trees. Mielitta

182

instinctively raised her bow, nocked an arrow and aimed at the retreating deer but stayed her hand. If she needed food, this was something she would have to learn how to do but she had no such need. She smiled, wondering what her teacher would say about shooting deer in the Forest. She pulled her arrows out of the tree, checked she hadn't split or spoiled them and stood still, watched, turned invisible.

The more she looked, the more she saw. A trail of ants was marching up the tree-trunk where her arrows had left sap oozing. *Making honeydew.*

A flash of brown alerted her to another creature startled by her presence but this one was smaller, sat up on its back legs before zigzagging madly away between the trees. Deer? *Not a deer. Hare.*

Something green coiled and wriggled along a thick branch out of sight. *Snake.*

An irritating whine from an insect near her face stopped for a painful second as it jabbed her. 'Ouch!' *Mosquito.*

And always birdsong. Long-tailed swoops over her head, red and gold, blue and white. Mielitta had never seen living feathers before and each bird's flight was as distinctive as had been the individual leaves. So much singularity was overwhelming and Mielitta found the word *drunk*, savoured it. Yes, she felt drunk on so much Nature.

If she hadn't shut her eyes to listen better to the birdsong, she wouldn't have heard the tell-tale snap behind her. In that second's warning she whirled round with an arrow ready in her bow. But it would be no use against a mage.

Jannlou.

'You shouldn't be here,' he began, moving closer, dominating her. 'It's dangerous.'

He couldn't say any more as Mielitta threw him to the ground with her full weight and held an arrow to his throat. So he was a mage. So what! She was going to make him work his hardest to take her, however strong his magecraft.

It would be easier if he shut his eyes but instead, he stared at her. She could see her own grimacing face reflected in duplicate. Twin blue mirrors, purple and silver ringed. Circles like the archery corkboard for target practice.

The longer she sat in this ridiculous position, astride a supine assailant, the more vulnerable she was to a quick knee-jerk from someone much stronger than she was. Her advantage was in surprise, in catching Jannlou off-balance, in darts and distance. Her hand was steady but her thoughts were not.

She should use the arrowhead. She could see the pulse below his Adam's apple, where the steel pushed against the skin, making a tiny discoloured dimple in the even pores. Even as a blunt instrument it could kill. She would only be defending herself. Not that she would ever be asked to justify herself. Nobody would know. But he kept looking at her with sunshine and her face in his eyes.

Clearly, Jannlou had come to the same conclusion. 'Are you going to kill me or not?' he asked her, not one cloud in his eyes.

'Don't try glamour on me!' she told him. 'I'm immune. It doesn't work.'

'No, it doesn't,' he agreed. 'But this does.' Inevitable as the Citadel's greylight, he bucked her off as if she were a feather and then he rolled, so Mielitta's half-hearted jab landed in the earth.

Then he was behind her, grabbed her arms behind her back, avoided the backward lunge of her head and bent her forward so she couldn't try it again.

'Vicious beast, aren't you,' he panted.

Bite your head off, thought Mielitta but she said nothing, saving her breath for her next move. She flopped, as limp as if she'd fainted, a dead weight in his grip. Then she back-kicked with both feet, using all her strength and aiming for his privates. As she'd hoped, he was startled enough to slacken his grip and jerk backwards to avoid her boots. She caught him higher up, enough to wind him and to give her the momentum to follow-through in a full flip out of his grasp. She was fit and flexible so she landed facing away from him. She turned, grabbed her bow while he was still doubled over and ran past him into the Forest.

'Mielitta!' he gasped.

From a safe distance, she called, 'I know, you're going to tell me I've got it all wrong. But it doesn't look that way to me!' She nocked an arrow, pointed it towards him.

He stumbled a pace in her direction and she loosed a warning. The arrow twanged into the tree-trunk beside him and Jannlou stood still. Her heart thumped as she waited for the blast of mage-craft that would surely come. Even if it was half the power of Rinduran's, she had no chance. And if she survived, she would have to kill him or she was doomed. Once he reported her to his father, her future was in ashes.

Jannlou was no deer but the same reluctance stayed her hand. Did she really need to kill him?

Hesitation would be the death of her.

'I followed you,' he yelled. 'I saw you at the water gate. Heard you use the password and I followed.'

'No kidding,' she yelled back. 'And I suppose you were trying to be helpful again.'

He tried moving another step towards her.

'Don't move or it'll be in your head next time.' Why was she still warning him? She even felt the urge to tell him what she'd overheard in the library, between Bastien and his father. As if she wasn't in deep enough trouble without meddling in mage politics. Jannlou would never believe her anyway, not when he'd witnessed her using a stolen password and committing trespass.

Then she realised what else Jannlou must have witnessed.

Outraged, she shouted, 'Did you watch me in the stream too?'

'Did you go in the stream? I waited before I tried the pass-word. Didn't want to bump into you the other side of the gate.'

She flushed crimson, wondering whether to believe him. She could hardly say, 'Did you watch me undress?' and whether he said 'no' or 'yes' she wouldn't know the truth. The only certainty would be that he'd laugh at her. That deserved an arrow in the head!

'It's the first time,' he called, his voice starting to regain its usual gruff, deep tones. 'I've never been in the Forest before. It's–' He was searching for words.

She had many words for the Forest but they were personal. 'It's not fake grass that cleans itself or greylight,' she told him.

'Why is it forbidden?'

'You tell me. You're the mage. Perfection forbids it, I suppose. You've been into the walls so you know the history.'

There was a silence. 'I drank the water. In the stream.'

'Then you know.'

'Yes. Every citizen should come here, should have the right to come here.'

'You're going to tell Daddy that when you go back?' she mocked.

'When the time is right.' Maybe he *was* working his glamour on her but she couldn't shoot him, not if there was even a tiny chance he was telling the truth. What if, in the future, the Forest could be visited openly? What if Jannlou could bring that about one day, when he took over from his father? And she would be the one who made it happen. *What if?* She lowered her bow and watched as he walked cautiously towards her.

CHAPTER TWENTY-THREE

The birdsong had stopped during their shouting and in the ensuing calm, tentative whistles and tweets queried whether the danger was past. Rustling began again in the canopy above the human heads.

'Will you show me the Forest?' he asked her. He was wearing his leatherette jerkin and britches, swordbelt, his knight's clothes. He must have abandoned his mage's robe as she had her lady's gown.

'I've only been here twice,' she said. *As a human.* Her bees thrummed their disquiet, before falling silent. 'But we could explore together. As quietly as you can.' She eyed his clanking apparel with disapproval but he just shrugged and put his hand on his sword pommel.

'It's like your bow. I need it with me. And you didn't notice me following you.'

'Fat lot of use a sword will be in the Forest!' She told him, 'Follow me, then, seeing as you're so good at it.' She shut her eyes, focused her bee senses and found the Forest mapped as she remembered, between the drinking-water of the stream and the beehive that was home. She recognised other landmarks: rock formations, trees and flowers, sources of nectar and pollen. There was one place she definitely did not want to visit, with or without Jannlou. Even as a human, she felt queasy at the thought of the drones gathering.

'What are you doing?' he whispered. 'It looks like you're consulting with the walls.'

'Hush,' she told him. 'Follow me and keep your eyes open.' Which was funny, given how well she could see with her eyes closed. Guided by the bees, she weaved in between trees, through pools of light and shade. She made a game of trapping the sun behind branches in the canopy, so that its rays were concentrated into sharp spikes, spearing one rock or one tree with light. Then she'd move and unleash the sun's full brightness in a blur.

She stopped by one tree and pointed, waited for Jannlou to see and understand. Bright green leaf-shadows stood starkly outlined on the grizzled trunk.

'How can shadows be green?' he asked.

Like their archery teacher, she led him to see. 'What are they shadows of?'

She watched him see what she had seen, the leaves that made the shadows, with sunlight filtering through them, catching the green colour in its joyous rays and painting leaf-shapes on the bark.

Jannlou touched the shadows, watched them change. He caught green leaf-shadows on his own broad fingers.

Verdigris on bronze. His brown skin shimmered green and Mielitta wanted to reach out, touch it. Instead, she stroked the tree bark, feeling its unique whorls and lifelines, like those on Jannlou's hands. She breathed in bitterness of bark and brown sweat, catching the acrid scents at the back of her throat, relishing them.

Time moved as slowly as a finger along a tree-trunk and Jannlou seemed no more rushed than she was. They watched a procession of ants at their feet, each carrying ten times its weight in seeds.

Work.

'Look,' she told Jannlou. In the direction of the ants' march was a whitish tower, a strange stone pillar. *Ants' nest.*

'That's their Citadel,' she explained. The pleasure of sharing the Forest with someone whose face expressed the same wonder she felt made her forget her mistrust.

Jannlou asked her, 'How do you know all this?'

'It's as if I was born with all this knowledge in my deep thinking.' *Damn.* Now she'd have to explain that.

But he'd been taught by Tannlei too and he just nodded, so she continued. 'I used to clean the library, when I was a servant, and I'd skim the books. Words sort of stick in my head. Then when I see something, the words that go with it come to me and I just *know* what it is. It's as if my experience is catching up with my deep thinking.' She flushed. 'That must sound stupid.'

'No, I know what you mean. I–' Whatever he was going to say next was interrupted by an anxious fluttering of birds, all rising from trees an arrow's flight away from the humans. There was a stillness in the air and Mielitta remembered the deer, frozen in fear. Some danger approached. They had been so loud in their fighting and talk. Every creature in the Forest knew they were here.

She put a finger to her mouth and nocked an arrow, faced the direction of the disturbance and braced herself. Now she was concentrating, she could hear it, as she'd heard the snap underfoot when Jannlou tracked her. But whatever was tracking her this time was much better at it. Four-legged and huge. And made the Forest hold its breath, each creature praying *Not me, not me.* Praying for invisibility. Mielitta remembered the feeling well but there were no walls here to hide her or give her strength.

You could run crazy with the fear or you could track it back to its source, waiting with a nocked arrow. Jannlou had unsheathed his sword, was shifting his balance in a warrior's stance. There was nobody she'd rather have at her side in a fight.

Their senses as tightly strung as Mielitta's bow, they couldn't have been more prepared but they saw nothing. Just stripes of trees and grass, sunlight and shadow. Stripes. The silence gathered itself to spring at them; a massive beast, striped yellow and black, broke cover and charged towards them.

Tiger.

Shock skewed Mielitta's aim and she missed.

Her bees were loud in anger and insistence. *Flight! Up the tree!*

In an instant, she leaped onto the most accessible branch and reached down to haul Jannlou up to safety. He shook his head, standing his ground in front of the tiger, which had not followed through – the stones be thanked! – but which crouched low in front of Jannlou, tail swinging, ready for a lethal spring.

What had Tannlei taught? 'Don't choose the companion who would fight a tiger with his bare hands.' The tiger clearly felt the same concerns about a man unafraid for his own life. Unfortunately, the hungry gold eyes shifted to Mielitta, no doubt considering her an easier prey. She climbed higher up the tree, aided by a thousand tiny wings. If she could only secure herself to a branch, she could use her bow but the branches were bouncing with her weight and even if they held, she couldn't guarantee shooting true. An enraged tiger would not think twice about taking the nearest prey and Jannlou was so close to the beast that, even with human senses, he must smell its foul breath, as she could.

Jannlou seemed to grow even taller and broader as he faced the predator but if that was all his magecraft could do, Mielitta wouldn't bet on his chances. Every time the tiger opened its mouth, issued a threat, she could smell its last victims.

Then the tiger made up its mind, roared and sprang. Only to land on nothing but pine cones. Jannlou had leaped too, reading the intention in the coiled muscles. He opened his mouth as if to roar his own defiance but instead he yelled, 'Stay in the tree!'

The tiger hesitated, then it saw what Jannlou had. Crashing through the trees, tearing off branches, came a growling brown monster. Clumsy but surprisingly fast, it attacked the tiger, raking its huge claws along the striped flanks. It reared up onto its back paws, a two-legged parody of Jannlou, before dropping onto the tiger and sinking its teeth into a writhing mass with equally dangerous teeth. Bulk against muscle, matched in tooth and claw, the giants wrestled with and gashed each other. Skin and hair made tattered fringes around bloody rips.

Mielitta clung to her shaking branch. She had never seen so much blood. Cuts, scratches and her own monthlies were the sum total of her experience and her stomach churned at this carnage. Jannlou stood like a charmed statue while the savage contest churned up the earth all around him.

Just when it seemed they would kill each other, in a ripple of black and yellow, the tiger freed itself from the bear's crushing grip and conceded defeat by running away. The bear reared up again, facing Jannlou. Mielitta screamed. Mage and bear were face to face for a long moment, then the creature dropped onto all fours again and set off in pursuit of the wounded tiger.

Mielitta threw herself to the ground.

'Are you all right? Was that magecraft? Did you summon the bear? Wasn't there a safer way to get rid of the tiger?' she asked Jannlou.

His eyes were distant and he still held the same warrior's stance but he seemed his normal size again. He focused on her slowly, measured his words. 'No, there wasn't a safer way to get rid of the tiger. I think we should go home now.'

But she wanted to check on the beehive.

Silly girl, her bees murmured. *If there was something wrong, we would know. Our people are fine. It's better the man doesn't go there.*

She could feel their suspicion of Jannlou and of course, they were right to be wary. But she didn't mind having human company as they walked back through the Forest together. She didn't even mind returning to the safety of the Citadel. At least she knew what dangers lurked there and if she had to choose between Shenagra's braids or a tiger's teeth, she wasn't sure which was worse. The Forest held its own terrors.

'I don't think I have the courage for this,' Jannlou admitted and she glanced quickly at him. Was he a soul-reader too? So often, he seemed to know what she was thinking and yet he spoke as if they were his own thoughts.

'Are you sorry you came?' she asked, remembering the wonder of leaf-shadows, now that the danger had gone.

They had reached the edge of the trees, where the meadow was split by the stream, where they could walk side by side. He took her hand and she let him.

'No,' he said. If he stopped, pulled her to him, leaned towards her, she would kiss him.

Aftershock from the predators' fight, she told herself, as he let go of her hand, moved away politely.

He indicated the water gate. 'I'll go in first.' Then he smiled. 'So you can get dressed with only the Forest watching.'

'You did look!' she accused him.

He just smiled but then the laughter left his eyes. 'It's too dangerous. You mustn't come out here any more.'

Dangerous because of creatures with teeth and claws or dangerous because it was treason?

'Thank you for not using magecraft against me, when we fought.'

'I can't–' he began, then he shook his head, started again. 'I don't think it works in the Forest.'

Lie. Evasion.

'Will you be my partner at the Courtship Dance?' he asked.

Stones. Everybody knew that was the prelude to marriage. But she couldn't afford to antagonise him, even if she wanted to say no. Which she probably didn't. *Courtship Dance. Which came after the Maturity Test. Drianne!*

'I haven't promised anybody else,' she answered, offhand. Not that she'd been asked! How Hannah and her friends would stare!

'Then you can promise me.' He smiled.

'Yes,' she agreed and rushed on before she could change her mind. 'I mean yes, I can. Maybe yes, I do. That is – yes. My friend, the girl I rescued from–' *Not tactful, Mielitta!* She corrected herself:

'The girl who went into the stones and lost her voice. She's going to be in the next Maturity Ceremony and I wanted to give her some words of advice. Is there any chance you can help me see her?'

If he wondered what advice she could give, when her own forging had obviously failed in such a spectacular way, Jannlou didn't say so. 'I'll do my best,' he said. 'Till then, may the stones be with you. And we have to try to fit in. You know we do.'

'Perfection guide our ways,' she responded, the formula ashes on her tongue.

CHAPTER TWENTY-FOUR

Perhaps she should have risked bringing Kermon. Mielitta studied Drianne's face, tried to read her eyes and felt inadequate. She'd not thought further ahead than seeing her friend and now she was here, she didn't know what to say. Especially as the other candidates for the Maturity Test were within earshot.

Jannlou had made good his half-promise and was hovering at a tactful distance but no doubt listening to every word she said. Mielitta had never been in the Candidates' Quarters and she looked around, gathering her thoughts. She and Drianne were in comfortable chairs at a small table. The others were seated likewise in chatty groups or helping themselves to drinks or sustenance at the end of the room furthest from the door. Which was locked by wards on the outside.

Drianne sat with her hands folded in her lap, pale, eyes downcast. She seemed folded in on herself, already a different person from the girl who'd played in the archery yard. This was no playground. She seemed distant even from the girl bullied by Bastien. This Drianne was in a place beyond tears. Or – Mielitta had to consider the Hannah and Georgette possibility – Drianne was in the place she considered to be her best option.

'I didn't think it would be like this,' Mielitta spoke the words aloud and found shadowed grey eyes raised to hers, questioning.

Maybe she would be able to communicate after all. If she started simply, she would find out. 'I wasn't part of a group,' she explained. 'Everything was different for me because I was a late starter. Like Mage Rinduran.'

There was no mistaking the way Drianne shrank in fear at the name.

Mielitta nodded to show she understood but kept her tone light. Just friends chatting, apart from the fact that one of them had been rendered mute. 'And the Maturity Mage for my Ceremony was Mage Yacinthe. Things might be different now that Mage Bastien is in charge.'

The grey eyes turned pebble-hard with loathing and the clasped hands turned white, peeping out from the overlong sleeves of her even whiter candidate's robe. If they had been alone, Mielitta thought Drianne might have spat. So, that answered the question of willingness.

'I was nervous before the Test,' Mielitta chattered on, 'so I thought I could let you know not to worry, that everything will be all right.'

Drianne jerked forward, grabbed Mielitta's hands, desperation in her eyes. One heavy sleeve fell back, revealed the word, 'HELP!' scratched on the pale skin and still oozing blood. The red was even more shocking in its colour-bleached context. A flick covered up the scratched skin and Drianne turned her gesture into a matey pat on Mielitta's back.

Smiling for the watchers, frothy for the listeners, Mielitta babbled, 'I'm so looking forward to watching you.' *I'll be there*, she told Drianne with all the force of her mind.

'The time before the Test is always a bit tense!' *That's when I'll make my move.* She watched Drianne to see if she'd been understood, hoped the slight nod and gleam of hope meant that she had.

She ploughed on, bubblier than fake mousse. 'And I can't wait for the Courtship Dance. Mage Jannlou has asked me to be his partner.' *Suck that up,* she told the invisible observers.

Drianne clapped her hands with suitable pleasure but her eyes held a wary sadness, hard to interpret.

Mage Jannlou's reaction was much easier to interpret. He glared at Mielitta and for a moment she felt ashamed of using their private relationship as a public smokescreen. The moment vanished. He *had* been listening. Good luck with reporting *that* conversation as treacherous. He could expose her any time he liked but he would have nothing on Drianne. However, it was safer to say no more.

'May the stones be with you in your Perfect future,' Mielitta told her friend as she stood up to leave.

Drianne placed her hand on her heart in dutiful response but it was unlikely that the love in her eyes was for Perfection or the stones.

Jannlou spoke the one-use password at the door and they left. Mielitta forced herself not to look back.

'I thought you were going to give her helpful advice,' her companion observed drily.

Mielitta shrugged. 'I could see she didn't need it. Just somebody saying it was fine, nothing to it. Girlish matters.'

'Girlish matters.' His look said he believed her about as much as the tiger believed a bear-hug was friendly.

'Thanks, anyway. Appreciated.' She turned her back on him, making it clear he was dismissed and it wasn't until she was back in her chamber that she realised how unwomanly her behaviour had been. Of course Jannlou saw through her. When she was with him, she forgot to put on an act, or, worse still, she behaved as a queen bee. If only she could read his eyes as easily as she had Drianne's.

Apart from her own invented coming of age, Mielitta had last seen a Maturity Ceremony when she was fourteen. No children were allowed to watch the Ceremony, in its enclosed courtyard, but Declan had been indulgent enough to let Mielitta sneak a view each year during her puberty.

She'd merge with the shadows in the back of the forge as the Maturity Mages led the procession of candidates through the forge and out the back door, followed by their adult family and supporters. Then Declan would watch proceedings through the spyhole and judge the moment that the new adults were due to emerge from the Barn. Was that why the Maturity Test was called forging? Because the procession went through the forge? Or was it just Declan who used the term because the smithy was his life and every human activity was like a forge process to him?

Declan would wink at Mielitta then join the Ceremony as part of his mage's duties. It would be Mielitta's turn to peek through the spyhole in the forge back door as the Maturity Barn's hidden exit was revealed and the new adults walked proudly out onto the greensward and were cheered by the crowds. In their women's gowns and men's leatherette jerkins they had seemed different people to the girls and boys Mielitta had known.

She'd been fourteen. This was the last cohort of her school-friends to mature and she hadn't even watched the Ceremony to the end but had turned to work for comfort, hammering metal on the anvil with all her young strength. Declan hadn't said a word but he'd understood. While he slipped out to perform his usual duties, she beat her frustration out on metal and stone. *They* made no comment on her ridiculous status.

Now, she wished she'd looked through the spyhole all the way through a ceremony, counted how many went in for a test and how many came out. She wracked her memory for details but they were fuzzy. Surprisingly fuzzy. She certainly couldn't remember any of the cohort from her year in school going into the Barn and not coming out. Not when she was eleven and the first friends achieved maturity, nor any of the four years she watched after that. But why was it called a Test if everybody passed? It made no sense.

She flinched away from later memories of contact with those same friends, when she'd been ignored as she pasted herself to the wall to let them pass. She'd waited on them at table without seeing any sign of recognition and even the memory of such humiliation made her cheeks burn.

Now, she was a woman in a lavender gown, standing among the other adults, completely normal apart from the bees in her head. She'd made a ladylike Perfect greeting to Declan and Kermon, gaining a nod of approval from her foster father and a puzzled stare from his Apprentice. She could afford to play the lady because she'd been up early enough to reorganise a corner of the Ceremony Courtyard, where some barrels and trays were ready on a trestle table for the celebration drinks. Having been a servant was proving to be advantageous: Mielitta knew the best places to hide a bow and quiver.

Father, daughter and Apprentice watched the procession together and it had been her turn to be surprised. Ahead of the Maturity Mages Bastien and Yacinthe came Rinduran, in full cere-monial robes, sporting the gold braid of leadership. Mielitta steeled herself not to shrink back as every instinct screamed that his one eye was burning into her, seeking her out. Or worse still, that they were connected through the poison dart in his blind eye, that he didn't need to see her to know where she was.

He doesn't know it's you, she told herself. But she shuddered at what he might do to her.

Why was he here anyway? Usually, the Ceremony was dele-gated completely to the Maturity Mages so it was a change in protocol for any other mage to be present. But that was a minor change compared with Rinduran's new robes. The only mage Mielitta had ever seen wearing the gold of leadership was Maga-ram. Mage Puggy's expression was grim but, instead of seeming to resent his father's interference, Bastien positively glowed with triumph.

Mielitta had no time to consider the implications of the mages' power games as she could see Drianne, trudging silently amongst the chatter of teenage candidates. She was more like a ghost from the walls than the earnest, stuttering girl she'd been before. The worst kind of maturity had already come upon her and what happened next could add to her suffering.

It was hard to hold back, say nothing, be as mute as Drianne. Mielitta bit her tongue and joined in the procession immediately after the last child in britches, so she could be at the front of the audience and work round to the trestle table, underneath which her weapons were hidden by a convenient tablecloth.

She wanted Drianne to know she was there but her friend's thoughts seemed to be directed inwards as she stood, swaying, her slim neck barely supporting her head. Heavy-headed, like a wild poppy, or like a human under a spell. If only Mielitta could send her a message.

The procession had stopped in front of the Maturity Barn, was gathering around the mages and from the way he puffed himself out, Rinduran seemed about to make a speech. Drianne was still lost in some other, nightmarish world. It was hard to believe she was the same girl who'd stroked the scout bee and smiled. Mielitta remembered the smile and wondered. Among the bustle and many distractions, was it worth the risk?

She looked again at Drianne's head bent in despair and she sought her bees.

One to fly and find Drianne. Settle on her hand just a few seconds and come straight home to me. She let them see her picture of the path and of Drianne but there was no need. They all knew her flower-friend and her special scent, from the past seeking.

Immediately, Mielitta felt a bee leave her, materialise and fly its looping path towards Drianne.

Hush, she told the scout and it stopped humming.

Luckily, all eyes were on the mage in his gold embroidery.

Rinduran began to speak. 'Our children are our future. When we established the sovereignty of the Citadel, built the barriers that keep us safe, learned the lessons of the walls, we created a world to make our children's future Perfect! And their children's future! And their children's children's future!'

Everybody cheered, Mielitta the loudest, waving her embroidered scarf in the air along with the other hands and scarves. But she dropped hers on the ground, muttered, 'Whoops, so clumsy.' As she stooped to retrieve it, she scrabbled around to bring the bow and quiver within easy reach.

Another such feint later would allow her to nock an arrow, whirl round and shoot. She'd practised loosing three in quick succession often enough and she had the advantage of surprise. The obvious targets were the three mages but she had no idea what wards protected them. Maybe she would be better wounding members of the audience, a more predictable target. A third option was to shoot in the air and let the stones decide where the arrows fell. Her heart hurt at the thought. But she would not abandon Drianne.

What is your target, Mielitta?

The best she could hope for was that she'd cause chaos and could make an escape with Drianne through the forge back door and out the other side. Her father would not stand in her way. Then they'd go down the passageways to the water gate. But it was a long shot indeed

'We have been too tolerant and our children are dying from allergy.' Rinduran's voice broke and Mielitta would have sworn he was sincere if she hadn't heard his words in the library. Besides, his child was standing there, suitably serious in mien but with a smug twitch of his mean lips showing how much he was enjoying his father's self-proclaimed importance.

Rinduran pointed at the candidates and repeated, 'Our children are dying from allergy! Will we continue to tolerate the traitors in our midst, the breach of our defences against sickness and death?' He paused dramatically but nobody was quite sure, it seemed, what the appropriate response should be. Clearly cheers wouldn't do and a few calls of 'No!' petered out in uncertainty.

'It has gone on too long and somebody has to take stronger action!' continued Rinduran, throwing out his arms, whirling the new gold edge to his sleeves, leaving them in no doubt as to who that somebody should be. Mage Puggy's face was a stormcloud; she opened her mouth to speak, then shut it again, frowning. Her face shifted in and out of its beautiful avatar appearance so that she wavered between her usual dumpy appearance and an Aphrodite, apparently struggling for stability, while Rinduran smiled.

Bzzz. Mielitta felt the soft vibration as her bee landed on Drianne's clasped hand. She saw the girl jump a little but not enough for others to notice. Slowly and gently, Drianne freed her bee-less hand and, as in the Council Chamber, stroked the tiny black and yellow body.

The bee thrummed with pleasure, preened itself. Mielitta could feel the hum of approval from the whole colony at such respect and tenderness.

As Drianne continued to stroke the bee, she stood taller. Her head lifted, her body shifted from its drooping misery to an archery stance, balanced and ready for whatever might come.

When Mielitta heard the voice in her head, she thought it must be her bees but the timbre was different, light, young, female and most definitely human.

It will be all right, the voice told Mielitta, light with something almost like laughter. *I will be all right now,* she clarified. Drianne raised her hand slowly to her mouth, let her lips touch the bee lightly in reverence, glanced towards Mielitta and nodded as she blew the bee lightly away, with a mind whisper. *The walls speed you, little honey sister.*

Drianne's transformation went unnoticed by the audience as they stared at the more spectacular one that was taking place in front of them. Mage Puggy went many shades of crimson as she fought to speak and at the same time hang on to her lank hair, her boils, her dumpy figure and thick arms. One at a time, each unattractive feature was replaced. First, silken blonde hair stopped its blurry dance and flowed in golden light around a face that settled into arched eyebrows, wide cornflower-blue eyes, symmetry of cheekbones and full lips. When she grew taller, showed every curve and dip of her body under a robe that clung as if wet, the men in the audience swallowed hard.

Mage Puggy's lips were full and sensuous but she could not speak. Mute as Drianne, she stood by Mage Rinduran. Lightning flashed in the sweetness of her blue eyes but hit nobody.

Mielitta received her bee safely back into her mind and watched Drianne resume her submissive pose as Mage Puggy was revealed as – or transformed into – a spellbinding beauty. Only she was no longer the one in control of the spells bringing that about.

'This,' declared Rinduran, 'is one of the problems. Women mages. I am new to the Council.'

Yes, yes, a late starter, thought Mielitta.

'So,' continued Rinduran, 'you can imagine my shock at seeing such a siren among the mages. How can we concentrate on our Perfect work with such temptation before us all the time? We can see Mage Puggy as she really is, as you see her before you now, without her trickery and misglamour. *This* is why we can no longer allow women mages in the Council, for their own sake and for that of the Citadel. If the Councillors had been able to concentrate on finding the traitor and protecting the Citadel, without such distractions, we would not be dealing with allergy.

'And the women mages could enjoy proper lives. Like the dear children before us today.' He swept an arm around to indicate the candidates for testing, who were looking very bored.

'Dear children, you are the new generation of Citadel adults and when you return from the Maturity Test, you will be ready to hear my plans for the future and to carry them out. Isn't this exciting?'

Apparently, it *was* exciting, to judge by the reaction.

Condemned to her beautiful exterior and universal contempt, Mage Puggy remained mute, while Rinduran beamed with the pride of new ownership. If she could speak, would anybody have listened? wondered Mielitta. Or would they have watched the movement of her breasts, outlined by the robe?

Now was the time Mielitta must reach for her bow, if she was going to, but she was even less sure that she should.

Drianne looked her way, gave a little shake of her head, smiled, turned to enter the glowing rectangle Bastien had opened in the Barn. He had clearly done his Apprentice work well and he looked smug as he stood by his father, watching the candidates disappear into the dark interior. Mage Puggy entered with them, her hips swaying lightly as she walked.

The new Maturity Mage spoke in his father's ear. Mage Rinduran's face darkened and he nodded grimly. Then Bastien turned to the crowd, made sure his voice carried and named one more candidate to enter the Barn. Mielitta's heart stopped but it was too late to use her weapons. Drianne was already inside. And so would she be.

The name Bastien announced was her own.

CHAPTER TWENTY-FIVE

'B ecause her forging was incomplete, Lady Mielitta will please enter the Maturity Barn with the other candidates, to repeat the process.'

Bastien's words rang in Mielitta's brain as people made way for her, murmuring the formula for good luck as she paced the distance to the entrance.

'May the stones bring you fortune.'

'As Perfection wills,' she replied, wondering why she would need luck if everybody passed the Test. Her temples throbbed and she longed to connect with her bees and take flight but she would not go without Drianne. As she passed so close to Rinduran she could have spat in his one good eye, she looked down demurely. She gathered her skirt in one hand, as if to enter the Barn with ladylike elegance but it was to avoid touching him with so much as a scrap of cloth. Both from repugnance and the fear he would detect an anomaly in her, she emptied her mind. She refused to feel Bastien's breath on her neck as he followed her into the darkness.

The glowing outline of the entry vanished at Bastien's command and only their breathing and scents revealed the presence of the candidates.

Mielitta blinked, reached for a hint of bee vision, and at once the interior of the Barn filled with dark blue human shapes. She was on one side among the girls, fresh-scented as apples. Among them was the heady perfume of Mage Puggy, an exotic orchid in their midst. Drianne's spring sweetness reached Mielitta from the furthest side of the group.

On the other side of the Barn were the boys. *Like the drones' gathering place,* thought Mielitta as she inhaled their adolescent pheromones. And something else. Sharp as vinegar, the smell disabled her nose and she quickly reverted to merely human senses. Bastien.

It didn't take wall magic to figure out who had told Bastien that her forging had not worked properly. She had only used that excuse to one person in the Citadel: Bastien's friend. Of course, Jannlou had betrayed her. She was glad she hadn't told him what Bastien really thought of him. Serve him right when his turn came! And his father's. Judging by Rinduran's speech, the new regime was poised to take over. But she'd only find out what horrors that meant for the Citadel if she survived this ordeal without losing her mind or being exposed as a traitor

Bastien was not among the boys but central in the Barn, at the focal point from which tiny glowing cups floated outwards to each candidate. Pink for the girls and blue for the boys, just as Hannah had remembered. There was something hypnotic about the rays of glowing cups and Mielitta shut her eyes to avoid their patterns. Even with her eyes closed, she still kept seeing something that made no sense. One cup had stopped in front of Mage Puggy's mouth, forced her lips open, emptied down her throat.

Then Mielitta's own lips felt the tap of her cup and the instinct to open her mouth. She had learned to override such reflexes during long hours training in the archery yard and she held back a moment to shut her bees and her suspicions into her deep thinking. Then she opened her mouth and let the liquid explore her mouth before slipping down her throat.

As tasteless as the usual Citadel water, the liquid was more viscous and it sparkled, tingling on the palate, anaesthetic. Mielitta's mouth grew numb and the insensibility spread, affecting her sense of smell, travelling up her nose, seeking her mind.

Pretty colour, lavender, she thought. *Maybe Jannlou will dance with me and then, if I'm lucky, we'll kiss... and more than that.* It wasn't ladylike to linger on the details of his body glistening with sweat as they fought in the forest, so she didn't. But something in her deep thinking fought to keep a memory of the salt tang of his skin, to know that it mattered in some visceral way. Somehow this diminished to *Wouldn't it be nice to have babies with him, to support him in his important work as a mage, to be envied by all the other wives.*

Her shallow thinking preened at the picture: Mielitta on her wedding day. Such a pretty gown. And herself, so happy, so safe, protected by Jannlou in a Perfect Citadel. All eyes on the beautiful lady and her desirable mate.

Drone, a voice suggested somewhere in the distance.

As Mielitta pleasured herself in such visions, swaying in a slow dance, she became vaguely aware of another intrusion in her mind. First, a warm spot glowed. She could see it reddening, feel it growing hotter, but there was no pain. In her dreamy state she enjoyed the strange sensation. She was an arrowhead in the forge, melting enough to be welded to the shaft. The rod turned the exact shade of cherry red required and she felt its touch on the compartments of her mind.

She was being forged. *Dancing in Jannlou's arms.* Her deep thinking was being sealed off forever by magecraft. *Such a happy life ahead. So pretty. In Perfection we trust.* Sealed off by the craft of a Mage-Smith.

That bastard, Kermon! Help me! she summoned her bees, fighting every fluffy thought that filled her head.

An angry buzz rose up as the bees joined the hive mind to hers, blocking out shallow thoughts of dances and perfect babies. She didn't want perfect babies. She wanted ones like her, wild and free. Still the welding rod continued its fiery work and she could feel something closing inside her, a future being destroyed.

Oil it, she commanded, giving the bees a picture of the implacable torch, and of their own special elaiophore glands releasing the floral oils that some had collected instead of pollen.

Work! the oil-collecting bees thrummed as they obeyed orders. Flying rank on rank, then retreating into the depths of Mielitta's mind, they oil-bombed the red-hot rod. It merely worked faster to close the access point through which fresh bees came to do battle.

More! Faster! she told them, digging her nails into the palms of her hands so that the pain would shake her out of the torpor. It wasn't enough. She unclasped the arrowhead from her neck and jabbed the inside of her arm. How fitting that she should fight Kermon with the help of a weapon he forged himself. A moment of refreshing clarity came with the pain and she directed the bees in a wave of attack.

The white halo round the red glow diminished, then the fiery heart turned black. Mielitta could see the texture of the rod, see the tongs holding it, the hand holding the tongs. The person to whom the hands belonged wavered into view through the smoke given off as the rod cooled but was gone before Mielitta could identify him. She didn't need to. She knew the soul-reader had penetrated her mind.

Panting with effort, Mielitta gradually regained feeling in her mouth, a sour taste. She could smell a false sweetness in the Barn, sickly, stomach-churning. Should she try to fly?

Drianne, she remembered, opening her eyes, glancing round cautiously. What in the stones' name had happened to the other candidates? She could see the girls around her swaying. *Imaginary dances with all-too-real partners,* she thought bitterly, part of her yearning still after the future she'd given up. What did the boys see?

Mielitta identified Puggy, her body moving like reeds in the wind, more erotic in her mature sensuality than the dreaming teenagers. There would be no help from that quarter. Beside Puggy was Drianne, indistinguishable in her movements from the others. With a start, Mielitta remembered to feign her own drugged state, to fit in, be the lady she could have been.

Maybe Drianne would be happier forged. Maybe that's what her words had meant, Mielitta mused as she swayed like a branch in the breeze. She'd be alone with her bees. She licked a salt trickle from her cheek, remembered the taste of Jannlou, who'd betrayed her. But the dream world was not real. She could not live there.

We are with you, her bees told her.

It will be all right, Drianne had said.

Around her, the candidates were jerking to a halt, returning to their senses – or rather to the new people they'd become. Mielitta copied the actions of those around. It was easy enough in the dark to blend in.

She glanced at the corner. Was the pile of ashes higher? She'd tried to count the candidates but the drink had wiped out her memory of the numbers and left only vague pictures of the procession, no faces other than Puggy and Drianne, who were both still here. Would their faces have been wiped from her mind too if they'd become ashes? If their forging hadn't worked? But she was still here. And still herself.

Jannlou would be pleased. Her lie was now true. She had been through a Maturity Ceremony and it hadn't worked properly. Of course she could never tell him. She would just have to lie better next time.

'From this day forth, you are ladies and knights, tested and found true to the Citadel. May the stones protect you in your Perfect lives as adults. May you have two forgeable children, lead faultless lives and be obedient to those in authority,' intoned Bastien. 'Lady Puggy, lead the ladies to the greensward and the Ceremony!'

The newly-demoted mage waited for Bastien to speak the password, open the glowing rectangle. The shaft of sudden daylight revealed no regret on her beautiful blank face. Her full, reddened lips parted slightly in what could have been either a smile or a gasp of pleasure as she took her first step into a new life. Rinduran was waiting and took Lady Puggy's arm, escorted her to pride of place in front of the audience, while the procession followed. Girls trooped out first, holding their skirts up above the sterile ground in a ladylike manner.

Mielitta eyed up the distance she had to cover to reach the table. She tried to catch Drianne's eye but was ignored.

The boys filed out, solemn with the weight of their new responsibilities. Finally, Bastien emerged, silhouetted against the open door for a moment, a giant bat in his fluttering robes. Even he looked changed, older, tired. At the first Maturity Ceremony he'd led, the Apprentice had presided over the forging of his own mentor, Puggy.

Bastien walked along the row of candidates, while the pink and blue flares enlivened the grey canopy in the traditional salute. Did the flares carry the same magecraft as the drinks? Prevent the waiting crowd remembering how many had entered the Barn? Let parents forget their own children if they didn't emerge as new adults?

Like grubs hatching. Nobody counts.

The Maturity Mage stopped beside Drianne, spoke a few quiet words and she flushed. Then she smiled prettily at him, a little girl playing grown-up, and she took his arm. Bastien was not playing grown-up and Mielitta knew what he'd said. Betrothal. Wife. Her stomach lurched as Bastien continued his inspection, moving towards her, Drianne at his side.

'Congratulations,' Bastien said to the beaming girl beside Mielitta.

Clever braiding, Mielitta's remaining brain fog noticed. *Rose ribbons wound through glossy black frizz. Wonder what hair treatments she used. Must have taken ages.*

Bastien and Drianne stopped in front of her. She looked down, her hands clasped in front of her, stilled all thought, whether shallow or deep. Not one ripple.

The Maturity Mage sniffed, looked puzzled, opened his mouth to speak but Mielitta would never know what he had been going to say as Rinduran's voice overrode his son's. 'Arrest her. She is vile, a traitor, riddled with Forest.'

There was a gasp at the forbidden word.

Mielitta lunged for the table. But Rinduran's order had not been to any person. The greensward itself had obeyed and was reaching upwards, curling tendrils of grassette around her legs like shackles. She was locked in place. She reached for her bees, thought of the glowing queen on her thigh but instead of communion there was absence.

Rinduran nodded at her, his eye patch black as stone death. Whatever he'd done had isolated her. She couldn't move, she couldn't fly as human or bee. In the flood of panic, she felt a connection she recognised, the eye behind the patch looking at her through her own powers, using them against her as she'd used Jannlou's own weight to throw him.

She was drawn by the black poison dart into that poisoned eye, into the putrescent milk of the cornea, where she floundered, alone. Her own inner darkness told her to give up. Death would be a relief. She should just let go, surrender.

'Throttle yourself,' she suggested. 'The crowd would enjoy that. A fitting end.' Her hands rose to her throat, felt a thin gold chain, hesitated.

'Break it,' she told herself but instead she reached for the arrowhead, knowing exactly how she'd stab herself, multiple times, until there was peace. But she was thwarted in the attempt to end her despair. Steelwing hurt her but did no further damage.

Then Rinduran laughed and the pressure on her withdrew in a mocking rush. She would have staggered if not bound in green chains. Instead she had no option but to listen to the mage's plans for the Citadel while facing her own execution.

'I promised you changes.' Rinduran's tones oozed a politician's sincerity. 'And, like this cohort of new adults, the Citadel will be born again, sovereign and Perfect, cleansed of the impurities that have wormed their way into our community.' His arms embraced all those who'd just passed their Maturity Test and then fixed the impure worm with a glare. All eyes were on Mielitta. So much raw hatred was worse than hands on her throat.

It was a relief when Rinduran drew the audience's attention to the woman at his side, holding her in what he probably thought was a loving embrace. 'It is with great pleasure that, on this special day, I can now announce my forthcoming marriage. Lady Puggy is to be my wife.'

Thank the stones, Mielitta no longer had to join in with the false cheers. 'Always make the best of things,' Declan would have said. If only she were still the little girl he'd comforted over a scratched knee or difficult schoolwork. She'd so wanted to be an adult and now she knew what it meant, she couldn't think of anything worse. She looked around for her father but Declan was nowhere to be seen. The back door to the forge was closed and unless you knew it was there, the spyhole was invisible. Maybe he was watching her, ashamed of what she'd become.

Rinduran was still droning on about the future. As long as he was speaking, Mielitta's death sentence was postponed, so she might as well listen. Anything to distract her from her own doom.

'For too long, girls afflicted with magecraft have lived unnatural lives, forced to join male mages in work and even in Council, unable to marry or to have children. My own betrothed, dear Puggy, suffered such a fate.' He kissed the ex-mage on the cheek, raised her hand and kissed that too. She seemed compliant, her vacuous half-smile never faltering. Bastien seemed less enamoured of his father canoodling with the new wife-to-be but quickly schooled his expression on hearing his own name.

'Things have changed! The new Maturity Mage Bastien has intervened during the Test to ensure that no woman will ever again endure such a fate. From now on, girls will have the curse of magecraft excised during the Maturity Ceremony, so they will all be able to live full women's lives.' Rinduran paused on a triumphant note and was rewarded with applause.

'Today is a great day for the Citadel and I want to thank Mage Bastien for his leadership in this new Ceremony and for saving

Lady Puggy with his skills. You will forgive me if I take pride in this achievement, for I am a father as well as a mage. So it is with personal pleasure that I want to introduce Lady Drianne, my son's betrothed. Their wedding, and our own, will be the symbol of the Citadel's renewed future!'

While the crowd yelled variations on 'Our saviours! Mage Bastien and Mage Rinduran!' Mielitta focused on her bee sigil, willing the queen to merge, so they could fly together. But there was no glow. No interior voices. No company. Just these hostile faces and shouting mouths.

Mielitta scanned the audience again. Not all those watching were enthusiastic. Or at least they did not display any enthusiasm. Declan wasn't present but his Apprentice was. *That bastard Kermon.* Hatred was a steel core and she used its hard certainty to hold back tears. She would not give him the satisfaction. But he wasn't even looking at her. His gaze never left Drianne, at Bastien's side, as cheerful and compliant as Puggy.

Then she recognised another mage and forgot Kermon as her unruly heart lurched. Jannlou. Taller than those around him and grim as she'd never seen him, not even when facing the tiger. Worried for his father at last, no doubt, having noticed Rinduran's high-handed words and gold braid. Mielitta could have bled laughter at his pain. He'd betrayed her to Bastien and he deserved everything that was coming to him. She stared at him, willing him to turn. When he did, she held his gaze, long and hard, then spat on the grassette, hoping the contamination with her spit would make it shrivel. No such luck. But Jannlou did not look down and in the end, she couldn't face him out. Not when she remembered what dreaming of a future in his arms had felt like.

CHAPTER TWENTY-SIX

'W hy are you keeping me alive?' Mielitta asked Rinduran, staring at his sighted eye so as not to look into the blackness of the other.

His eye flashed daggers. 'Enjoy your accommodation while you can.' He sketched a mocking bow and indicated the open door. She knew she could either walk into whatever awaited her in some room or be dragged in there by the floor magecraft.

The first time the greensward tendrils had withdrawn from her legs she'd tried to escape and immediately she was clamped in place. After two more attempts, she realised that Rinduran had activated the ground against her, throughout the Citadel. She could be held or dragged, propelled or shunted by grassette ropes or shifting cobblettes. Her only freedom was to walk where she was herded. So she walked into the room and the door clanged behind her. There was no chance that this room was ward-protected to keep others out. She tried opening the door, just to make sure, but neither handprint nor voiceprint, with any password she could think of, made the slightest crack appear in the sealed rectangle. There was, of course, no handle.

Mielitta didn't need to make an inventory of the room's contents. There was a bed and a door to a functional washroom.

Given the choices available, she took off her boots and lay on the bed. That raised her above the floor. So, if she could widen the door, make the bed fly along the corridors and out through the underground passage to the Forest, without being noticed, escape would be easy. Hah!

She could wait until Rinduran came to gloat, rush him and stab him with her arrowhead. Hah! She was still shaking from his casual suggestion that she might want to kill herself. If he made the command serious, she would do it without hesitation and feel she was leaving the world a better place. She could feel the power in his dead eye, absorbing all hope, all life.

She could pass the time making ever more ridiculous escape plans but they were little better than the Maturity Test fantasies. Why *was* Rinduran keeping her alive? Maybe if she knew the answer, she could keep herself alive longer. While she was searching for an answer, exhaustion overcame her and the temporary peace of sleep cradled her till dawn's greylight.

A yawn caught her attention.

What she'd thought was a wall, swayed and became a transparent partition between her own room and its twin. A tousle-haired girl sat up in bed in the mirrored bedroom, looked through the veil at Mielitta.

'So Daddy caught you,' she said, running her fingers through long, strawberry blonde curls. 'He said he would.'

'I'm Mielitta,' she stammered, as the other girl got out of bed, threw a robe over her shift and peered at her. It was like being a specimen in a school study but without knowing who was the observer and who was the specimen.

Now she was out of bed, the girl's childish frame and elfin face suggested that she was about Drianne's age. 'Your name doesn't matter. You're the traitor.'

'Perhaps that depends on your point of view,' Mielitta suggested. 'Who are you?'

After a long pause, the girl condescended to reply. 'I am Mage Rinduran's daughter, Verity.'

'Bastien's sister!' Mielitta spoke the thought aloud. She hadn't known of a sister, didn't remember her from school or the archery yard.

'*Mage* Bastien's sister,' came the reprimand. A coughing fit spoiled the attempt at hauteur. Verity doubled up and wheezed as she took the time needed before she could speak again.

'I am dying of allergy,' she explained calmly, 'so I live within the Perfect protection of my room, to keep me alive as long as possible. Your room is the same. My mother died in there last week.'

Mielitta blinked. Rinduran hadn't wasted time in his pursuit of Puggy. She screwed up the bedcover in one fist, trying not to think of the room's previous inhabitant. Things under the bed were bad enough but a ghost *in* the bed was even worse.

'You killed her.' This time the girl's voice trembled. 'You brought the Forest into the Citadel and it came into her room on the air. Every time somebody comes to see us, we die a little bit. I mean, I die a little bit. She's died completely now.' Another coughing spasm wracked her.

'I told Daddy I wanted to see you, tell you what you've done, call you a murderer. *Why* did you kill Mummy? And why are you killing me? We've never done anything to you.' Her face was white and severe, an angel's in judgement.

'I did not kill your mother!' Mielitta's vehemence was doubled by a nagging suspicion that she might have. Who knew what effect her bees had on the Citadel? Or what had come in with them. A fly that had died and wrecked the magical fabric of the library floor. *Stones*, she wished her bees were with her now.

'Daddy said you had creatures inside you. Insects.'

Mielitta said nothing but the girl nodded.

'Thought so,' Verity said. 'And Daddy said you want the canopy ripped open so sun destroys us all.'

'Sun doesn't destroy! It's warm and gentle!' Mielitta retorted.

'See.' Verity was smug. 'Daddy was right. You're evil.' Another coughing fit interrupted her speech. She wiped the blood from her mouth and showed the red wetness on her hand to Mielitta. 'This is what you did. And when Daddy and Bastien have finished wiping you clean, nobody will have allergy again.'

'But you're talking to me now. If,' she couldn't bring herself to say 'your Daddy', 'if Mage Rinduran is right, this should be making you worse. Maybe I'm not so bad after all.'

'But I told you.' Large brown eyes opened wide at Mielitta's stupidity. 'Our rooms are protected. Both of them, separately. Mummy and I could see each other through the partition but it's clean. Nothing gets through except sound and light. It's the doors that allow bad air in, the *badness* that you brought.'

Mielitta tried. 'I'm sorry that you're ill. I don't want anybody to have allergy.'

The brown eyes appraised her in sceptical accusation.

Mielitta ploughed on. 'I just think… maybe… if we could learn to live with the Forest, it would be better, people would be better… maybe there would be less allergy.'

'Daddy said you thought you knew better than everybody in the Citadel. Better than the walls and centuries of Perfection. One stupid, evil girl destroying the whole world. And Mummy. And me.' Verity's breath came in pants and sobs as she lost control. She lay back down on the bed, curled up like a foetus, her back to Mielitta as she breathed in great rasping shudders that raked Mielitta's conscience raw.

Was this her punishment? Watching Verity die of allergy, an accidental target killed by Mielitta's loose arrows? What had Tannlei said? *The archer and the target must become one, linked by the arrow's flight.*

Mielitta tested the floor's tolerance with one cautious foot, then the other: walked a couple of paces. There was no hindrance to her walking around the chamber. She stooped into a back exercise, extended it to stretch her calves, then upped the pace on her workout until she built up a sweat.

Her pulsing temples covered any sounds of ragged breathing from the other room and driving her body to work harder stopped thoughts that hurt worse than her muscles ever could. Verity would never know the exhilaration of running through the woods, turning a backward flip, loosing arrows. But did that mean Mielitta shouldn't do it? Did Perfection mean that people like herself should be stunted to save people like Verity? Did people always live full lives at others' expense? There must be another way!

She ran on the spot another fifty times, lifting her knees high to increase her heart rate. She paused then repeated the exercise. Then some jumping jacks and, followed by fifty squat thrusts. And again, until sweat dripped into her eyes.

Then she took a shower. While the water did its job, she remembered the wild joy of bathing in the stream. What was wrong with her? Why couldn't she settle for the Citadel life?

There was no movement now from the other side of the veil. Verity must be asleep again. One dull day after another. Mielitta paced the floor. She hadn't eaten for twenty-four hours but she'd drunk water from the washroom. It tasted the same as every other kind of water in the Citadel. She remembered rain pelting down in the Forest, drumming against the hive.

Pacing up and down, she measured out the steps she could take in each direction, wondering how long she could stay sane, whether she *was* sane. Without her bees, she didn't know what to think.

She lay down on the bed, shut her eyes, drifted into the rustle of leaves and chatter of goldfinches. Someone's hand was smoothing her brow and calm rippled inwards from each movement. Her mother's hand. She must have had a mother and now, when most needed, her mother was here, giving her strength.

'There, there, darling,' soothed the voice.

Mielitta opened her eyes, looked straight into the bloody cauldron of a damaged eye with a bee-sting black in its centre. Her instinctive recoil was mirrored in Rinduran's as he stepped backwards from the bed, placing a safe distance of flooring between them. Too late now to jab him and run.

To her shame, the loss of her imaginary mother flooded her with grief and overspilled in heavy sobs.

'There, there, darling,' Rinduran mocked, as she rocked on the bed, shaking. 'You wondered why I kept you alive? For the Citadel of course. We can learn from you.' His voice softened, almost to the tones she'd mistaken for parental love. 'And for Verity.'

At the sound of her name, the girl through the partition roused, raised herself up on her elbows and looked through the partition. Like Mielitta, she'd woken and seen Rinduran.

'Daddy,' she said with a sleepy smile. 'Are you going to fix things?'

'Yes, sweetheart,' he replied, then returned his attention to Mielitta, who could not control her tears.

'How did you bond with these creatures?' he asked, as if enquiring politely about her daily routine. But with the words came the same stab of power she'd felt when linked to him by the bee, pulling out words she didn't want to speak. This time she was alone, no bees, no friends; betrayed and abandoned. And so, the interrogation began. Smooth and considerate questions, accompanied by needle-thin spikes of pain that left her sweating, panting and talking.

She told him everything. The bee attack, the sigil, the summons to the hive, the beauty of the Forest. Worse than that, she told him how she felt about Jannlou. Amid her shamed tears, he smiled, the kindly uncle of a girl's nightmares. If she'd written a private diary and been forced to read it aloud in public, *this* was how it would feel. With jabs and prods of power to shock her into continuing.

'Don't,' he warned her gently as she thought of her arrowhead, wondered once more if she could hurt herself back into control. She yelped as a blast immobilised her hand. Without her bees, she was nothing. Just an ordinary girl.

Just when she felt she could bear no more, Rinduran's attention wavered. His sighted eye lost focus as if seeing something outside the room. She avoided looking at the other eye.

'Other business calls me,' he told her, apologetic. 'You have been very helpful but I have more questions before proceeding to a more physical dissection of your aberrant brain. Unfortunately, further discussion must wait.'

He looked over at Verity, who took it as a sign she could speak. What had the girl seen? Mielitta wondered but she knew the answer. Just her Daddy asking civil questions to a freak, who jumped and shrieked, cried and shivered for no reason.

'Do you think you can find a cure for allergy?' Verity's eyes showed that her life hung on the question.

'Yes, little Vee,' he assured her. 'We'll have to experiment but I think we can extract a substance from this girl that might change everything. I need to consult the walls. I'll be back tomorrow.'

'Promise?' Verity asked.

'I promise,' Rinduran said, looking at Mielitta.

She curled up in a ball, hiding her eyes, didn't watch him leave.

Never again, she told herself. *Never again.* Whatever she had to do. Although she told herself she would not sleep, her body decreed otherwise, in fits and starts, wakening always into sickening fear. What she feared most was the glamour of a gentle voice, the deception and mockery. So when she heard such a voice again, her instinct was to hide.

There was nowhere to hide and the voice was insistent.

Mielitta. Watch!

She had prayed to the walls so many times to open to her but since the time she'd hidden from Shenagra after the Council Meeting, the stones had been inert. She'd thought her birthday gift, with the cryptic verse, had come from the walls, but if so, there had been no explanation. Just consequences. She was tired of mysteries and she was alone. She should ignore this new torment but how could things become worse?

Mielitta. Watch!

Wary but incapable of doing otherwise, she obeyed.

Now, one wall shimmered and settled, screening a large image: the Council Chamber, with a meeting in full session. And every word was audible, at least to Mielitta. She glanced across at the bed in the other room but there was no movement. Verity seemed unconscious of the drama playing out, with her father at the centre.

Mielitta touched the wall, expecting her hand to move through it, for this to be the moment she could finally enter the walls, but the stone remained cold and solid, as if it had no pictures or sound flickering across it.

Although he was still at the head of the table, wearing his leader's braid, Magaram was no longer exuding the confidence she remembered in him. Shenagra was at his side but she too seemed diminished somehow, her braids waving a plea for help rather than threatening to dispense judgement.

The voice booming out was Rinduran's, his gold braid glittering more than Magaram's as he waved his hands to emphasise his words. Puggy's place had been filled already – by Bastien – a clear indication of where power lay now.

'No mage greets his own retirement with pleasure and we all appreciate what you have done in your time, Mage Magaram, but we need new blood to deal with new dangers and it is your time to step down.'

There was no shock visible around the table, not even from Shenagra, who moved closer to Magaram. Some mages shuffled, looked away, but nobody spoke against Rinduran. He and Bastien had obviously made their moves as planned, gained more than two reluctant brides from their manoeuvres.

Looking grey, old, in need of retirement, Magaram could still command respect. 'I do not accept.' His voice pulled at any strings of loyalty left around that table but nobody spoke up.

He addressed his usurper. 'So this is what *late starter* means? A man who hides his magecraft and bides his time, lays the explosive that will destroy the building then steps into the breach to

QUEEN OF THE WARRIOR BEES

save it? A man who whispers slander in each ear, tailor-made for the listener, until all believe they will see a better world with Rinduran the master of it?'

He glared at each member of the Council who dared look his way. 'Make no mistake – if he wins, he will be a tyrant and you will find out the lies he's sold you. The Forest will be the least of your problems when the enemy within the Citadel achieves his own ambitions. Mage Puggy is only the first of his conquests and an example of how he treats his peers.'

'Lady Puggy,' corrected Rinduran. 'And we all know that mage work is too much of a strain for women, how much they sacrifice to wield magecraft. It's not fair on them and, let's be honest, they are struggling to compete with men when they lack the capacity. They shouldn't have to struggle! We have strayed from Perfection and our women have paid the price. Now we'll restore them to their proper place and protect them as we should. I spent enough years studying the lessons of the walls to know what resulted from women trying to behave like men. Assault. Rape. Incest. Child abuse. Child neglect. All because men felt diminished and women didn't care about their proper responsibilities.' Each word came out like a stab to the guts.

Shenagra's braids turned white-hot as she blazed up under Rinduran's words. She was the only woman in the room. 'Maybe that's up to men to do something about,' she muttered.

'Oh, we are, my dear. We are.' Rinduran's smile twisted the knife.

'Shenagra,' ordered Magaram and Mielitta knew what was coming. The braids hissed and snaked towards Rinduran, heedless of anyone or anything in their way, oozing poison. There would be no question of acceptance. He was condemned. The Chief Mage's face drained of all colour in some invisible battle of wills as the tendrils of hair reached inexorably for their target.

'What's your target?' murmured Mielitta and suddenly she knew Magaram's mistake. *He* was Rinduran's target, not Shenagra, and while all his concentration was on reinforcing their attack, he was open and vulnerable. And he was Jannlou's father.

Mielitta called, 'Magaram! Beware!' Maybe his blue eyes flickered in response or maybe not. The paralysis hit him too quickly to be sure. The Chief Mage was turning to stone in front of his colleagues' eyes and nobody except Shenagra moved to help him.

'Appropriate, I thought,' commented Rinduran as he built up layer by layer of wall where there used to be a man. Feet, ankles, knees, thighs disappeared within tight-packed dry stone.

Shenagra's braids rushed back to the growing wall, ripped ineffectually at it and were tangled in the construction like black ivy.

When the stones had transformed Magaram up to his eyes, Rinduran told him, 'She loves you. That's what is killing her, not me. So blame yourself. As I said, female mages are too emotional, incapable of government.'

In a screaming rush, Shenagra was consumed in the braids as they drew her into the wall that had once been Magaram. No lovers could be closer than the stone and the black creeper intertwined in every layer. Then the wall and its partner crumbled to dust.

'Now,' said Rinduran. 'Let's get to business.' He moved to his place at the head of the table, brushed a speck of Magaram's dust off the sparkling braid. 'This traitor girl. We need to penetrate her, find these creatures that have appeared in the Citadel, eliminate them and then, when we are sure she's clean, eliminate her.'

Bastien spoke up. 'I have an idea.'

Then the sound stopped, the pictures whizzed and blurred, and the walls were only stone.

Mielitta kicked one in frustration. 'The Forest take you!' she told the wall, without one thought as to what was ladylike, or for the sensibilities of the girl on the other side of the veil, who jammed her fingers in her ears.

CHAPTER TWENTY-SEVEN

W hen the door opened on her second morning in captivity, Mielitta hoped for Declan. Surely her father would visit her. Instead, a tray slid through and the door closed too fast for Mielitta to see who'd brought a bowl of sustenance. Through the veil, she saw the door to Verity's room open and the process repeated. Again, the door was opened and shut as quickly as possible, presumably to minimise contamination. Being protected and being captive looked much the same on the surface.

Mielitta wolfed down every scrap of sustenance while Verity barely pecked at hers, coughing and swallowing with difficulty. Had there been some deterioration in two days or was Mielitta imagining it? If she hadn't already finished her food, so hungry that its blandness was irrelevant, the noises from the other chamber would have put her off. Sickness was disgusting. If Verity was a bee, she'd be carried out of the hive entrance and dropped on the ground outside to die, so she didn't weaken the hive. And she would not question her fate.

But humans did not behave so and Mielitta forced down her instinctive repulsion, imagined what it must be like to live as Verity did. When the girl had stopped eating and coughing, leaving almost as much on the plate as had been there to begin with, Mielitta asked, 'Is it worse today?'

'I'm fine,' Verity replied. She lay back down on the bed but was facing Mielitta this time. An invitation to talk?

'I don't want anybody to be sick. It must be horrible.'

'I'm not just sick, I'm dying.' Verity merely stated the fact. 'And I have allergy because the Forest is brought into the Citadel by traitors. People like you.'

Mielitta's heart leapt. Were there other people like her, other traitors? She recalled the execution of 'the traitors'. The mage who'd enjoyed the beauty of the Forest, the citizens who'd been unmasked in the Great Hall. There had been no real treachery and no traitors but her. No, there was nobody like her and lone honey-bees died quickly. She searched again for her bees but the only buzzing was of her own thoughts and the sigil was cold.

'Well I'm going to die too.' Mielitta was also matter-of-fact. Facing imminent death made them equals and for the first time in her life, she could say anything she liked. 'What if they're wrong? I mean, what would happen if there were no barriers, if the Forest could come and go from the Citadel, if people could come and go from the Forest?'

Verity did not turn away but she didn't think twice before answering. 'Then more people would get allergy and die. Daddy saw it in the walls, the time when children got more and more allergic, before they made the barriers, made safe food and drink, protected people so everything is Perfect.'

'But what about the people who didn't have allergy?' *Especially the weird ones with bees in their heads.* What was it Jannlou's mother had said? *Existing not living.* 'They could have lived with the Forest and they had to give up so much.'

'You would rather I died than you give up the Forest and live a Perfect life,' Verity accused Mielitta.

And you would rather thousands of people were crippled, instead of living full lives, just so you can exist. A bee would rather die. But Mielitta did not speak such thoughts aloud. It seemed that she couldn't say anything she liked, after all, unless she wanted to end the conversation. Did it have to be her life or Verity's?

Even if most people could live with the Forest, perhaps *needed* to live with the Forest, did that justify killing dozens of people like Verity? Shouldn't the whole Citadel live in such a way as to keep everyone alive? A bee would sacrifice herself willingly to keep the community strong. Was it she, Mielitta, who was sick and had to be ejected from the human hive? Perhaps Rinduran was right. She should be executed.

Her forehead tight with frowns, Mielitta said, 'There has to be another way.'

'There isn't. Daddy spent years in the walls, studying Perfection.'

In the following silence, Mielitta started her work-out. Physical exercise was the only way she knew to stop the treadmill her mind was running on. Her head was up and her back starting to arch during her two hundredth push-up, when she noticed the door outline glowing.

'Someone's coming for you,' murmured Verity. Then her voice warmed in recognition and she called out, 'Bastien!'

On the threshold of Mielitta's room, the new Maturity Mage greeted his sister gently, the sly lines of his face relaxing into a smile. 'Vivi. Not like you to be so lively first thing in the morning.'

She giggled at the pet name and fraternal teasing. *Like any normal brother and sister* thought Mielitta, wondering what it was like to have siblings, what it was like to know one of them was dying of allergy.

'I'll come and see you afterwards,' he promised, 'and I want you to meet somebody.' He stepped into Mielitta's room, as did the two people behind him. She readied herself to attack but she sensed the reaction in the flooring, as it tensed to anchor her to the spot.

Bastien still spoke to Verity, bringing forward the girl who accompanied him. 'This is my betrothed, Lady Drianne,' he told his sister. 'She can only speak through this soul-reader,' he indicated Kermon, 'so I've brought him too.'

He hugged Drianne tight and kissed the top of her head. As he released her, his robe flapped open and Mielitta could see his knight's belt, boasting a new trophy, the padlock of betrothal in metalwork. Crafted by Declan? Or Kermon?

Bastien's attention was still on his sister.

'She was in danger and she suffered terribly when she had to go into the walls but I rescued her. I know you'll get on so well. In fact,' he teased again, 'I chose her because she reminded me of you.'

Again the giggle, marred by the first cough since Bastien had entered. His face clouded but he gave no acknowledgement of his sister's ill health. Drianne's expression was as serene as when she'd come out of the Maturity Barn but pity flickered in her eyes as she looked through the veil. Did Drianne also hold Mielitta responsible for those afflicted and dying of allergy in the Citadel?

Some silent exchange took place between Drianne and Kermon – *that bastard!* – and the soul-reader spoke. 'Lady Drianne says she is happy to meet her fiancé's sister and sorry to disturb your morning. She hopes that today will be one of your good days and looks forward to hearing your stories of her lord's childhood.'

Eyes gleaming with mischief, Verity said, 'Oh yes, I have *lots* of stories you should hear!'

It wasn't that Mielitta wanted Drianne to snub a sick girl but she felt the clanging of doors in her heart. Bastien had a plan, surely to kill or even torture her; Kermon had tried to forge her and then exposed her; and now Drianne seemed more interested in her future sister-in-law than in her friend. If there *was* still any friendship after the forging.

Bastien still had laughter in his eyes from his sister's threats when he gave his full attention to Mielitta but then all smiles faded. 'My lady wanted to see you and I can refuse her nothing. She said that from the friendship you once shared, she wanted to give you a chance for redemption.'

Drianne nodded agreement at her future husband's words.

Oh stones, thought Mielitta. *I'm to be one of Bastien's experiments and rescues.*

'And Apprentice Mage-Smith Kermon is not just here to speak for Lady Drianne. If you repent and comply, following all the steps required, he is willing to marry you.'

Kermon nodded agreement, his expression pleading as if he was the innocent suitor he pretended to be. Her hands slipped to the arrowhead around her neck, tracing the Damascene whorls of Kermon's master-work. *The bastard, abusing such skill! Forging children's minds!*

'I'll kill him first!' she burst out. 'He's not penetrating me twice!'

'I d-d-don't understand,' stammered Kermon, flushing.

Bastien's mouth was a moue of distaste. 'I hope you will change your mind,' he said, 'for the sake of your friends, whom I respect. But I always feared it would come to this. You never learned your lesson.'

Mielitta remembered Bastien's lessons all too well but she wouldn't give him the satisfaction of knowing how scared she'd been of him and the gang. Of Jannlou. *Just one more betrayal,* she told herself. *Forget him.*

'This will be your last chance. If it doesn't work, my father will have his way. Believe me, you don't want that.'

Mielitta shrugged. 'I'm busy this morning. Get on with whatever it is and go.'

Even then, Bastien kept his temper. Maybe because Verity was watching her big brother with wide-eyed hero-worship. As was his fiancée, who gave Kermon an intense look, one Mielitta recognised as the prelude to speaking through the soul-reader.

'Lady Drianne is sad to see her archery friend fallen so low,' began Kermon. 'She urges Lady Mielitta–'

'She's not a lady,' interrupted Bastien. 'She failed the Maturity Test.'

'She urges Mielitta,' corrected Kermon, 'to listen to the Perfect wisdom of Mage Bastien. Then we can become friends again, two married ladies enjoying full lives in the safety of the Citadel.'

His switch to first person confused Mielitta and his eyes seemed to plead for her friendship with *him* not just Drianne.

While Kermon pontificated about ladylike behaviour and vague sentimental nonsense, she was startled by a voice in her head. Not her bees but Drianne, exactly as she'd been just before the Maturity Ceremony.

Ignore the tissue of lies Kermon is spinning for me. We agreed what he'd say, beforehand, so I could speak to you properly. I don't know what you've got against him but he'd do anything for you! Anyway, we can argue about all that once you're free. No time to tell you the details but your bee woke my magecraft.'

I don't trust him and neither should you. Mielitta responded in her mind, as she did to the bees but Drianne showed no signs of having heard and made no reply. As the silence became awkward Mielitta said aloud, 'I don't believe you.'

Drianne nodded vehemently.

Believe it! All I know is that I tingled all over, felt a rush of power, hard to put into words but you just know what it is. Magecraft! And it was strong enough to keep me hidden during the Test. I could feel Mage Puggy with me, giving me her strength, her own magecraft, and then she was gone.

Bastien frowned. 'You have to trust somebody, to be saved. Drianne and Kermon are telling you the truth.'

Stones! This was complicated. 'I am thinking about what you say,' was the best she could come up with to fit both conversations.

You don't have to reply to me, just listen. We will come back, Kermon and I, use magecraft to rescue you. But you need to trust us both.

'I think I see,' said Mielitta slowly. But *they* didn't. They only saw her prison room, which was not what bound her. They didn't know about the magecraft in the ground, transmitted through the whole Citadel. They couldn't fight that and she would still be trapped, while they would be discovered. If Kermon didn't betray them all before then. She didn't trust him, couldn't trust him. She knew the smithwork involved in the forging and he was the only one capable of it, apart from herself. Unless there had been some other apprentice of whom she was ignorant.

But this was her only chance, if she could think of a way to escape the alertness of the ground itself, tensed to clamp her for one wrong step. As a bee, she could fly, but her connection was completely dead and she couldn't shift shape any more. If she could walk out on a tightrope or clinging to the walls, she'd be above the ground.

If the walls would let her enter here and leave at the water gate, she'd be free. But the walls were capricious and she had no idea what they would do or what they meant by it, goodwill or spite. They could send her a note in spidery green handwriting or show her the Council Chamber when they chose but their interventions were outside her control.

She'd been over these thoughts before and dismissed them all. Maybe she should just hope her friends' magecraft would be strong enough to break the floor spells. It was hopeless. The entire Citadel was constructed on floor magecraft, which had no weaknesses.

Except for the one she had introduced. What if? And how on earth would she communicate what she needed?

'There is something you should know. I do lack self-control,' she confessed.

Bastien's eyes narrowed.

She continued, 'I always have. You remember our old archery tutor, Drianne, how she complained about my self-discipline and told us about stance.'

'Lady Drianne says that archery was part of your childhood and, like her, you must leave those memories in the past,' Kermon rebuked her.

While Mielitta heard Drianne's real response. *Make the ground your friend not your enemy by how you stand and move. Is that it?*

'Yes, yes, exactly so.' Mielitta willed Drianne to understand. She rubbed her foot along the woodette floorboards, as if nervous.

The ground! You're trapped by the ground!

'Yes, I know.' Mielitta looked down. Bastien thought so little of women's intelligence, and so highly of his own, he would be motivated to believe her act. 'I need a service from you, one that will help me control myself and then I will try my best to be Perfect.' She rushed on, so Bastien couldn't interrupt her. 'There is something in the library.' Too vague. 'A motivational cutting, to help me get my self-control back. It's under a pile of books, beneath a stool. Just a cutting. But it would help me a lot. To read it again, I mean,' she finished.

We'll get your cutting, promised Drianne. *And we'll be back as soon as we can manage.*

'Lady Drianne asks your permission to visit the library, to get this text for her friend,' Kermon told Bastien. 'Maybe you can save her,' he added. 'You were right to try. And you know I will make her behave in future, inspired by your example.'

Verity was hanging on every word and it was to her that Bastien glanced, as if considering and approving his reflection in her eyes.

'These are dangerous times,' mused Bastien, 'and I don't want my lady outside the mages' quarters without my personal protection. I'm too busy with Citadel affairs to go to the library on such a trivial errand but if you want to go, Kermon, by all means. The door will admit you to bring this text to this headstrong girl and I hope you're right, that we can bring her to her senses, and that you can be as happy in your mate as I am in mine.'

Drianne smiled and allowed herself to be drawn into an embrace. *Until later,* she told Mielitta. *This is the last time he'll touch me, I swear. Whatever happens.*

'Until later,' echoed Mielitta to Kermon. 'With the cutting.' She didn't dare to emphasis cut any further. She had no idea whether the soul-reader could hear the thoughts Drianne sent to her or not, nor whether either of them had a clue as to what to do in the library. She could only hope they would see the damaged floor and guess the rest.

'You have an angel for company,' Bastien told Mielitta. 'If anybody can bring out the best in another person, it is my sister, as beautiful in spirit as in body.'

What hurt Mielitta most was that he spoke the truth, his truth. Nobody in that room could doubt the love between brother and sister, the family bond. And still Declan had not come.

CHAPTER TWENTY-EIGHT

With no distractions, the waiting hung heavy on Mielitta. So she was almost relieved when the wall shimmered and the Council Chamber came into view again. First, she saw Rinduran speech-making at the head of the table, Chief Mage now. Then she heard him. And her relief vanished.

'...traitor is contained, it is time to destroy the enemy. Only Magaram's weakness has allowed the Forest to exist on our doorstep, to invade our sanctuary over and over. To infect ever more people with allergy. The Forest will kill the human race if we don't destroy it now! Hamel, report to the Council.' Rinduran sat down.

Tiny, pointed and green, Hamel was now occupying what had been Shenagra's seat, on the right hand of the Chief Mage. His high voice whined like a mosquito. 'I too have spent years in the walls and can support every word Mage Rinduran says, with evidence from the past. You can watch a little girl die of asphyxiation, choking in the effort to breathe, turning scarlet, because the Forest touched her.'

Rinduran blanched as he listened, his hands clenched in front of him on the table.

'You can hear the pleas of our saviours, begging us to ensure

JEAN GILL

our society maintains the ways of Perfection, not to make the same mistakes again. We have carried out every prescription but one. We have not ended contact with the Forest. I have said it in Council before and been mocked for it, as I've been mocked for my odd physique and funny voice.'

Nobody laughed.

'I don't see those who've mocked me around this table now. And this time when I speak of policy, my words will be heard. Mage Rinduran is right. Can anybody here give one reason we need the living Forest and its vile creatures?'

Silence. If somebody had spoken up, who would have executed them, now that Shenagra was dead? Had Hamel taken her place in every way? He was rumoured to have unpleasant skills and Mielitta doubted whether he – or Rinduran – would worry about their colleagues' willingness to have their thoughts policed. She knew how it felt to have your mind forced and she shuddered. To Mielitta's relief, the silence endured. She had no wish to see more executions.

But *her* mind was still free. *I am not as contained as you think! I need the Forest*, she thought. *I am one of those vile creatures.*

Hamel continued, 'The Citadel is self-sufficient. If we kill the Forest and everything in it, we lose nothing! We can switch to woodette when we've used up all the wood, and until then we can collect it in complete safety! We can cleanse not only the Citadel but the environment. If I tell you that Mage Rinduran knows exactly how to kill the Forest and win this war so we never have to fight it again, will you support us?'

Rinduran jumped in before anyone could answer. 'I believe we must do this if we love our children and want a future for them and for *their* children. That's the purpose of a Perfect society! But you should have your say. Let's put it to the vote in the accustomed manner' Rinduran's open arms welcomed them all into the decision-making process. 'Motion: that this Council is henceforth in a state of war with the Forest and will proceed immediately to

236

hostile actions, which will cease only on the death of the Forest and all life forms in it.'

'Aye,' said Hamel.

The result was a foregone conclusion, one 'Aye' following another around the table, with no life-threatening hesitation.

'This is how we do it,' Rinduran began, with the beatific smile of a prophet whose time had come.

Heart pounding, Mielitta swore she would unpick the walls stone by stone if she lost sound now. *Let me know how they're going to do it,* she prayed, *please!*

'The walls showed me how it was done. Our ancestors used chemicals and the physical destruction of habitat; we use mage-craft on the small creatures and let the Forest destroy itself. Insects create the very fabric of the Forest. We scramble their senses and communication so they can't find food or each other.'

My bees. If Mielitta was struggling to cope with their absence, how would they deal with isolation from each other? Confused, their sense of smell destroyed, unable to find flowers, unable to dance, to return home. This wasn't just hive death. It was crippling, killing despair and she could feel its blackness growing in her already. *No bees.*

Rinduran grew more and more enthusiastic, sharing the fruit of his years of research in the walls. 'We cut down the trees, which will give us wood. We kill everything that moves. And we replace all natural ground with the Citadel's base network: stones with cobblettes, grass with grassette greensward and woodette flooring.'

There were gasps at the scope of the plan but nobody said it couldn't be done.

One mage risked a question. 'We'll be exposed to impure water and sunlight?'

Rinduran nodded. 'We need to purify the water. Maybe in the future we can build a new Citadel and a second Canopy but for now we will have to endure sunlight if we venture into our new territory –

just as the logging parties have been doing – but there will no longer be any risk of bringing Forest back into the Citadel. Sunlight cannot be brought into the Citadel so is only a risk to those who venture out.'

Even the water will be dead, thought Mielitta, remembering the taste of the stream. *No leaf patterns on tree bark. No sunlit canopy. No birdsong. No thunderstorm or tiger fight.* All things that were most alive would be dead. No. She couldn't let it happen.

'For our children,' Rinduran was saying. 'We do this for our children.' Then the wall rippled and the Council Chamber faded from view.

Mielitta looked at Verity, apparently asleep in her bed through the veil. *Yes, she told herself. Let's do this for the children. For all the children.* She had an idea.

Two meal trays came and went, raising Mielitta's hopes and dashing them again, before the door outline glowed. Her heart pounded and she clenched her fists, determined to throw herself at the mage if it was Rinduran, force him to kill her. She couldn't withstand his attacks on her mind.

Two shapes materialised. Drianne and Kermon, the latter carrying a bow, a quiver and a large rectangle of floor fabric.

I saw Bastien claim the bow and where he hid it, so I stole it back, said Drianne. *He likes trophies.*

'Thank the stones!' Mielitta didn't waste time in greeting but grabbed the piece of fly-damaged floor and inspected it. 'Can you cut it into pieces large enough to cover the soles of my boots?' She quickly untied her laces, passed Kermon the boots as a template.

He nodded, pulled out the knife a smith always carried, no doubt one of his own making. He snapped it open, scored a rough outline and then cut the flooring in its sole shape.

Through the veil, Verity stirred in bed and coughed a little. She was always restless. Now was not a good time for her to wake up. Mielitta worked fast, ripping the hem of her gown into strips.

She was about to bind the floor-sole onto her boots when Kermon held out a hand to stop her. She jerked back as if she'd been burned and she saw the hurt in his eyes.

'The cloth will be in contact with the floor,' he explained. 'It won't work. You'll be restrained.'

'The moment I go through the door,' she realised, chewing her lip. Now what? She looked at the cut-out soles, the discarded bits of woodette, the ugly bump of the fly's body, covered in sticky orange goo. Propolis! The bees' miraculous glue.

There was no time to lose. Rinduran would be back any moment, Bastien might notice his wife-to-be was behaving oddly and Declan might choose the wrong moment to visit her. She wouldn't want to divide his loyalties. Once she was free, she could explain, make things right.

She smeared propolis onto each sole, held the strip of cloth onto one and applied as much pressure as she could to glue it in place.

'Let me,' offered Kermon, taking the first sole from her while she attached the second cloth ribbon.

'Thanks,' she said gruffly, then explained her plan in a low voice while she tied her makeshift soles onto her boots, praying the propolis and cloth would hold.

Her voice wasn't low enough and Verity asked, 'What are you doing?'

Mielitta only just heard the girl through the buzz in her head. The moment her feet were isolated from the Citadel flooring by the flawed piece from the library, her head swarmed with bees. Their anxiety, their understanding, their joy at the reunion made her whole again and she had no time to be gentle with Verity.

All of you, go outside me, cover all of my head but my eyes and mouth, buzz loudly, she ordered.

Work agreed her bees happily, forming a dense cloud around Mielitta. She could feel the tiny wings tickling her cheeks and forehead, her ears and hair. As ordered, they left her eyes and mouth clear so she could see Verity through her own eyes, speak clearly.

'These are my bees,' she told the girl, who was cringing in the furthest corner, her mouth open in a silent scream. 'Make one

239

sound, call for help and I will set them on you. I am their queen and I can order your death now, if you call for help. Death by a thousand stings, each one more painful than the one before.' The bee cloud shifted as individual bees darted out then returned. Verity whimpered.

Mielitta! Drianne objected. *That's cruel! And you don't need to hurt her!*

In a whisper, Verity said, 'Daddy was right. I knew Bastien was too kind to you.'

Whether she meant Mielitta or Drianne wasn't clear and both reacted.

'Yes, Daddy was right about me.' Mielitta was venomous.

I'm sorry, said Drianne. *Truly. Kermon, tell her.*

'Lady Drianne says she is sorry,' Kermon told Verity but the bees spoke louder, a menacing buzz.

'We haven't got time for this,' Mielitta said. 'Shout for help and I let the bees out again, through the veil next time.' She recalled the bees until the last buzz disappeared from the room but she could still feel the comforting thrum of their presence inside her.

She looked at the girl, still huddled in a corner, so afraid. *For all the children,* Mielitta thought, hardening her heart and resisting Drianne's objections.

'It's the only way,' she said. 'Verity, you have to come with us.'

'I'll die,' said Verity. 'You said you weren't a murderer but you are.'

'That was before your Daddy declared war.'

Verity opened her mouth to scream but Drianne was quicker. A shaft of power streaked through the veil, ripping it open and stopping Verity's mouth, closing it. Then the sick girl shut her eyes, slipped into a deeper sleep than she'd probably known for years, slumped to the floor.

Mielitta gulped. She had not realised the strength of Drianne's power.

'Have you killed her?' she asked.

No. She's asleep and I've given her sweet dreams. Is this really necessary? What if Rinduran's right and she dies in the Forest?

'She's dying anyway. And she's Rinduran's weak spot. We must use it. And what if the Forest offers healing for her?'

You don't believe that. She has extreme allergy.

'Kermon, take the girl through the water gate to the edge of the Forest. Use whatever glamour and excuses you need if you're questioned. Nobody apart from her family will recognise her, so some story tale of a faint and of her being your betrothed will work fine. You're known so you'll get away with it easily enough. Drianne and I will meet you after we've been to the schoolroom.'

While Kermon walked through the ripped veil and gently settled Verity's slight form onto his muscled shoulder, Mielitta asked, 'Drianne, can you disguise me?'

You should have asked me that before you ripped up your gown. Such a waste! But yes. A little glamour will repair your clothes and change your face, without tiring me.

Mielitta restrung her bow and slung it over her shoulder. She'd check the rest of her equipment later. 'And hide my weapons?' she asked, belting her quiver around her waist. She accepted Drianne's cloak as a rough cover-all and hoped that glamour would refine the effect. Then she gave Kermon the water gate password and wished him good fortune.

He meant it, said Drianne, when Kermon was gone. *What he said to Bastien. He would have married you. He loves you too. He's a good man.*

'Maybe,' acknowledged Mielitta. 'But I'm not a good woman.' She didn't have time for all these complications or for tact. 'And I have my bees to think about. Let's go.'

CHAPTER TWENTY-NINE

W alking on the cut-out soles was clumsy but Mielitta was getting used to them. *Like wearing snowshoes,* her book learning told her. Short, ladylike steps beneath the gown hid her bizarre boots and Drianne kept to the slow pace, adding to the illusion that two ladies were going about their normal business.

'I can't wait for the Courtship Dance,' burbled Mielitta as they nodded to a chattering group in bright gowns and passed them by, treading the familiar passageways towards the schoolroom.

Flowers, commented the bees.

Noisy flowers, she agreed, her heart blossoming in the renewed contact, whole again. Even when they obeyed her order to hide, quietly, so she could concentrate on Drianne's telepathic words, she could feel the hum of happiness throughout her body.

Drianne was less wholehearted about the plan. *You have become hard,* she told Mielitta. *Remember these are children and be gentle.*

The weight of her weapons was as comforting to Mielitta as the hum of her bees. 'I know what the target is, Drianne. And I am the arrow. You'll have to be the gentle one.'

Number chants in high voices told them they'd reached their destination. Mielitta wondered what she looked like wearing glamour. Not like the divine incarnation of Puggy, she hoped, although it would be fun to see Jannlou's face if that was the case and then he realised it was actually her. But Jannlou was one of the many trains of thought she refused to follow, banished from her mind as distractions from what mattered. One target. Save the Forest. Nothing else mattered, and she would give her life in the attempt, as would any bee.

They can't hear me, Drianne told her. *You and Kermon hear me but I don't think anybody else does. Not that I've noticed anyway. And I don't know what my magecraft can do. I've had no training. It just comes. So I think you'll look like Mage Yacinthe and I can bend their minds enough to accept a day with you. They'll realise later that it doesn't make sense.*

'How much later?' asked Mielitta.

I don't know. I've never done this before.

The door into the schoolrooms glowed in outline and opened in response to Drianne's touch; Mielitta flounced in, feeling the float of glamour covering her more effectively than the borrowed cloak. It had been years since she'd been here but you never forgot your schooldays, nor the classrooms.

Seven rooms opened off a quadrangle, where a class of little ones had reached their ten times table, the chant they'd heard from outside. When the chant finished, the children were dismissed for break-time, to play tag and let off steam, while the teacher watched. As Mielitta had done once, with the friends who were now forged, the enemies who were now mages. Jannlou had pulled her braids. Why did boys do that? And Bastien had tripped her up, mocked her.

'Mage Yacinthe! This is unexpected.' The teacher had noticed them, her mouth a severe pink line of disapproval.

How did you make a teacher too concerned about her own performance to question authority?

'The stones be with you, Lady Belinda,' began Mielitta. At least teachers couldn't be demoted under Rinduran's new rules, although they were all female. They'd never been valued higher than ladies and no mage would stoop to teaching. 'Maturity Mage

Bastien is implementing a new programme of school inspection and I have been tasked with this, along with my library duties.'

The pink line thinned further. 'Of c-c-course,' stammered the teacher on outside duty. 'I can select some children if you want to see what they've learned today?'

The best, no doubt, thought Mielitta cynically. Drianne urged her to hurry up. As if she didn't know that Bastien might discover them missing, any minute.

'Another time,' she told the teacher, whose shoulders relaxed in relief. 'We will visit each class in turn to collect all the children for a visit to the library. This is my Assistant Librarian, Lady Hannah.'

Mielitta stalked away from the quadrangle towards the classroom where the oldest children were taught, the twelve-year-olds. Until her selection as a witness, Drianne had been a pupil in this very class. Now she scurried in her friend's wake, apparently subservient, and, hopefully, well-disguised.

'The stones be with you, Lady Fidelity,' boomed Mielitta and repeated her cover story, with the same success. This time, however, she and Drianne took all the children out with them, ready for their day in the library.

'Bring your lunchtime sustenance,' Mielitta told the children. 'We shall have a jolly picnic together.' Well-trained, the children proceeded to the quadrangle to wait, each carrying his or her little lunch-box.

Five times, the self-declared school inspector entered a classroom and emerged with all the pupils. The quadrangle was now somewhat crowded and the children's anticipation of a day out mingled with the teachers' hopes for a day off. Their wishes were all granted.

'If you line up the children, we will take charge now,' Mielitta told them. The teachers only too happy to organise their charges and watch them leave in a long crocodile, following her. The littlest ones held hands in pairs and Drianne brought up the rear.

My persuasion must be strong! Drianne thought to Mielitta. *How in hell do they think all these children will fit in the library?*

'Let's hope it doesn't wear off before we get out the water gate.' Mielitta muttered to herself.

Twice, Mielitta led her small procession past knights and ladies and exchanged courtesies.

'Day out.' She smiled and moved on swiftly, without looking at them. She wouldn't recognise them anyway in these dark corridors, which was a reassurance. Her own disguise would be more secure too. Drianne would do what was necessary to smooth any suspicions. It did not occur to Mielitta that one of the knights might excuse himself to his companions and join the children in the middle of the party, hidden from view by the two adults as the corridors twisted through the Citadel.

Just before the path downwards narrowed to single file and became slippery, Mielitta made the children stop. She walked the whole length of the crocodile, giving instructions and messages of caution.

Somewhere in the middle of the group, a little girl with shining brown eyes said to her, 'Where did the man go?'

'What man?'

'A nice man, big and friendly. He held our hands and walked with us.' The brown-eyed girl's partner held up her left hand as proof.

'And he didn't have a lunch-box but we said he could share ours and he said thank you.'

Could they have been tracked? 'When did you notice he'd gone?' Mielitta asked sharply. Too sharply.

The little girl flinched and her answer was hesitant. 'I d-d-don't know.' After a moment of reflection, she added, 'I remember now. He went all shiny and vanished. Poof!' For good measure, she completed the picture. 'In green smoke.'

Mielitta smiled. How easily children made up stories, encouraged by the walls' tricks.

'Sharing is good,' she told the two girls. 'I'm very pleased with you.' That's what Declan would have said. Then she dismissed the story of a nice man and worked her way to the back, where Drianne was waiting for her.

'We both need to be at the front. You go through the water gate and collect them on the other side. I'll help them get through from this side and come through last. I've told them what we're doing and that they are going through a door into the library world where books come to life.'

That's good. They won't be scared if they think they're in stories.

'Why should they be scared? I wasn't.'

Drianne said no more and the two adults made their way to the front of the crocodile, leading the children in single file down to the wet rockface and the water gate. This was the most dangerous part of the access. What if a child slipped and fell into the river? What if a child panicked and started them all crying? But she'd forgotten that the path was wider to a child than to an adult. In fact, they could easily have continued walking two-by-two. Sure-footed and excited about their journey into the unknown, they saw marvels in everything new, from wet rocks to running water.

'This is what forging kills,' she told Drianne. 'All those stupid ladies and brutish knights were once as open as this. If Kermon is responsible, I can never forgive him, whether he was forced or thought it was right. Never.'

He didn't do it. Drianne clearly believed what she said but then, she would. She had a connection with Kermon.

'Radium,' pronounced Mielitta clearly and the rainbow gate appeared, drawing awed gasps from the children who could see it.

'May the stones be with you,' Mielitta told her friend. Drianne jumped onto the sill, waiting to catch the children each in turn, see them safely through the gate. One by one, each eager child landed safely. Clutching their lunch-boxes, they were helped through the gate by Drianne and then they vanished. They had strict instructions to wait on the other side and they behaved like Perfect little citizens. Then it was Drianne's turn and she too leaped through the rainbow, leaving room on the stone for Mielitta to land and follow.

Maybe the Citadel flooring did not extend as far as this water-soaked passage but if the river was purified and the gate warded, Mielitta was taking no chances. When the ground had clamped her, it had done so in seconds, with no escape and she'd not come this far to lose everything. She dared not remove the cut-out soles but they hampered her movement when walking. How much more difficult they would make the jump across to the iron gate.

She steadied herself mentally. She'd made so many jumps far more difficult than this one. 'Make the ground your friend,' she murmured and leaped. Her left foot landed safely and she tried to throw her weight forward, gain purchase, but the tip of her right cut-out sole caught on a rock edge, bent and pulled the boot with it. For a moment, she teetered, her body weight see-sawing between the sill and the foot that dangled over the water-race below. Then a force slammed her sideways, onto the sill and through the rainbow gate.

Jannlou.

CHAPTER THIRTY

On the other side, Mielitta arced, ready to buck and free herself but Jannlou had already rolled away and sprung to his feet, leaving her short of breath but very much alive. And surrounded by giggling children, who ran barefoot, splashed each other in the stream. Little sign of their Perfect education was evident as they rolled and played in the meadow or the water, clothing discarded as they went. If the children reacted so spontaneously to Nature, maybe her plan would work.

Where was Drianne? Then Mielitta spotted her friend, barefoot and balanced on a rock, being tugged in all directions by squealing children until she slipped laughing into the water. She choked as she took a faceful of water, swallowed, recovered and laughed. She was no older than the top class of students and smaller than many of them as she acted her age for once.

Mielitta swore loudly and the nearest ring of children giggled.

'That's the nice man,' the brown-eyed girl told her in reproving tones.

'Not in front of the children,' Jannlou admonished her but she was in no mood for jests and she prepared to launch herself at him. *Self-defence*, she told herself. Then she saw his red-rimmed eyes and held back, just as somebody who

Jannlou's equal in strength if not size came hurtling towards them from the edge of the forest, where she'd asked him to carry Verity and wait.

'Kermon,' she yelled. 'I don't need to be rescued!'

The Apprentice Mage-Smith stopped dead but all three of them were poised, ready for a fight. There was no time for this!

'And I didn't need you to rescue me either.' She glared at Jannlou.

He interpreted her words for Kermon. 'That's her way of saying thank you.'

Mielitta ignored his irritating smile and spoke to the perplexed Apprentice Mage-Smith. 'I don't know what Jannlou's doing here but if we keep him with us, he can't betray us.' Another daggers look. 'A second time.'

Jannlou looked back at her without flinching. 'Yes, I told Bastien your Maturity Test hadn't fully taken. He recognised you, kept asking questions, why you were working in the library, why you were still… different. He was pushing for answers and I thought it would get him off your back.'

He shrugged. 'And he's my friend. We always shared things. I never thought he'd summon you to do it again.' His voice shook. 'You really think I knew what they had planned? Bastien and his father–' He choked on the words, couldn't say more.

'I'm sorry,' Mielitta told him. 'About your father.'

Both men gave her a sharp look. 'How did you know?' asked Kermon.

Mielitta told the truth. 'I saw it.' Jannlou's eyes blackened with pain and she forestalled any questions. 'And I don't want to talk about it. Kermon, where's Verity? You haven't lost her?'

'No, she's resting in the shade at the tree-line.'

'Right, let's round up this lot and take them to the beehive. Then we can talk.'

The children had let off enough steam to accept the idea that there was more fun to be had deeper into the forest. With help from an apologetic Drianne, clothes and lunch-boxes were recovered and the children marshalled into a dishevelled version of their previous order.

They were having so much fun, Drianne justified the chaos that was not part of the plan.

Mielitta didn't need to shut her eyes to see the bee-map danced into her mind, showing her the way home. She headed up the procession with Kermon, entrusting the nice man to the two little girls who'd taken a shine to him. This time, Drianne knew he was there and would keep watch over him using her magecraft. Whether she was stronger in her powers than Jannlou remained to be seen but for the moment he seemed harmless, entertaining his little fans.

Kermon stooped to pick up Verity from her resting-place at the fringe of the Forest, her face a pale oval dominated by watery brown eyes, full of accusation.

'Did you drink from the stream?' Mielitta asked her.

'I'm not allowed,' responded Verity.

'You should have tried it. But here, take this. It's from the Citadel, purified.' Mielitta passed over a leatherette bottle.

'How do I know you're not lying?' asked Verity.

'You will know by the taste, the lack of taste. You're thirsty. Drink.'

Kermon flashed a look at Mielitta. Perhaps Drianne was not the only one who thought her hard. But Verity took a much-needed drink, then they walked onwards, weaving through the trees.

'See the shadows of the leaves, the sun burst through the canopy?' Mielitta asked. Nobody could say she didn't try.

'It's too bright. It's bad for my eyes,' was the sullen reply.

'See how tall that tree is? Each ring in its body is a year's growth. Imagine how many years old it must be.'

'Daddy told me about trees. That's a week's wood for the Citadel.'

How could people's perceptions be so different? Mielitta's bees sang of home and work. Her mouth still fizzed with the taste of the Forest water, drunk upstream from the area turned into a children's playground. Goodness knows what flavours had been added by the schoolchildren.

She saw flashes of feathers overhead, heard warnings of their approach tweeted and barked by the Forest-dwellers. Despite the threat of war, Mielitta felt the Forest working its peace inside her, its natural forces drawing her home. When she reached the glade and saw the beehive humming with activity, her heart melted, sweet and golden, as soft as Drianne could wish.

'We camp here,' she told Kermon. 'Can you tell Drianne to help settle the children down, calm their spirits, tell them to open their lunch-boxes but wait for the order before eating. We need to keep them all here. Rinduran would never dare to attack the Forest while the children are with us.'

Kermon's face showed the concentration that Mielitta now recognised as communication with Drianne, who knew the plan already.

Loosed, Mielitta's bees flew dizzy loops around her as she walked towards their home. Humming gently, ignoring the inner circle of wide-eyed children and the three adults who'd joined her in the glade, she removed the roof from the hive, revealing the top box full of honeyed frames.

Surrounded by the bees, she hummed her news and her request, waited while the scouts told the workers, while the workers took word to the Young Queen and while the hive danced in debate. Their anger at the prospect of war was a roar. Their attitude to the children was a confused buzz that settled into understanding of what Mielitta needed. And their trust in Mielitta was the respectful dance of those who guard their queen, unconditionally.

Patiently, in mind-pictures, in a dance, she showed the bees what must be done. The first bees repeated her instructions, hesitant, but as she approved their response, confidence grew and soon, the hive was of one mind and intention.

Feed the human grubs, they agreed.

Mielitta punctured the caps on honeycomb and each worker bee collected its load of honey, flew to a child, and regurgitated the honey onto the sustenance in the open lunch-box. This work was repeated until each child had a layer of honey spread on the usual Citadel bread-substitute. Then Drianne released the children's waiting spell and let their hunger instruct them.

Each bee observed her designated child eating the honeyed sustenance and the forest around the glade hummed with contented bees. Equally contented, the children let bees alight and tickle their open hands while they munched. All the children but one.

Pale and as isolated as she had been in her partitioned room, Verity would not touch the honeyed sustenance Mielitta offered her. The bee who'd been charged with feeding the girl hovered anxiously.

'I'm not allowed,' said Verity, swiping at the bee with her arm. 'Make it go away!'

'She made the honey and brought it to you,' Mielitta said. 'Bee grubs are given honey, pollen and water. She would bring you pollen if I ask her. You could try it.'

'I'm dying,' said Verity.

'What if you're not?' asked Mielitta. 'What if it's the Citadel life that's killing you?'

'You're wicked!' Worried by the tension, Verity's bee buzzed closer to her, settling on her hand, asking what was wrong. Verity smacked one hand on top of the other, forcing the bee's sting through her skin, fatally.

'Ow,' screamed Verity, flicking the dead bee onto a heap of pine needles and staring at the tiny dart still sticking in her hand.

The bee's death buzzed black in Mielitta's head, souring the smell of happiness everywhere else in the glade. She reached over and pulled the sting out of Verity's hand.

'It's killed me,' the girl whimpered, nursing the reddening bump on her hand.

'Good!' Mielitta spat back before she could help herself.

Drianne moved between them, inspected the girl's hand, told Mielitta, *It feels sore but not dangerous. You should tell her. It's not going to kill her.*

Mielitta maintained a stubborn silence and it was Kermon who passed on Drianne's words to Verity. The girl didn't believe him, just cried harder. 'Daddy will come for me,' she sobbed. 'And then you'll see.'

To keep some control, Mielitta walked around the glade and soothed herself by watching the other children. Under the effects of Drianne's magecraft, the children were all calm and as curious as their bees, which flew or settled on their skin, inquisitive, asking questions with their wings and antennae, amused by the answers.

'Why couldn't you do that to Verity?' she asked Drianne bitterly, as her friend joined her.

'I don't know. The others are all open to the Forest, to new experiences. They've not been forged. You saw them at the stream, just following instinct.'

'I saw *you* at the stream.' Mielitta smiled weakly, still grieving for one dead bee.

'I think, maybe, Rinduran has changed something in his daughter. His fears are her reality. She clings to the idea of her own death.'

'And if she doesn't die it will kill her to admit Daddy could be wrong!' Mielitta's laugh hurt. 'I thought maybe your magecraft wasn't working in the Forest.' Then she realised what she'd said, recalled why she'd thought that and looked around for Jannlou.

He was sitting with his fans, making little creatures out of pine cones by squashing them into each other and gouging out pieces to make eyes, legs, beaks or claws.

She went over to him, fuming. 'You said magecraft didn't work in the Forest!'

He smiled at her and her stomach butterflied. How could a man do that to you, even when he was in the wrong? *Especially* when he was in the wrong!

'I don't have any,' he told her. 'Magecraft.'

This was outrageous. She was prepared to swallow his excuses for betraying her to Bastien but she wasn't a fool. 'Of course you don't. All those years studying magecraft, the times you and Bastien used it against me – of course the Council got it wrong, your teachers got it wrong and you don't have any magecraft at all! And I'm the Queen of the Citadel!'

'Bastien covered for me. Right from the start. Everyone expected me to have magecraft because of my– because of my father. *He* expected me to have magecraft. People see what they want to. And I wanted to please my father. Wouldn't you?'

'I'm a girl.' Mielitta remembered Declan's reactions to her hopes of becoming a smith.

'Well, anyway, it started as a game. Bastien was so powerful he could throw his magecraft, make it look as if I was doing it. We practised until we were really good. Everyone thought we were inseparable so it was easy. If I was with my father nobody expected me to show my talents – he did everything. And then it was too late for me to say it was all Bastien. He never let on. But things have changed.'

They were silent, thinking of all that had indeed changed.

Mielitta flushed. What a fool she'd been. 'B-b-but you've been using glamour, with all those girls…'

His grin was a Perfect demonstration of charm. 'No, I haven't. No magecraft, no glamour.'

Mortified, she rushed off to find somewhere in this Forest to cool her burning face. She sought refuge in the beehive glade but when she reached it, there was no balm for her soul. Quite the opposite. The war had begun.

CHAPTER THIRTY-ONE

Darkness panicked the bees and Mielitta urged them all back into the hive. Any dribbled honey from the top box had been cleaned up with lightning efficiency and the colony was at fighting strength. *It needs to be,* thought Mielitta as a wave of black obliterated the sun, like the sleeve of a mage's robe sweeping across the sky. In its wake lay only the void. Darkness indeed.

It begins? the bees queried.

'Yes,' she told them. 'I will call you when you can help.'

This was no thunderstorm but a blackness that drained all light, all hope. Mielitta had faced this twice before when he entered her thoughts but Rinduran's power had grown. Maybe he'd added Magaram's and Shenagra's strength to his own, as Drianne had gained Puggy's. Ravished minds, ravished power – consent was irrelevant to Rinduran.

'He will play on your fears,' she yelled to the others, hoping that Jannlou and Kermon were hidden. Then the wave of unnatural darkness descended, enveloped her, cut her off. Drianne had wrapped the children in a sleep-binding that should preserve them in a honeyed dream while the war raged around them.

When the voice came, it grated like a knife on glass, pared her.

'This is your doing.' The blackness dissolved, allowed her to see the ashen wasteland in which she was the only life-form. Leafless trees raised their agonised branches to an indifferent grey sky and throughout the bare Forest, Mielitta saw only skeletons, four-legged and two-legged, big enough to be bear or tiger, or small enough to be birds.

Her heart thumped as she looked everywhere for her friends, scanning the barely recognisable places where she'd last seen them. Drianne and Kermon, white bones against a tree. Why torture herself further by looking for Jannlou?

'Bees?' she queried.

Shivering, huddling together, they were still there but their crushing despair brought her to tears. Through their eyes, she saw the hive empty, no queen, no adults, only grubs dead from starvation. The dance directions in their heads whirled, nauseating, and their sickness was terminal. She was sucked into their vortex, black as an eye-patch.

No home they whispered. *No food. No flowers. Nothing.*

Mielitta was weeping, knew there was no hope. It was almost a relief to let go. There was no place for her or the bees in this sterile Perfect world. The pine needles at her feet were already changing into grassette, an extension of the Citadel's control, of Nature's loss. Rinduran had won and Verity would be safe. Sterility had won.

Something about that train of thought was wrong. She reached for her lucky arrowhead in her habitual nervous reflex and the touch of the steel cleared her head for long enough to think straight. Something about sterility, being sterile... her thoughts zigzagged like bees desperately seeking flowers. Sterile... sterile meant no children. But there should be children here. Where were the children? There should be hundreds of them, or their bones, lying around.

Even as she thought of them, pictured Jannlou's little fans, the brown-eyed girl and her friend, the landscape around her gained a green tint, brown on tree bark, dancing shadows. Human shapes shimmered into view. The children were all there, safe, sleeping, with a taste of honey in every mouth. Not just the children. She could see–

And then she couldn't. The scene blacked out completely but now she knew the mirage was only that, a misglamour. And she would fight until the end.

'You can't do it, Rinduran,' she yelled. 'Your children have the Forest inside them and if you loose the destruction you planned, they'll all die.'

The blackness rippled, as if gathering strength, suffocating her. 'I know you, Mielitta. We've talked before. We've connected before. You recognise who I am, what I am. You enjoy killing, don't you?' the voice grated. 'Even children. Because they have what you don't. They're normal. They have parents who love them. Of course you want to destroy them and their home.'

'Bees,' Mielitta sought the solidarity to protect her against Rinduran's vicious darts but her bees still huddled, shaken by her vision of a dead world. Rinduran had not wounded them to near-death with his misglamour. She had. She'd pictured the nightmare and shared it with the creatures she most loved. They would never recover. Maybe Rinduran was right.

'I spy with my black eye, a foul bug, unwanted child, friend to no-one, traitor, riddled and contagious. Do you know her, foundling? If you don't trust me, the walls can show you, your beloved walls. Look.'

Stones appeared in the blackness. Mielitta could not move, as if the ground was indeed the Citadel's fabric, rooting her to the spot. She could not see beyond the walls that now surrounded her. The walls could never lie. They wavered, just as they had done to show her the Council Chamber.

'They gave birth to you, foundling. Remember?'

Her favourite story came to life as she saw the baby coming through the walls. Only this time the baby oozed insects that crawled all over her, vanishing into her eyes when the smith heard the crying and stopped. He didn't know what evil creature he was adopting, the honest, kind smith. As he picked up the baby, Mielitta could see the scurrying of insect legs in the baby's smile, but the smith noticed nothing. He was too good to see the evil being he harboured, nurtured for years, who would reward him by killing his whole community.

'You see her, don't you, and you know her. You know this is the truth.' The voice stabbed at her, prodding, searching for weak spots, for more weak spots, rejoicing at the pain it caused.

Mielitta sat down, rocked back and fore, hugging herself. She felt the glow of the bee sigil, her inner queen.

Are you ashamed of us? asked the bee.

Unable to answer, Mielitta rocked to and fro.

The walls showed Declan again. The poor smith was sitting in the forge, weeping, knowing now the terrible scourge he'd brought on his community. The Maturity Ceremony was outside, Rinduran's voice was saying that he had an important announcement to make later, when the new adults came out of the Barn. What should have been a wonderful day was the worst of the smith's life because he'd found out the truth about the freak he'd brought up as a daughter. The truth about what she'd done.

Mielitta stopped rocking. The walls wavered, uncertain, then turned black again, the visions gone. Her bee sigil glowed ever brighter.

'No,' she said, 'I'm not ashamed of you.'

'Tell me,' she yelled at the blackness that was only a mage's eye patch, whatever the misglamour he used. 'Tell me, how did Declan know so much about his daughter's condition *before* the candidates came out of the Maturity Barn?'

The black shimmered into walls again, showed Kermon at the spyhole and Declan learning about the Test from him. But Declan did not cry. If this was when he found out, he would have cried. This picture did not match the one before, did not fit the story.

'Fake!' she cried. And if one bit was fake, so was the rest.

Either the facts or the way of seeing. What had Drianne said about Rinduran? '*You* are the infection in the Citadel! You have infected your daughter with your way of seeing, with a desire for death! She could live if you let her. The Forest could save her. But you'll never find out, will you, because you prefer being certain she'll die. You prefer to blame somebody else!'

The fake walls were leaking light, not blackness but sunlight, pouring in and destroying the misglamour, until Mielitta was free again, glowing with the natural force the bees gave her. She could not see her three partners but that didn't mean they weren't near. They must fight their own battles. In front of her stood Mage Rinduran, glowering in his gold braid and temporary defeat. Beside him, as she'd dreaded, was Declan.

What's the target? she asked herself. *Make the ground your friend and use the arrows of light.*

'It was you,' she stated. 'Not Kermon. Forging people, all these years.' Her tone dripped contempt. She drew three arrows from her quiver, kept talking. 'You knew I hadn't taken the Maturity Test because if I had, you'd have been involved. You just watched and waited for your moment to betray me, your unnatural daughter.'

'No daughter of mine.' Declan's face was hardened steel, his eyes flint. 'I watched you for the Council, from the moment you came through the wall.'

She felt red-hot steel probing her mind but her bee-self danced round it, let her workers douse it in oil. She zigzagged round the hammer and the clumsy tongs attempting to grip her.

'You should have respected my smithcraft more,' she told Declan as she blocked his invasion. 'You've betrayed yours. You don't even smell of the forge any more. You smell of nothing. You *are* nothing. How many children have you mind-raped?'

He flinched. 'Helped,' he told her. 'I helped them become Perfect. I wanted to help you but they warned me your sweetness was a glamour, that you didn't fit and never would.'

His hand sneaked behind his back. Always reluctant to waste

magecraft and he was on his own now. Rinduran had vanished. She would deal with the Chief Mage afterwards. He must be tired after his wall stunt if he was letting Declan finish the job.

But Mielitta also knew how to time her move. She screamed high, the death song of a queen about to be murdered, and she fused with the glowing sigil so that she was in bee form when the thrown dagger passed through the space where her head had been.

'You always were full of yourself. Try this for smithcraft! Forged from your own mind and can't miss, so zigzag away, little bee.' Declan hurled a fine thread of seek-spell towards her, with the command, 'Steel, kill!'

Steel? She looped high to evade the seek-spell but Declan was right. The magical tracker merely turned and headed for her again. Her bee-body wavered and she reached instinctively for her lucky pendant. Steel! She dived down and the seeker whizzed overhead, turned towards her again. Visualising her human body, Mielitta transformed enough to unclasp the arrowhead that was about to kill her. It thrummed in her hands as she held it out. Each Damascene blue line vibrated like the bees' wings she'd imagined in her design, so beautifully executed by Kermon. Steelwing. She pointed it at the white light spearing towards her.

The seek-spell was too quick for her human form to duck and, in a blinding flare, it hit the arrowhead. The glowing steel jerked itself from Mielitta's hand but, instead of pursuing Declan's command, it stayed true to its forging and to its maker Kermon's whispered injunction. 'Steelwing, know one master, Mielitta; one aim, to protect her; one revenge, reverse all harm.

Welded to the seek-spell, the arrowhead traced the spell's reverse route. The deep wavy Damascene lines took on a life of their own and an escort of glittering blue bees accompanied the weapon honed against himself by the words of the Mage-Smith.

Declan tried to swerve and run but he had cast a seeker-spell too strong to counter. The arrow-head pierced him, buried itself so deep in his heart Mielitta could no longer see it. Her father's cloudy eyes repeated Rinduran's words as he crashed to the forest-floor, clutching at his chest. *Unwanted child, friend to no-one, traitor, riddled and contagious.*

'No!' she cried, dropping to the ground, searching for signs of life. Her father was gone. *Had never really been,* she told herself. Rinduran's doing all along.

Channelling her self-pity, her grief, her outrage, she forged all the flaws in her raw material into a weapon against the Chief Mage. She would find him. She was the arrow. Her bee sigil glowed as she transformed once more.

Now she called her bees. She felt them stagger, then respond to her need, grow stronger as they felt her passion. Then she connected them to their hive, their home, and fifty thousand bees responded, *Ready.*

Now she called the creatures of the Forest. *Now* she called to the Forest itself.

She focused on her bee sigil, merged with the queen into a flying warrior, with infinite arrows in her quiver and all of them poisoned. Then she drew her natural forces together and led the attack.

All glamour had lifted from the Forest and, adjusting to communal bee-sight, Mielitta spotted the remaining enemy mages as ten ghostly faces in black robes, scentless. As if their lives no longer touched them or marked them, left no smell.

Even if they threw off their garb, their lack of scent distinguished them clearly from Drianne and Kermon. She and her bees could smell Drianne-flower and smoke-Kermon. And Jannlou. Mage or not, his earth pungency told her his position as clearly as any map.

I'll hold the children and block all attacks on us, Drianne told her. *Don't worry about me. Kermon is going to pick them off one at a time, blend in to confuse them. They don't know he's here.*

Ten thought Mielitta. Why were there still ten? The Council had lost Shenagra but if Declan was the new member, there should be nine left. If only she could tell Kermon there were ten. And Drianne had said nothing about Jannlou. They were all separated now, each in a different world. She looped a swaying twig in dizzy flight and told herself, *Concentrate*. This was her domain and she must fight her own battle.

CHAPTER THIRTY-TWO

Ducking streaks of power that flared up violet in bee-vision, Mielitta collated the surveillance from hundreds of scout bees. They presented her with a map of the Forest and the enemy positions, which she passed on in mind-pictures to their force of thousands.

At the heart of every mind map was the home hive, almost empty now, containing only the drones and a bodyguard of workers to reassure the Young Queen.

'Keep laying eggs,' Mielitta told her. 'We know you're working and that creates positive vibrations.'

Do you have to take so many? fretted the Young Queen.

Yes, answered the workers, gathering round Mielitta in a volatile swarm. *We have danced this question and if we lose this war there will be no home, no Forest.*

The mages had failed with glamour and were now using focused power, seeking Mielitta with hurled fireballs that streaked out, screaming her name and intent on killing. If the seek-spell found a Forest creature in its path, it exploded. The Forest shrieked with dying animals. Trees cracked and fell in the unnatural storm. Birds no longer warned of danger but had flown away or died. Panic drove all away from the last attack, bringing unlikely companions together, bear and tiger, fox and rabbit, but they were as likely to flee towards their deaths as away.

As the bees buzzed their frantic fear of fire, scrambling to re-form a tightly packed ball, Mielitta danced confidence until a few bees tried her dance, tapping and waggling on top of the others, then more tried the movements, until fifty thousand bees shared the same conviction.

Then they shared one word, one thought, one flood of angry banana scent. *Attack.*

As one army, they zoomed at an enemy they saw as purple-faced in black clothes. Mielitta didn't even identify the mage except that he was not Rinduran, nor of the greenish hue of Hamel. This one crossed his gauntleted hands as he wove a spell that cloaked him in chainmail, allowed him to taunt a bemused stag with a spear before plunging the point into its side, again and again, as the deer toppled, its eyes lightless.

They said *she* enjoyed killing? More bee than human, she roared as she took handfuls of arrows, jabbed them into the chinks in his badly-forged armour. The rage of bees was its own volition. When the front ranks had buzzed to their own deaths, piercing every gap in the metal links, wave upon wave followed, berserk with the scent of bee-deaths, finishing what their comrades had begun.

Mielitta was everywhere, stabbing, screaming, buzzing her grief at their losses, defying the last feeble streak of power that singed the top of her head. She felt no pain.

'Next!' she yelled as the mage crumpled, slipping down to lie in the blood of the dead stag.

Bite his head off, responded the giant rage of tiny creatures. Their flight was not the playful zigzag of pollen-gathering but the purposeful loosing of an arrow. Mielitta pictured the next purple face, steered this living weapon she wielded and another duel began.

As bees died, so their anger grew and made them an unstoppable force, whereas the mages grew weaker with each death, each loss of magecraft, too selfish to pass on what they never thought to lose. Until it was too late.

Four left, thought Mielitta, stabbing a book that had been dropped on the Forest floor. A book entitled *The Proper Education of Girls in Perfection.* A book that screamed when pierced by a thousand darts before transforming into a dying mage, slumping into a human heap. What a foolish refuge! Bee-senses had ignored the shape and colour, fretted at the alien object and its lack of smell, while human sense had read the title and recognised the shape of mind that could create such a work.

Scout bees brought her updates, told her of the three that Kermon had disabled, attached to trees with his magecraft. And of the rage in the Forest itself, which had used the power flaring wild in its domain, against the wielders. Three trees had grown in diameter, fifty rings in fifty seconds instead of fifty years, until their screaming victims were silenced, part of bark history, like flies in amber.

Four left. And no sign of Rinduran yet. Nor of a mage with greenish skin.

'Where are they?' Mielitta consulted her scouts again. But the answer came from the hive, in the voice she hated most.

'Say goodbye to all your little friends,' Rinduran rasped.

Mielitta saw the giant hands through the sharper vision of drones' eyes, but it was the Young Queen's anguish that racked her as a frame of brood was lifted out of the open hive.

Our babies! The bees' collective keen paralysed the colony and Mielitta couldn't move her warriors. They dropped to the ground, dizzy, lost. But she would not give in to the monster. She flew on alone, to certain death.

'I'm sorry,' she yelled aloud, her human voice tiny in her bee body. But the trees raised up a wind and the loose magic blew it harder, faster so that Mielitta's words grew loud and large. When she heard the echo of her own voice, she knew sorry wasn't good enough and she summoned all her strength. She could not do this alone.

'Help me,' she shouted and every tree in the Forest fanned her plea into a command that roused the very stones to resistance.

Mielitta burst into the glade in time to see Rinduran stamp on the first frame, crushing the unborn bees with his boot. He was torturing the bees with old-fashioned violence, no doubt saving his magecraft to use against her.

'I'm here,' she yelled. 'Take it out on me!'

The Forest roared, 'I'm here. Take it out on me!' but it was not Mielitta's voice that roared defiance in her words. She whirled off track in a sudden gust of wind as a gigantic bear stormed past her and rushed Rinduran.

Bear, panicked the bees, roused once more to attack by an enemy traditional as fire. *Eats honey. Eats baby bees.* They rose from the ground and from the hive, once more a fighting unit, one Mielitta could either join or watch. They were beyond her direction in their fury at the open hive, their dead babies, the damaged Forest.

After the initial surprise, Rinduran spoke some words of power and blazed white. The stench of hot, singed fur filled Mielitta's nostrils and underneath was a more familiar scent. She couldn't quite place it.

The bees were attacking both bear and mage randomly but the beast took no notice. He reared up on his back legs, twice the height of Rinduran and batted away the shafts of power fired at him as easily as he swatted at the bees with his great paws.

'For my father,' the bear growled and closed with the mage. Fur hung in tatters, blood oozed from the dark brown skin but the bear took Rinduran into a smothering grip, dug his claws into the mage's back and crushed the man to his chest, tighter and tighter. The bees made a furious halo round the opponents, buzzing their own anger.

Finally, the bear released Rinduran, lifted his snout to the blaze of sunny sky and roared, 'It is ended.' Even the bees faltered in their warnings, confused by the strangeness of the bear's behaviour.

Mielitta felt her sigil glow, felt her instinct transforming her once more until she could run as a human to the beehive. She straightened the damaged frame as best she could. Rinduran had not killed all the unborn bees and some brood was still capped, so she slipped the frame back into the hive, put the roof back on, recalled her bees.

'It is ended,' she told them. How could she explain the temporary alliance between Forest creatures, that the bear was on their side in this war?

'Like when there's a fire.' She showed them the purple-faced black-robed mages, their shafts of destructive power. 'They're like fire.' She pictured the fox and the rabbit, together, hiding. Then the bear and the beehive. They grew anxious, rejected her dance but she showed them again, insisted. 'Like when there's a fire.' She showed them home, the hive, safe.

The bear had dropped to all fours, watched with hard brown eyes. Was she so sure it wouldn't charge them, follow its nature and pillage the beehive? She inhaled singed fur, bear stench and an earthy smell she knew well, peaty and male.

Yes, she was sure the bear would control itself, she told her bees. For now.

Then, one of the remaining mages ran through the trees, screaming, 'Father!' as he attacked the bear. The beast reared up on two legs again and let the mage run into his lethal embrace but the claws did not so much as scrape the skin of the mage's back.

Mielitta could only watch as Bastien struggled to hurt the enormous creature that held him too close for any weapon to be used. Little spikes of fire had no impact on the bear, which showed all the concern of a wall being kicked by a child in a temper.

'Bastien,' a voice gasped, breathing with difficulty.

Mielitta had forgotten the sleeping children and the fact that one of them was as impervious to magecraft as she was to the Forest. Verity was sitting where she had been all along, opposite the beehive, watching everything that happened. If she'd spoken at all, the Forest must have dismissed her words. If she'd tried to move, the Forest must have held her, gently, without the judgement passed on the three mages held prisoner.

At the sound of Verity's voice, a change came over Bastien. He stopped trying to fight the bear, stumbled as he was abruptly released and began to sob, gulping ugly sounds. Controlling himself with difficulty, he walked over to his sister and took her in an embrace as vital as the bear's.

'We're orphans now,' she said to him. 'So we must look after each other. Daddy would want that.' She looked at Mielitta. 'You've won. You've killed our father. Are you going to kill me and Bastien too?'

'No,' whispered Mielitta, her eyes on the bear, which glared back at her, dropped to four feet and lumbered off into the Forest. 'No.'

CHAPTER THIRTY-THREE

'Call the other mages here,' Mielitta told Bastien. 'So we can talk.' She consulted her scouts. 'You have enough to contact them? There are three left. And don't try anything silly. The Forest is still angry.'

Four-footed shadows prowled around the glade, striped with sun and shade. Or just striped. But they came no closer. Oblivious to all danger, the children still slept. *Hostages*, Mielitta reminded herself. Winning the war was a responsibility she hadn't fully considered and she should not make decisions alone. Bees would never make decisions alone.

'Drianne,' she called and her friend became visible, sitting against a tree, a dormouse and two rabbits snuggling on her lap. She tenderly lifted the creatures onto the ground and they scampered off. Then she stood up, glided towards Mielitta as if the rough ground was smooth as a dance floor.

A shaft of sunlight caught her face and Mielitta gasped at the changes. Bastien stepped back, held his sister tighter. A silver network like a spiderweb was etched over the fine young skin of her face, puckering it, distorting her features so that one eye was higher than the other, her nose tipped sideways and her mouth skewed, one half laughing, the other sour.

'What have you done to her?' asked Bastien, eyeing his young fiancée with revulsion. 'She was so pretty!'

'What should I say?' Mielitta asked Drianne, ashamed that her instinctive response was the same as Bastien's.

Tell him I belong to the Forest and chose to bear its mark. I release him from his vows. He doesn't need to know I kept my magecraft despite his Test. Let him pity me.

Hamel and another member of the Council joined them in the clearing. The metallic sheen of the second mage identified him as Veebo, the keeper of the water gate. He'd been so keen to take the position vacated by Crimvert and now he was responsible for the biggest breach of its defences the Citadel had ever suffered. Mielitta should thank him.

Instead, she transmitted Drianne's words to Bastien, whose face smoothed in relief then darkened again as Jannlou came through the trees. And joined Mielitta and Drianne.

'In this place, Mielitta is our Chief Mage,' Jannlou said, his deep voice carrying as if by speechcraft in the Great Hall. 'Let this be our Council Chamber. If I can put my grievances aside to discuss what is best for the future, so can all of you. The children sleep and we adults can sit and talk.'

Mielitta's body obeyed his courtier's gesture and she sat first, as a queen should. Cross-legged in the dappled sunlight, she weighed her options, as one after the other, all the adults sat. Somehow, the very act of sitting diffused some of the tension. The prowling beasts distanced themselves further and the trees stilled, as the wind died down. A child burbled in sleep, a honey-dream sound.

On her right hand, Jannlou looked at Mielitta, giving her leader's status. He was his father's son and more. But she must not think of fathers or three hearts would break, four including Verity, who also had a place at this Council, leaning on her brother, her eyes sharp, unforgiving.

Bees give me strength, prayed Mielitta as she chose her words.

'We have stopped you destroying the Forest. That was all we wanted, not to destroy you.'

The silence told her the power she held and she continued, 'You are destroying yourselves. The stronger the barriers you erect against the Forest, the more fragile you are, the more people have allergy.'

Verity interrupted her. 'That's a lie! Daddy has kept me alive.'

'And you're here,' pointed out Mielitta. 'And you're still alive. Maybe Daddy caused your allergy. Maybe he wanted an enemy so he made the Forest into one, so he could imprison you. You're the perfect example of Perfection and where it leads!'

Bastien shushed his sister gently, then spoke up for her. 'That's cheap, even for you. Lashing out at a sick girl and sullying the memory of a man who can't defend himself. You haven't studied the walls, understood why the Citadel needs defences. Not only my father, but his father–' he nodded at Jannlou '–and all the Councils for centuries, have dedicated their lives to our protection. And you think you know better?'

Mielitta swallowed. 'All those centuries eliminating people like me,' she said. 'All those centuries forging people's minds, making *men* and *women*, against their natures! I could have been a Mage-Smith. I would have been happy, found a compromise within Perfection.'

She was glad Kermon had not shown himself. She had enough complications to consider. But Jannlou *was* here so she added, 'Centuries where people survived but never lived.' His mother's words. 'Is that what you want for all the people of the Citadel? Are you happy that only mages keep their minds? Sorry, I mean that only *male* mages keep their minds? And everybody else is mentally raped.'

Hamel sneered, the effect diminished by his evident discomfort sitting on the grass, pointed boots stuck out straight in front of him. 'You exaggerate, over-emotional like all women. History has shown what happens when women wield power. Nobody is happy with the violence that ensues. You pontificate about mental rape – such emotive language! But you've never risked physical rape. Perfection has kept you safe in your room, until you should marry.'

Mielitta opened her mouth to argue but Drianne's words stopped her.

You're being drawn onto their ground. We know marriages can be sanctified rape, that my marriage would have been so, but they will never understand that. You're wasting words. Keep to the point.

Drianne was right. 'We will live by our rules not yours. We hold all your children.' Mielitta was cold, precise. 'And these are our terms for their release. You will return to the Citadel and make changes there. Your Maturity Test will cease. Forging will no longer take place. Nobody will die because of affinity with the Forest. Those who choose to leave the Citadel may do so. Women with magecraft will have the right to be mages. All women will have the right to marry or not marry, to have children or not have children.'

'And men? What will their rights be?' Hamel asked sarcastically.

'You'll figure that out,' Jannlou added his weight to Mielitta's words. 'Real men will manage just fine.'

Mielitta said. 'But that won't be your job. You've never been Chief Mage and your hostility now suggests you're too emotional for the job.' For the first time, she turned to the man who'd grown up heir to the Chief Mage, the man who'd fought at her side.

Jannlou didn't hesitate. 'There are two natural heirs to the position of Chief Mage and we should only keep the Forest to this pact if Bastien and Verity are equal leaders in the new regime.'

'But she's not even a mage!' objected Hamel, his fingernails unsheathing, digging holes in the ground beside his little legs.

'Then she can represent those who aren't,' snapped Mielitta. 'I don't like either of them but I trust Jannlou's judgement of Citadel politics. If he thinks Bastien and Verity can bring about the changes I demand and stay in power, I'm willing to negotiate with them in future.'

'No, you have to negotiate now. I hope never to see you again after this,' Bastien told her, then glanced at Jannlou. 'Or your friends. What's to stop us giving our word and then going back on it once the children are returned?'

'You signed a blood oath,' said Jannlou quietly.

'Like the one we made to each other!' Bastien spat. 'After all I did for you. I m–' His attempt to speak died in a choking fit. He clutched his throat, eyes bulging and face red.

'He cannot tell you because he swore on a blood oath to keep this secret but I will,' Jannlou spoke quietly. 'It is my secret to tell and reflects only honour on Bastien. You should take this truth back to the Citadel. I have no magecraft and Bastien, my friend, covered for me by using his.'

'Not possible!' exclaimed Hamel. 'Shenagra would have noticed! Your father!'

Sweaty and smeared from battle, he outfaced the mages' hostility. His face was chiselled flint as he spoke.

'Nobody examined the Chief Mage's son too closely. Bastien and I were inseparable and his magecraft was so strong–'

'Is so strong!' wheezed Bastien, recovering his voice. 'Oath-breaker!'

Jannlou shook his head. 'I have not broken the oath of friend-ship. But we also owe loyalty to different causes. And people. My reasons are my own business.'

Mielitta recalled the conversation in the library between Rinduran and Bastien. Hannah and friendship in what Bastien had done for Jannlou? Or expedience, to gain power in secret before the take-over that killed Jannlou's father. Whatever her own thoughts, Jannlou would never believe his friend to be so calculating, so there was no point telling him.

'Your requirements are not impossible,' Bastien told Mielitta. 'But I have some too. The boundary remains. The Citadel stays Perfect, purified and sterile, so that my sister and those like her can live.'

They have different beliefs, Drianne reminded her. *You can't convince them.*

Mielitta bit her lip but said nothing.

'And,' continued Bastien, 'those who leave the Citadel, who choose the Forest, are exiled forever. Including you. We don't want you.' His scathing glance swept all three of them: Jannlou, Drianne and herself.

She shivered. It was what she wanted, wasn't it? Not the cosy chamber in greylight. Not safety. Not the Courtship Dance and marriage to Jannlou. But four-legged prowlers and storms.

'And if you need to discuss boundaries?' asked Jannlou.

'Then I will let you know.' Bastien was curt, his expression making it clear how unlikely such an event was.

'You will let Lady Mielitta know,' Jannlou corrected.

'Oh, I don't think she's a lady any longer,' Bastien said.

'If not, then she's much, much more.'

'Enough of swapping petty insults,' Mielitta told them, uncomfortable that she was enjoying the exchange. 'I agree to your terms.' Drianne and Jannlou nodded. 'When the new Chief Mage has signed his blood oath, you may go. The children will return before nightfall.'

Watched closely by Jannlou, Bastien drew his knife, scored his hand and swore by the blood beads to enact each of the demands Mielitta had made.

'Is the wording tight? Can he wriggle out of any of our demands?' she asked Jannlou quietly.

He shook his head. 'The blood oath merges words to intention. Any attempt to twist or renege, poisons the oath-breaker. If he's a Mage,' he added. And she knew that Jannlou was not a mage, as Bastien had known for years. She could only guess what they had sworn to each other.

Jannlou spoke low, for her ears only. 'I keep my promises, without being forced.'

It was none of her business. 'Go,' Mielitta told the mages. 'If you come back, come in peace. I hope one day you will be open to the Forest.'

'One day,' Verity told her, 'I will find you and kill you for what you've done.'

'Then you'll still be alive,' Mielitta replied, 'and I will be pleased for you.'

The mages vanished, Bastien carrying Verity, as Kermon had done earlier.

As if summoned by Mielitta's thoughts, the Apprentice Mage-Smith appeared through the trees, his pace heavy as a man three times his age. His face showed no strange marks of Nature bar those of years lived, too many years, in one day. He held something tightly in his hand and his mouth worked as he tried to speak to Mielitta.

'I got this back for you,' he told her, holding out the object to her. When she'd taken it, he sat down hard on the ground and wept.

Mielitta unclenched her fist but she had known straight away what she was holding. The Apprentice Mage-Smith's masterwork, its Damascene steel bee-wing patterns sparkling clean, lay in her hand. Steelwing. Kermon had retrieved her arrowhead from his master's body and taken its defilement into himself. She could not refuse such a gift though her heart bled a dirty signature oath for all of them and what they'd suffered this day. And must yet suffer.

'Thank you,' she told him. 'I thought– I thought it was you. That you'd done… those things… in the Maturity Ceremony.'

He looked at her, his face ashen. He touched the arrow-head in her hand, uttered words that cut like a sharpened blade. 'And now we know the truth. And it's worse.'

She shook her head, blinked back the tears, hardening herself. 'We must make one more decision. One of us must go back to the Citadel with the children. And live there. For the sake of the Forest and the future.'

CHAPTER THIRTY-FOUR

T he children all ate some honey, carry the germ of love for
the Forest, but you heard Bastien. Their life in the Citadel
will nurture only hatred for all of this.' Mielitta waved her arms
round the glade and a visiting party of bees skittered wildly then
settled back on her shoulder, nuzzling.

She didn't need to convince her friends of the Forest's vitality.
'One of us has to make sure their nature flourishes. Without
support, it might wither and die. With one of us to keep their
minds open, these children might open the Citadel to a different
way, one day.'

The future of the Citadel lay asleep on pine-needles, tree
stumps and warm rocks, while shafts of sunlight played on the
soft down of their cheeks and arms. In the golden glow, the children looked like cherubs, pastoral images plucked fresh from the
walls' images of paradise. How did such children grow into ambi-
tious, spiteful haters? Did forging do all the damage or had
Declan merely worked with the material he was given, shaped
and cut what was already there?

You had to believe in a better future. Mielitta looked at the
grime-streaked faces of her comrades, loved each one beyond her
own life. As bees do.

'So I will go back,' she told them. 'Bastien and Verity will accept me if I go with the children, offer them allegiance. It will be a coup for them.'

The protest was immediate.

'Verity has sworn to kill you.'

'Bastien won't stop her!'

'What about your bees?'

Our people, the bees queried, anxious. *The Forest needs you.*

'They will understand,' Mielitta said. 'The children are my people too. I can't abandon them to the life I grew up in. Now that Rinduran has gone, I can talk the mages round. I was born for something. They know that! They'll be curious, want to know what the walls mean by their actions.'

She could see their scepticism. 'It's not self-sacrifice.' She grinned weakly. 'I could go into the walls. I'm sure they'd let me now. I can find out where I'm from, maybe meet my real parents. The walls are part of the Citadel too and we know so little about them.'

Us, pleaded her bees.

'No,' said Kermon. 'You are needed here. I'll go.'

No, he is too gentle, Drianne objected. *I'll go.*

Jannlou's deep voice cut in. 'I'm the best choice. Neither Bastien nor his sister can hurt me. You should not be the one to judge what is best, Mielitta. You can't see all the options clearly.'

Like house-hunter scouts, commented the bees.

Mielitta shook her head, besieged on all sides. Human leadership was not easy in a bee democracy. 'I don't want to but I owe it to you all to discuss this. Even the bees are harassing me so we'll do it their way. I've had my say. We should take turns to say why each of us is the best choice, like bee scouts do when they're house-hunting.

'Each one reports on the potential home she's found, dancing the details, describing how well it fits a hive's needs. The swarm considers the dances, the reports, and copies the strongest dance until they all agree. They choose the home that really is best. And

Kermon's right.' She sighed. 'One bee can't choose, especially not the queen, who's never foraged or scouted. The swarm doesn't leave the branch until all the bees dance the same decision, until they all agree. So let's do this.

Each of us will start with the same number of scout bees, dancing for us, showing how good our proposal is and when everyone has had a say, we'll know who's the best choice, by the reaction of the swarm.'

She sent out all her bees in a humming swarm to hang from the nearest low branch, told them to send scouts to investigate each person. She welcomed her own scouts, reminding them of her arguments, making them waggle with enthusiasm, dancing on her behalf.

When Jannlou, Kermon and Drianne were each hosting several scouts, Mielitta was ready. 'Drianne, go next and Kermon can translate your speech for Jannlou to hear.' She glared at the Apprentice Mage-Smith. 'And remember I can hear every word she says so don't cut or embroider!'

I'm the youngest so it's easiest for me to stay with the children, be one of them, gain their trust, Drianne began, stroking a scout bee that almost purred on her hand. *I have magecraft so I can learn how to use it in the Citadel, become a mage, maybe even a Councillor. Looking like this, I'm safe from unwanted attentions and my magecraft is strong so I can look after myself.*

So enthusiastic were the bees dancing on Drianne that three of Mielitta's gave up supporting her to join in the new dance.

'But you can't speak without Kermon or me,' objected Mielitta. 'So one of us would have to go back with you.'

Drianne's bees faltered a little and one took up Mielitta's moves again.

She asked the question that had been troubling her since she first saw her friend's marked face. 'Did you use your power to change your face?'

Yes. Drianne was defiant. *I learned from Puggy. She knew what happens to women who are beautiful.*

'But what if a man loves you? And can't see past the strangeness? Do you need to make it as difficult as that?'

Oh you're so obtuse sometimes! I don't want a man to love me!

Kermon stopped interpreting Drianne's words in order to make his own objection. 'Bastien isn't going to forgive Drianne so easily. There would be conflict from the start when we want healing. Drianne going would be just as bad as if Mielitta did. And women aren't going to suddenly be equals overnight, which means fighting for your rights all the time.'

The bee dances paused, taking in the information, waiting for the next proposal.

'I'm best suited to go back.' Jannlou's voice was grave, stating an absolute truth and his bees were suitably impressed before he'd even given a reason. 'Bastien and I have history so he would accept me as he would not accept any of you. He is angry now but we know each other and I could explain... The other mages would accept me because of my father and they would see me and Bastien working together as healing, exactly what you want to make the Citadel more open.' All Drianne's bees and most of Mielitta's had migrated to Jannlou's dance now, waggling furiously, much to the chagrin of the two women.

'And I'm a nice man,' grinned Jannlou. 'Ask the children. I don't see a problem in staying in touch with them, supporting them as they grow into new adults.'

The bees seemed as smitten with Jannlou as the children had been and Mielitta felt chilled. Maybe he wanted to leave her. She'd assumed they were all willing to sacrifice themselves for the greater good, for the future, but maybe Jannlou *wanted* to go back. Would that be for his own good?

'No,' she said, 'if I can't go back, you can't go back. We're the same, you and I.'

His eyes pleaded with her not to say more but bees did not hide the flaws in a proposed home. All the advantages and disadvantages were open.

'You're not like your father, you're not even a mage,' Mielitta said, weighing her words. 'And Bastien won't cover for you any more so you can't go back to how things were. Drianne would have more chance than you of making changes, exactly because she would be invisible. You would always be Magaram's son and how long do you think you could hide your true nature?'

She challenged him with her eyes. He knew exactly what she meant and she would say it aloud if he didn't back down.

'I've hidden it until now,' he said quietly.

'*Now*,' she retorted, 'you have the Forest in you and cannot go back.' Then she realised what she'd said.

'Like you, Mielitta,' said Kermon quietly. The bees hovered or settled on the people they had to judge.

'Don't you see,' Mielitta burst out. 'I don't want any of you to go back. After what we've been through today, we don't need signature blood oaths to bond us. We shouldn't be split up!'

'But as you said, one of us must go back, to nurture the Forest in the children, quietly, without drawing attention to the fact, or getting into fights. Who do you think is best suited for that job?' asked Kermon. His bees began to dance, not as enthusiastically as had Jannlou's but methodically, repeating their movements over and over, as if they could do so forever.

'I am a mage,' continued Kermon, 'and now that Declan is d-dead, I will surely become the Master Mage-Smith. I will enjoy returning to the forge, making new patterns.' His voice betrayed his lie. 'I can control the materials that come into the Citadel, spot any abuse of the agreement, or attempts at forging children. I will be ideally placed to teach the children, to enable little girls to learn smithcraft.' His eyes sought Mielitta's. 'So they don't resent young male apprentices.'

Her eyes filled up but the bees danced relentlessly in Kermon's moves.

'You're too soft,' Jannlou told him, sparking the first ugly moment Mielitta had seen between them.

'This isn't work for a brute!' Kermon retorted. 'But I don't think a smith has to prove he has muscles, if that's what you want to see! Do you want us to fight for the privilege?'

Jannlou's bees all deserted to Kermon's, joining in the dance that was more of statement of fact than a frenzy.

'Truthfully, I'd rather serve Mielitta by going back to the forge than stay here and watch you together,' Kermon said, his colour high.

The bees stopped dancing, completely confused by emotions they didn't understand. But Mielitta understood well enough and flushed.

'This shouldn't be about me! It's bad enough when the bees treat me as their queen and fuss over me. I don't want people fighting over me too!'

See, said Drianne. *Beautiful means complicated. But you have to deal with that. I don't.*

'You'd be alone,' Mielitta told Kermon. The bees waited again. 'None of us want to go, all of us have strengths and weaknesses so, as I seem to be Queen of this Forest, whether I want to be or not, it's my responsibility. I should be the one to go back to the Citadel. Then there would be no disagreements here.' She glared at Kermon and Jannlou. 'I've listened to everyone's point of view and I still think I should be the one to go.'

The bees showed no sign of being impressed by this argument and continued with Kermon's patient dance movements. Mielitta searched desperately for a clinching argument. 'I've saved the beehive, I've always found a way to survive in the Citadel, I've shown I can do what I set out to do! Kermon hasn't proved himself. I have!'

'So where do you think the Queen of the Forest is most needed?' asked Jannlou.

How will the people who stay here survive without you? asked Drianne.

All the scout bees rose up and flew over to the swarm, dancing the four options on top of their fellow workers. There was little enthusiasm conveyed for Mielitta's dance, more for Jannlou's and

Drianne's but within seconds there was no doubt. All of the scouts were dancing the best proposal: Kermon was to return to the Citadel.

'You can't!' Mielitta flung at him.

'They don't even know I was with you,' he pointed out. 'I can return with the children as if I'd never fought against them.'

'Verity knows,' objected Mielitta.

'She'll believe I was just here to protect the children, under duress. And nobody saw me in the battle.' He picked up the backpack he'd brought with him from the Citadel and passed it to Jannlou, who took it in silence, with a curt nod.

Mielitta thought of the three mages who would remain forever silent as to Kermon's role. She knew he was right and she had no arguments left to prevent him returning to the Citadel, apart from the lead weight in her guts.

Drianne was already waking the children and the debate was over, whether Mielitta liked the outcome or not. She swore she would never use the democratic process again. She hated bees.

You will, her inner queen told her. *And you don't.*

The children skipped and prattled, keen to get back home and tell their parents about their adventures, while the adults disguised their heavy hearts in more practical concerns. A little one fell over a tree root and cut his knee, requiring some of Drianne's healing magecraft. Several had to be retrieved from explorations into the wild, inspired by a toadstool or a birdcall.

Finally, the Citadel's children were all in the meadow. Mielitta allowed them one last play in the stream. When, if ever, would they play in sunlight and fresh water again?

Kermon had the intense look on his face that meant he was communicating with Drianne but their thoughts were closed to her. Then it was time to say goodbye. She wished she'd been less spiteful when they'd first met, more sensitive to his feelings. And now she was choked up, with no time to say anything that mattered, when he was walking into his prison. Would she ever see him again?

JEAN GILL

'Don't worry,' he said, clear-eyed. 'I'm not as soft as he thinks.'
The attempt at a grin was too much for Mielitta and she hid her
tears against his chest. She hugged him tight, her voice muffled
against the leatherette that smelled as it should, of smoke and
smithcraft. Of her childhood that had been stolen from her.

'I do care about you,' she mumbled. 'Like a brother. What are
we going to do when we can't talk to each other?'

He disentangled her gently. 'I'm going to make another arrowhead, a twin to Steelwing. Then I can reach you through our
arrowheads, so we can stay in touch. You and me, the Forest and
the Citadel.'

'How?' she asked. 'How can you do that?'

'Magecraft and blood,' he whispered. 'I kept some.'

Her fingers went automatically to her pendant and she shuddered, knowing whose blood had been cleaned from it.

'Not so soft after all,' he told her, straightening his back and
holding her away from him. He drew her pendant up from her
bodice by the chain, kissed it. 'Still beautiful,' he told her. 'Never
doubt it.' He hesitated. 'He did care about you. Declan. Even
though he wasn't supposed to. But he was Perfect to the core, a
fundamentalist, couldn't accept what you were.'

She didn't know what to say and there was no time left.

Kermon dropped the arrowhead gently down into its
customary place and summoned the children, who reluctantly
lined up in their crocodile. Mielitta watched until the last child
vanished through the rainbow.

Her last chance to plead with the walls was gone, her last
chance to find out what they knew about her origins, her last
chance to talk to Kermon. What if he couldn't make a twin arrowhead, couldn't give it powers? He'd be locked in the Citadel,
couldn't speak to her ever again. She wanted to touch the walls,
ask them for a last message. Surely, they'd tell her something
vital? She wanted to have one more conversation with Kermon,
say all that she hadn't said, talk about Declan.

'I'll just be a minute,' she told Jannlou, already running to the

286

water gate. 'I'll come straight back. Just–' She reached the gate, which had already lost its colours. She yelled 'Radium!'

But the water gate hadn't just closed. It had locked. The last child through had triggered some change of password or more. The Citadel was closed to them all forever.

For a long moment, Mielitta remembered a chamber that she could lock, where she could be alone and safe. Then she turned to her companions, wondering what they would miss. Not sustenance and purified water, not greylight and mind rape.

'What was that all about? With Kermon?' asked Jannlou, his eyes fierce.

'Communication,' replied Mielitta and sighed inwardly. *Drones.*

They stumbled back as far as the Forest's edge but Mielitta could see her own exhaustion mirrored in her companions' ashen faces. The lengthening shadows showed that day's end approached. 'Let's rest here,' Mielitta suggested. 'I don't think I can go any further today.'

As if her words had given them license to give in to their own fatigue, Jannlou and Drianne dropped at once to the ground, rearranged a cloak and a backpack as makeshift pillows. Mielitta wrapped her britches around her quiver and used that as a bolster, thinking of all the provisions they should have brought with them. Instead, all they knew about survival outside the Citadel was what she'd digested from a library book.

Too tired to sleep, she lay awake, worried instead of triumphant. Today, they'd saved the Forest, defeated Rinduran, all she could have hoped for, but they'd lost everything they knew. The unknown did not seem like an adventure any more.

It seemed years since she'd opened the mysterious birthday gift, read the note, worn the perfume, been attacked by her bees. The golden sigil tingled, part of her now.

She remembered the words of the prophecy. Did they make any more sense now?

When the bottle is empty, you will be full.
No life ends while The One lives.
In the year of the prophecy, choose well.

She considered the cryptic lines. She was full of bees. They called her the One. Had she chosen well? 'No life ends' wasn't true. So many lives had ended!

But 'No life ends' echoed in her mind. There was a different way to read it. What had Jannlou's mother said? 'This is no life'. What if 'no life' in the Citadel should end? Because of what they'd done?

'Drianne, are you awake?' murmured Mielitta.

Yes.

'What did you really see, when you went into the walls.'

A pause. The reply came slowly, a voice in the gathering blue. Twilight looked like bee-sight.

Rinduran told the truth when he said it was too much for me. But he didn't understand. When he went into the walls, he saw people stroking animals and all he thought of was germs and allergy. I felt soft fur, companion spirits, the bond with pets. He saw people with animals, as food and as friends, and he was disgusted. I saw that people are animals. There was no disgust in her statement, rather an acceptance.

You were right to infect the children with honey, with Forest, because one day you will be able to say what you did and they will understand your words. They will never understand the truth that I saw in the walls. They all have Forest in them. Their own bodies need the work of millions of creatures, tinier than bees, to keep them healthy. When they try to keep the Forest out, they are killing themselves.

Mielitta thought about her body, occupied by thousands, millions, of tiny creatures. 'So everybody has bees.'

Drianne's laughter rang in her mind, gentle, not mocking. *No, only you have bees. These other lives in our bodies do not impinge on our consciousness. Unless we think about them. But they are there. And we need them.*

'Could that be what's wrong with Verity?'

Only the walls know.

Again, Mielitta felt her loss. There was so much she didn't know. And now she never would.

'Can't we tell the people in the Citadel? That they can't keep the Forest out. That it's inside them.'

When I stood in front of them in the Great Hall, spoke through Kermon, I had the chance. But the walls showed me much. What is true and what people can accept as true are two different things. Kermon understood. He spoke for me and I was muted.

Mielitta must have dozed because the sky was black when she opened her eyes again, with thousands of sparkles and one pale curve of light. She had to share this with her companions on their first night outside the Citadel's grey canopy.

'Jannlou, Drianne, look!'

I know. Isn't it beautiful?

'It's your bow,' Jannlou told her. 'Shining in the sky, a symbol of the new world we're going to make.'

If you enjoyed this book, please share your thoughts in a review, however short. Reviews help other readers find my books.

Anyone who reviews one of my books can have his/her dog featured in the Readers' Dogs Hall of Fame on my website

Contact me at jeangill.com

I love to hear from readers.

Acknowledgements

Many thanks to:

my editor Lorna Fergusson of *Fictionfire Literary Consultancy* for believing in my bees and for sterling work (if you've read *The Troubadours Quartet* you'll fully appreciate the word 'sterling');

my cover designer Jessica Bell with cover art by: art4stock, Michel Angeloop, Ales Krivec, Teddy Kelley;

Babs, Claire, Karen, Kristin and Jane for all your constructive criticism and creative genius. This story began as a suggestion from Babs that buzzed around my head until I had to start writing and see what happened;

Maurice Rossetti, the beemaster, who inspired me to run around a Provençal hillside in a white suit. Thanks to his patience over three years on his beekeeping courses, I have tasted honey from my own workers, produced in our beehives *Endeavour, Diligence* and *Resolution* (named by my husband);

Long-Suffering Husband who did not foresee thirty-odd years ago that he would be running around aforementioned hillside in Provence with me, both dressed in white suits (inevitable, some would say);

and the reader who told me about her little sister's habit of stroking bees and who inspired Drianne's reaction to bees.

Tannlei's archery teaching owes much to the most famous philosopher-archer: Confucius.

My research on honeybees includes
Inspiration from the work of Dr Klaus Schmitt, Weinheim, Germany, on Reflected UV Photography – UV Remapping / Differentials. Thanks to his photographs comparing the way human, butterfly and bee vision would perceive the same flower or other object, I was able to imagine bee-sight. All scientific errors are mine not his.

Selected reference works:
The Buzz About Bees – Jürgen Tautz
Honeybee Democracy – Thomas D. Seeley
L'Apiculteur – a monthly French journal for beekeepers

ABOUT THE AUTHOR

I'm a Welsh writer and photographer living in the south of France with two scruffy dogs, a beehive named 'Endeavour', a Nikon D750 and a man. I taught English in Wales for many years and my claim to fame is that I was the first woman to be a secondary headteacher in Carmarthenshire. I'm mother or stepmother to five children so life has been pretty hectic.

I've published all kinds of books, both with traditional publishers and self-published. You'll find everything under my name from prize-winning poetry and novels, military history, translated books on dog training, to a cookery book on goat cheese. My work with top dog-trainer Michel Hasbrouck has taken me deep into the world of dogs with problems, and inspired one of my novels. With Scottish parents, an English birthplace and French residence, I can usually support the winning team on most sporting occasions.

www.jeangill.com

f facebook.com / writerjeangill

🐦 twitter.com / writerjeangill

📷 instagram.com / writerjeangill

g goodreads.com / JeanGill

If you enjoyed this book, I recommend

SONG AT DAWN

Book 1 in the award-winning *Troubadours Quartet*.

***FREE** to members of Jean Gill's Special Readers' Group. Sign up at jeangill.com*

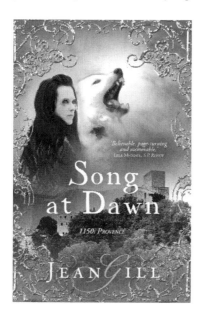

'Historical Fiction at its best.' Karen Charlton, *the Detective Lavender Mysteries*

Four Discovered Diamonds Awards

Historical Novel Society Editor's Choice

Winner of the Global Ebooks Award for Best Historical Fiction

Finalist in the Wishing Shelf Awards and the Chaucer Awards

Set in the period following the Second Crusade, Jean Gill's spellbinding romantic thrillers evoke medieval France with breathtaking accuracy. The characters leap off the page and include amazing women like Eleanor of Aquitaine and Ermengarda of Narbonne, who shaped history in battles and in bedchambers.

SAMPLE: SONG AT DAWN

She woke with a throbbing headache, cramp in her legs and a curious sensation of warmth along her back. The warmth moved against her as she stretched her stiff limbs along the constraints of the ditch. She took her time before opening her eyes, heavy with too little sleep. The sun was already two hours high in the sky and she was waking to painful proof that her choice of sleeping quarters had been forced.

'I am still alive. I am here. I am no-one,' she whispered. She remembered that she had a plan but the girl who made that plan was dead. Had to be dead and stay dead. So who was she now? She needed a name.

A groan beside her attracted her attention. The strange warmth along her back, with accompanying thick white fur and the smell of damp wool, was easily identified. The girl pushed against a solid mass of giant dog, which shifted enough to let her get herself out of the ditch, where they had curved together into the sides. She recognized him well enough even though she had no idea when he had joined her in the dirt. A regular scrounger at table with the other curs, all named 'Out of my way' or worse. You couldn't mistake this one though, one of the mountain dogs bred to guard the sheep, his own coat shaggy white with brindled parts on his back and ears. Only he wouldn't stay with the flock, whatever anyone tried with him. He'd visit the fields happily enough but at the first opportunity he'd be back at the chateau. Perhaps he thought she was heading out to check on the sheep and that he'd tag along to see what he was missing.

'Useless dog,' she gave a feeble kick in his general direction. 'Can't even do one simple job. They say you're too fond of people to stay in the field with the sheep. Well, I've got news for you about people, you big stupid bastard of a useless dog. Nobody wants you.' She felt tears pricking and smeared them across her cheeks with an impatient, muddy hand. 'And if you've broken this, you'll really feel my boot.' She knelt on the edge of the ditch to retrieve an object completely hidden in a swathe of brocade.

She had counted on having the night to get away but by now there would be a search on. If Gilles had done a good job, they would find her bloody remnants well before there was any risk of them finding her living, angry self. If he had hidden the clues too well, they might keep searching until they really did find her. And if the false trail was found but too obvious, then there would be no let-up, ever. And she would never see Gilles again. She shivered, although the day was already promising the spring warmth typical of the south. She would never see Gilles again anyway, she told herself. He knew the risks as well as she did. And if it had to be done, then she was her mother's daughter and would never – 'Never!' she said aloud – forget that, whoever tried to make her. She was no longer a child but sixteen summers.

All around her, the sun was casting long shadows on the bare vineyards, buds showing on the pruned vine-stumps but no leaves yet. Like rows of wizened cats tortured on wires, the gnarled stumps bided their time. How morbid she had become these last months! Too long a winter and spent in company who considered torture-methods an amusing topic of conversation. Better to look forward. In a matter of weeks, the vines would start to green, and in another two months, the spectacular summer growth would shoot upwards and outwards but for now, all was still wintry grey.

There was no shelter in the April vineyards and the road stretched forward to Narbonne and back towards Carcassonne, pitted with the holes gouged by the severe winter of 1149. Along this road east-west, and the Via Domitia north-south, flowed the life-blood of the region, the trade and treaties, the marriage-parties and the armies, the hired escorts sent by the Viscomtesse de Narbonne and the murderers they were protection against. The girl knew all this and could list fifty fates worse than death, which were not only possible but a likely outcome of a night in a ditch. What she had forgotten was that as soon as she stood up in this open landscape, in daylight, she could see for miles – and be seen.

She looked back towards Carcassonne and chewed her lip. It was already too late. The most important reason why she should not have slept in a ditch beside the road came back to her along with the growing clatter of a large party of horse and, from the sound of it, wagons. The waking and walking was likely to be even more dangerous than the sleeping and it was upon her already.

The girl stood up straight, brushed down her muddy skirts and clutched her brocade parcel to her breast. She knew that following her instinct to run would serve for nothing against the wild mercenaries or, at best, suspicious merchants, who were surely heading towards her. She was lucky to have passed a tranquil night – or so the night now seemed compared with the bleak prospect in front of her. What a fool to rush from one danger straight into another, forgetting the basic rules of survival on the open road. To run now would make her prey so she searched desperately for another option. In her common habit, bedraggled and dirty, she was as invisible as she could hope to be. No thief would look twice at her, nor think she had a purse to cut, far less a ransom waiting at home. No reason to bother her.

What she could not disguise was that, common or not, she was young, female and alone, and the consequences of that had been beaten into her when she was five years old and followed a cat into the forest. Not, of course, that anything bad happened in the forest, where she had lost sight of the cat but instead seen a rabbit's white scut vanishing behind a tree, as she tried to tell her father when he found her. His hard hand cut off her words, to teach her obedience for her own good, punctuated with a graphic description of the horrors she had escaped.

All that had not happened in the dappled light and crackling twigs beneath the canopy of leaves and green needles, visited her nightmares instead, with gashed faces and shuddering laughter as she ran and hid, always discovered. Until now, she had obeyed, and it had not been for her own good. Fool that she had been. But no more. Now she would run and hide, and not be discovered.

She drew herself up straight and tall. No, bad idea. Instead, she slumped, as ordinary as she could make herself, and felt through the slit in her dress, just below her right hip, for her other option should a quick tongue fail her. The handle fitted snugly into her hand and her fingers closed round it, reassured. The dagger was safe in its sheath, neatly attached to her under-shift with the calico ties she had laboriously sewn into the fabric in secret candle-light. She had full confidence in its blade, knowing well the meticulous care her brother gave his weapons. As to her capacity to use it, let the occasion be judge. And after that, God would be, one way or another.

By now, the oncoming chink of harness and thud of hooves was so loud that she could hardly hear the low growl beside her. The dog was on his feet, facing the danger. He threw back his head and gave the deep bark of his kind against the wolf. The girl crossed herself and the first horse came into sight.

Dragonetz considered their progress. They had been seven days on the road since Poitiers, and many had objected to the undigni-fied haste. Such a procession of litters, wagons and horse inevitably travelled slowly but they had kept overnight stops as simple as possible, resting at the Abbey and with loyal vassals, strengthening the ties. Apart from Toulouse of course, where Aliénor had insisted on a 'courtesy visit', her smile as polite as a dog baring its teeth. It had taken all his diplomacy to talk her out of instructing her herald to announce 'Comtesse de Toulouse' among her many titles and she had found a thousand other ways to throw her embroidered glove in the young Comte's face.

It was no easy matter to be in the service of Aliénor, Queen of France, but he would say this for her; it was never dull. The Lord be thanked that she had decided to insult Toulouse by the brevity of her stay or he could not answer for the casualties that would have ensued. Two more days of travel should see them in Narbonne and safe with Ermengarda and then he could relax his guard to the usual twenty-four hour check on every movement near Aliénor.

He was aware of the bustle behind him, wheels stopping, voices raised, and he slowed his horse almost to a standstill, antic-ipating the imperious voice beside him. Aliénor had tired of the litter and, mounted on her favourite palfrey, reined in beside him. He declined his head. 'My Lady.' Queen of France she might be but like all born in Aquitaine, he had sworn fealty to Aquitaine and its Duchesse, and France came second.

'Amuse me,' Aliénor instructed her companion, her pearl ear-rings spinning. The Queen's idea of dressing down for travelling might have included one less bracelet, a touch less rouge on her exquisitely painted face, and a switch of jeweled circlet, but there was little other compromise. The fur edging her dress could have been traded for a mercenary army. And that was exactly as it should be, she would have told him, had he questioned the wisdom of flaunting her status on the open road. She might have been spoiled as a child but she had been taught that a Lord of Aquitaine commanded respect as much through display and largesse as through a mailed fist, and she had learned the lesson

SAMPLE: SONG AT DAWN

well. In Aquitaine, she was adored. France, however, was a different country and they did things differently there.

'Once,' he began, 'there was a beautiful lady with red-gold hair, riding a white palfrey between Carcassonne and Narbonne, unaware of the danger lurking on the road ahead...'

She laughed. The pearls on her circlet gleamed and the matching ear-rings danced. Some red-gold hair escaped its net and coils under her veil. Everything about Aliénor was impatient for action. 'We have travelled more dangerous roads than this, my friend.' She was referring to their trek two years earlier, when they took the cross and the road to Damascus, the road paved with good intentions and finishing as surely in hell as anything either of them had ever known. A Crusade started in all enthu- siasm and finished in shame. Each of them had good reason to bury what they had shared and he said nothing.

She rallied. 'Wouldn't you love to deal with monsters, dragons and ogres instead of Toulouse and his wet-nurses?' Her smile clouded over again. 'Or the Frankish vultures, flapping their Christian piety over me. Do you know how Paris seems to me? Black, white and grey, the northern skies, the drab clothes, the drab minds. All the colour is being leeched out of my life, month by month and I cannot continue like this.'

'You must, my Lady. It is your birthright and your birth curse. You know this.'

'I cannot exercise my birthright when I am relegated to embroidery and garden design. It is insufferable.'

'Power does not always shout its presence, my Lady, and each of the two hundred men armed behind you on this road represent a thousand more ready to die at your command. Every word you speak has the weight of those men.'

'Tell that to my husband, the Monk!' was the bitter reply. Her companion knew better than to reply to treason, especially when it came from a wife's mouth. 'Oh to be free of Sackcloth and Ashes, to hear a lute without seeing a pursed mouth or hearing that bony friar Clairvaux invoke God's punishment on the ways of Satan.'

'Clairvaux,' her companion mused, 'Bernard of Clairvaux, now what was that story about him? No, I mustn't say, not to a lady.'

'But you must, my wicked friend, that's exactly what I need, gossip. The more scurrilous the better.'

'Scurrilous gossip? About the saintly Clairvaux? How could that be possible? Anyway it's an old tale so you'll have heard it before,' he teased.

'I want to hear it again,' she ordered.

'As my Lady commands. But don't blame me if you have nightmares.'

LEFT OUT

If you like Young Adult books that are enjoyed by adults too; if you're left-handed or know a leftie, try *Left Out*

"A compelling story about friendship, its strength, and the unusual ways it develops." Rebecca P. McCray, The Journey of the Marked

Being different isn't easy but it can be exciting!

How well do you know your friends? Are they left-handed or right-handed? Are they left-brained or right-brained? And what difference does it make?

Shocked at discovering how left-handers are persecuted, Jamie ties her hand behind her back for a public protest in school. This does not go down well with the teachers. Her best friend Ryan joins in but just when their campaign is working, Ryan's mother drops a bombshell. She's whisking him off from Wales UK to live back in America.

There he faces bullying at its most deadly.

FORTUNE KOOKIE

Can dreams take over your life? Although it is Book 2 of the series *Looking for Normal*, the book stands alone.

Shortlisted for the Cinnamon Press Novella Award

"Jean Gill brings her magical storytelling skills to teens, to weave compelling and thought-provoking stories that will linger on in their minds well after the last page is read." Kristin Gleeson, author and children's librarian

Jamie's mother is hooked on fortune-tellers, and running the family into debt. To cure her, Jamie decides to investigate the psychic world. Their research causes havoc in school and they are drawn deeper into the very world they are investigating.

Jamie's dreams of walking a medieval battlefield are so vivid that she feels compelled to resolve a historical mystery that starts at Kidwelly Castle in South Wales, where Princess Gwenllian once lived.

SOMEONE TO LOOK UP TO

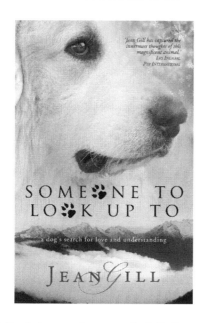

If you loved Mielitta's bees, try *Someone to Look Up To,* written from a dog's viewpoint.

Top Pick Award from Litpick Student Reviews. By IPPY and Global Ebook Award Winning author. For all dog-lovers!

'Jean Gill has captured the innermost thoughts of this magnificent animal.' Les Ingham, Pyr International

A dog's life in the south of France. From puppyhood, Sirius the Pyrenean Mountain Dog has been trying to understand his humans and train them with kindness.

How this led to their divorce he has no idea. More misunderstandings take Sirius to Death Row in an animal shelter, as a so-called dangerous dog learning survival tricks from the other inmates. During the twilight barking, he is shocked to hear his brother's voice but the bitter-sweet reunion is short-lived. Doggedly, Sirius keeps the faith.

One day, his human will come.

Jean Gill's Publications

Novels

The Troubadours Quartet

Book 5 Nici's Christmas Tale: A Troubadours Short Story *(The 13th Sign)* 2018

Book 4 Song Hereafter *(The 13th Sign)* 2017

Book 3 Plaint for Provence *(The 13th Sign)* 2015

Book 2 Bladesong *(The 13th Sign)* 2015

Book 1 Song at Dawn *(The 13th Sign)* 2015

Life After Men: *Book 1* The Silver Sex Kittens

co-authored by Karen Charlton *(The 13th Sign)* 2018

Someone to Look Up To: a dog's search for love and understanding *(The 13th Sign)* 2016

Love Heals

Book 2 More Than One Kind *(The 13th Sign)* 2016

Book 1 No Bed of Roses *(The 13th Sign)* 2016

Looking for Normal (teen fiction/fact)

Book 1 Left Out *(The 13th Sign)* 2017

Book 2 Fortune Kookie *(The 13th Sign)* 2017

Non-fiction/Memoir/Travel

How Blue is my Valley *(The 13th Sign)* 2016

A Small Cheese in Provence *(The 13th Sign)* 2016

Faithful through Hard Times *(The 13th Sign)* 2018

4.5 Years – war memoir by David Taylor *(The 13th Sign)* 2017

Short Stories and Poetry

One Sixth of a Gill *(The 13th Sign)* 2014

From Bedtime On *(The 13th Sign)* 2018 (2nd edition)

With Double Blade *(The 13th Sign)* 2018 (2nd edition)

Translation (from French)

The Last Love of Edith Piaf – Christie Laume *(Archipel)* 2014

A Pup in Your Life – Michel Hasbrouck 2008

Gentle Dog Training – Michel Hasbrouck *(Souvenir Press)* 2008

Printed in Great Britain
by Amazon